COMES THE AWAKENING

by

C. K. PHILLIPS

Comes the Awakening is a work of fiction. Names, characters, places, and incidents are either the product of the author's imagination or are used fictitiously. Any resemblance to events, locales, or any person, living or dead, is entirely coincidental.

DEDICATION

Comes the Awakening is dedicated to the many people who helped me and gave me suggestions for making the book better. Thanks to the early readers and reviewers: David Pollock, Steve Robinson, Nancy Lewis, and Joy Yates. Your thoughts were invaluable to me. A special note of appreciation also goes out to Cheryl Dalton who read the book and encouraged me.

I could never repay the help and advice that I received from Joe Spencer. Joe knows more about what makes a good story than anyone I know. He is an avid reader with a great collection of books which has served as a lending library to many of us. My choice of my first reader, he encouraged me to pursue the process.

The last person I want to thank is my wife Cindi. She is also a passionate reader and probably the most intelligent person I know. She has a keen sense of characterization and was a great source of advice in how to bring my characters to life. At crucial points of my plot when I was stymied, she said, "Do this or do that"—and it worked.

* * * * * *

Cover Design: Kent Holloway

PROLOGUE
LA ROCHELLE, THE COAST OF FRANCE –
SEPTEMBER, 1307

The huddle of men sitting around the makeshift table paused in their whispering as the knock sounded on the door. Omar put his finger to his lips and hissed, "Shhh" and pointed to the door. They all drew their knives or swords as they looked at each other and moved toward the locked entrance. The pattern of the knock was repeated twice, followed by a pause, and then was repeated once more. The men relaxed some as they recognized the signal, although they kept their weapons ready. Omar moved to the door and easily removed the heavy plank that served as the lock. The visitor stood in the opened door and provided the sign that kept him from being quickly killed, then slowly entered the room. It was Baullier from Corbeil and one of the Order's members. He removed his cloak, flicked the rain water off it, and sat down at the table. His beard dripped as he pointed his grave eyes at each of the three men in turn.

"Bad news," he whispered. "The King is planning to disband the Order and eliminate all of the members.

"We thought that there may be trouble brewing," Omar replied, looking around. "We were just discussing plans. How did you find out?"

"Lucius contacted me two days ago; I left immediately to come here." Lucius was a member of King Philip IV's court in Île de la Cité and was a secret knight in the Order.

Baullier spoke up, "The Pope will protect us, won't he?"

"Lucius said that the King has influenced Pope Clement to go along with him, so it looks like we are on our own. Why's the king doing this?"

Omar looked at Baullier and said, "Philip does not want to pay the debts he owes us. He's also placing his relatives in positions of power—he doesn't want to share that power with us. Did he give you any details?" asked Omar.

"He told me that the attack is planned for October thirteenth. It will take that long for the King to gather his troops to carry out the purge."

"That's only three weeks' time!" spoke up Landreau.

Omar replied, "That's not a lot of time to make our escape. It's a good thing we have procedures in place to contact our members; we need to call them together—immediately!" They discussed various timelines and considered what they should do. Although Omar would have liked to have all the member knights to gather for the escape, he realized that those members that were in the far reaches of France may not get the word quickly enough to meet here. "Not everyone can get here by the time we leave," he said.

"What do we tell them?" asked Baullier.

"Tell them to leave the country at once and make their way to the Templar lands in Scotland."

"Will they know where those lands are?" asked Landreau.

"Tell them go to Pitfundie in the sheriffdom of Nairnm, between Brodie on the East and Penick Map and the woods of Lochloy Map on the west," replied Omar. "They should be safe there. Advise them to stay there until someone comes for them. Also tell them that if they are captured, they will be tortured until they admit heresy and then they'll be burned at the stake. Philip is getting a reputation for that." He looked at the men nodding that they agreed with his assessment.

"It's no wonder the people are beginning to call him the Iron King instead of Philip the Fair," Baullier snarled.

"That settles it," said Omar. "We'll meet back here in six days' time. We all know who we need to contact to get the message out." As he spoke, the others began to move about collecting their coats. There was no time for idle talk; the meeting had lasted no longer than thirteen minutes before all four had mounted their horses and silently moved off into the night, each going a different direction. Each man rode from one contact to another, attempting to be as discreet as possible. As soon as a new connection had the word, he was off to spread the message to others. At the end of two days, the original four turned back toward the rendezvous spot, needing to be the first there in order to get preparations moving.

After six nights, the group began to gather, coming one or two at a time; each person that knocked was considered an enemy until he could prove his allegiance to the Order. Unlike other gatherings, there was no sign of casualness, as each face reflected a heightened sense of purpose. This was not a group that feared anything; however, they somehow knew that this could foreshadow a turn of fortunes for the Order. Coming from communities all over southwestern France, each man had established a reason for his extended absence from his workday. This gathering had to be kept a secret from King Philip and all his informers.

When it appeared that all were there, Omar called the meeting to order. "I am sure that most of you have heard what the King has planned for us. He is gathering his forces now and will torture and kill all knights that he can capture."

Gerard de Villiers yelled out, "Let him try—his men are no match for us!" There was a great murmuring of agreement in the group.

Omar replied, "I agree . . . as long as the numbers are close. But he is assembling an army to carry out his orders. The numbers will just be too great for us to survive. It is time we moved on. France is no longer our friend."

"Where will we go?" came from the back of the room.

Another shouted, "How long do we have?"

Omar replied to the second man, "We have only two weeks to make our escape. We have eighteen ships in port now that we can use. But we'll have to be careful; we can't let them know what we are doing."

"Just how are we supposed to do that? How can we keep it a secret that we are loading all the boats? Someone will see us and report us—and the King will attack earlier than expected." Master Jerar de Poitous asked the questions that many of them were thinking.

"We'll sleep and work normally during the daytime and load them during the nights. There shouldn't be anyone around in the dark; nevertheless, we'll post guards. If anyone sees us, his fate is sealed." Omar was definitely in charge of the meeting.

"Where will we go? You did not answer my question." It was Guillaume again.

Omar replied, "I will answer that in a minute. Any other questions?"

One of men from Marseille spoke up. "Are we going to split the treasure up or send it all to one place?"

"We'll put it all on the five boats we send to New Scotland. As you know, we have a place there where we have established a colony just as a precaution if this would happen. They should have a hiding place created for the treasure; we'll bury it there. Baulliere will go with me in that group. Other boats, we'll send to Scotland and England and set a time when we will all meet again. Landreau will lead the five boats to

England and Guillaume will take his group to Scotland. We have lands in those countries where we should be safe." He looked at Guillaume as he said this.

The rest of the meeting was taken up by planning how to secretly load the galleys and setting the timeline for the escape. The men were designated to twelve-man teams and each squad was assigned to a boat. It was almost daylight before they finished and they all lay down on straw to sleep.

The next two weeks were a flurry of activity—all at night. During the day, the men slept and took their turns at watch or work. They were all fit and they quickly gathered and loaded all they planned to take with them. Each day, they received updates on the king's armies; it seemed as if every man not with them had been drafted into service and they were coming from all of France to join the purge. On the night of Friday, October twelfth, the knights assembled for the last time.

It seemed as if someone were watching out for them as the fierce storm kept the night completely dark except for the occasional streak of lightening racing across the sky; the wet wind coming off the ocean was numbing, but they were happy for the storm, as no one would venture out during this type weather. The men were assigned ships and they quietly took their places. The only sounds heard were the shuffling of boots and hooves as they led their horses up the long gangways. They secured their mounts with the canvas slings that would protect them in rough and rolling seas. They used oars to quietly propel the boats away from the shore. As each ship unfurled its sails, every man stood on the deck shivering, watching the darkened shoreline disappear into the blackness. They would sail due east until they cleared the Ile de Re' and then turn north toward their destinations.

Omar stood beside his friend. Baullier raised his hand and pointed to the shore. "Will this be the last time we set foot on France?"

In the darkness, Baullier could not see Omar, who slowly nodded his head. "I am afraid it is. May God grant us safe journey."

Chapter 1
Nova Scotia—September, 2013

As I stepped onto the deck, Cyndi asked between sips of her coffee, "Did you have a good run?" Noticing the look on my face, she asked, "What's wrong?"

"We have to call the police," I replied. I sat down at my computer and began to look for the telephone number.

As I searched the local sites, she said, "Just dial 9-1-1."

"They have 9-1-1 here?" I asked.

"Of course; they're civilized." I know she had a smug grin even though I couldn't see it.

As I grabbed my cell phone and began to dial 9-1-1, Cyndi questioned me. "What happened?"

"I found a man dead on the shore."

"Did you recognize him? When do you think he drowned?" She fired questions at me before I could even answer the first. Even if she had waited for answers, I had none to offer her; I had no clue why the body was there. Did the boat really drop it or had it washed ashore during the storm yesterday and last night? It was not unusual for me to find objects along the cove following these late summer storms. But a body? That sure was a first! I quickly explained my discovery to the receptionist who answered the phone. She did not seem as excited about the body as I was but she said someone would be here shortly.

"I don't think he drowned; I believe he was murdered." I filled Cyndi in on the morning's events . . .

I love to work early in the morning, with just the darkness saturated with the pre-dawn fog. Waves crashing below—dew fresh on the grass. A cup of coffee and my computer. This day had begun just like all the others. The final draft was going well. My mind was clear and the early morning was so peaceful after last night's storm that I seemed almost one with the setting.

Suddenly, the silence was broken—but by what? I couldn't identify the sound, but I knew it was there. I looked at my monitor; it was not yet five-thirty and I knew my wife would not be up yet. I sat up straighter and listened. Nothing! I strained to hear anything unusual. *My book's getting to me*, I thought.

No, there it was again—just a slight sound that shouldn't be there; it was a deep bass and I could feel it more than I could actually hear it. I got up and went out on the deck. I felt the pressure on my leg and looked at Chelsea; she was growling low in her throat and the hair was standing along her neck as she pushed in closer to me. "What's going on, girl?" I scratched her ears as she continued to snarl.

Then, between the breaks of the waves, I made out the sound of a motor. Although it was just past idling, I could tell by the deep sound it made that it was a powerful engine. I willed my eyes to see into the still-blackened waters.

Finally. *There it is!* Just a ghostly shadow, a shade darker than the surrounding sea. I watched as it slowly inched out of the cove. *Why don't they have their running lights on?* I wondered.

I stood there quietly for some time, thinking. *Just looking for a nice fishing spot or a good place to camp,* I thought. However, I'm not sure that I believed that. The shadow of the boat that I saw did not really look like any of the local fishing vessels that worked out of these Canadian waters.

After a while, as the dark began to give way to the first light of the day, I went back inside. It was time for my daily run on the beach and as I put on my worn shoes, my mind continued to mull over the early morning visitors. I normally went for days on end without seeing another soul. The beach cottage here on the Nova Scotia shore was ideal for my work. Providing the quiet inspiration I needed for my writing, the cottage also offered me the satellite internet reception needed to let me keep in contact with the outside world; this is the only way that I could have hoped to continue teaching my online classes. We had been here for the past two months and I was almost through with what I hoped would be my final draft.

As I made my way down the winding steps to the sandy beach, Chelsea stayed close behind me. She enjoyed these early morning jaunts. She was almost ten years old now and although she was beginning to have some arthritis in her hips and back, the exercise was keeping her active; her buff color was beginning to mix with gray. She had more problems with skin allergy than anything else.

I paused at the bottom, looking around at the dunes and then out to the sea. Although there were clouds and dampness in the air from the thunderstorm, it was still among the most beautiful settings I had ever seen. During a vacation to the area a couple of years ago, my wife and I fell in love with the peaceful coast. Peggy's Cove and Lunenburg were postcard-perfect. We vowed then to return here one day. When we got a chance to rent the cottage on the eastern end of Lunenburg County, we jumped at the opportunity; although isolated in its own water inlet on Mahone Bay, it retained the idyllic setting of the coastal towns. I had a deadline for my new novel and needed some place quiet to complete it and I could not envision a more perfect setting. The owner was in Florida and would not return until the spring, so we could stay until then if we wanted to; however, our plans were to leave sometime before Thanksgiving.

I started my run, slowly working through the stiffness that age and sitting at a computer brought to me; the only sounds were the continuous breaking of the waves and the soft padding of the cocker spaniel following me. After about a mile, I turned around and began my jog to the other end of the cove; I made this five-mile jaunt at least five times a week and was in the best shape I had been in the last twenty years. The runs along the coast gave me time to reflect and freshen my mind. A little past the spot where I had begun my run, Chelsea began to snarl. I slowed and looked around. What I saw next completely shocked me.

It was a body and I knew immediately that it was dead. My mind flashed to the boat that had been there earlier—*was there a connection?* As I thought this, I involuntarily shuttered. While Chelsea shrank from me, I bent over the body to confirm what I first thought—he was dead! Being careful not to disturb the body or the area surrounding it, I backed quickly away and made my way back to the house.

We continued to discuss the finding while we waited for the sheriff. After about twenty minutes, I decided to go on back to the beach. This time, I left Chelsea at the house with Cyndi. Cyndi could not easily negotiate the steps down to the shoreline. After having her back surgeries, she was forced to enjoy the setting from the deck overlooking the cove. Standing on the sand at the bottom of the steps, I debated whether or not to wait for the sheriff there or go on to where I had seen the body. My curiosity won out and I moved off at a slow jog. I had told the sheriff how to get to my house and Cyndi would direct him how to find me when he arrived.

I had my iPhone and I began to take pictures of the body and the surroundings. And then it struck me. The body was more than half covered with sand. If the crew on the boat was responsible for it, they must have tried to conceal the body and had to leave before they finished. *I wonder what scared them away,* I thought as I moved back down the beach to meet the authorities.

"What's going on here?" The deep voice startled me and I jumped even though I could see two men moving cautiously toward me. "Are you the person who reported the body?"

Breathing a sigh of relief, I recognized the men approaching me. Although I did not personally know them, I had seen them when I visited the town. Holding out my hand, I said, "I'm Phil Kent and, yes, I am the one who called you."

"I'm Shaun Pfieffer and this is Jacque Roget. Let's look at that body?" As he grasped my hand, I sized him up. He was a big man—no, big was not the word. He was huge, about six and a half feet tall and must have weighed close to three hundred pounds. His short hair was just beginning to show signs of gray; dark eyes seemed to be looking right through me. The graying mustache and goatee provided an extra air of strength. Although he had a slight French accent, his English was good.

Jacque, however, was another story. He was of normal size and I could barely understand his broken English when he asked, "What are you doing on this beach and how did you find the body?" He looked at me suspiciously as he spoke.

I led them to the site and pointed at the man lying there. "He is dead—I confirmed that when I found him. Other than checking for a pulse, I touched nothing."

Shaun knelt to verify the man's death. "You're right— dead!" Looking at Jacque, he said, "Better call this in; get Locky down here. Every once in a while, someone will fall from a boat and wash ashore." As Jacque moved away from us and pulled his cell phone out, Pfieffer looked at me and said, "I'm the local sheriff. Tell me what you know."

"My wife and I are leasing the cottage up there. We've been here about two months now. I get up early every morning, work for a while, and then come down to the beach to get in my daily run. Chelsea—my dog— runs with me and she is the one that found the body." I explained the events to him and then remembered the visitors to the cove as Jacque rejoined us. "I don't know whether or not this has anything to do with the body, but there was a boat in here this morning. I was working on my computer about five-thirty and heard something. I went out to the deck and saw a boat. I barely could see its outline as it left the cove; it had no lights at all, not even running lights. I could tell it was a pretty big boat—probably about thirty feet; the motor sounded like one of those big, powerful engines even though the boat was slipping away at just above an idle."

"It looks like he has been here for several days as much as he is covered," Jacque said, pointing at the body.

"That's one of the strange things about it; I know it was not here yesterday morning or I would have spotted it. Maybe the people on the boat had started burying it in the sand and got scared away before they finished. I don't think the storm last night would have pushed it that far up the beach and covered it with that much sand."

As we talked, we were interrupted by a siren. "That'll be Locky," said Shaun. "He's the local medical examiner; you'll have to come down to the station and make a statement. Give us some time here and come to my office this afternoon. If I am not there, have Lucinda call me."

It was only about five minutes until a couple more men came shuffling across the sand. As one of them walked up to us, Pfieffer said, "Locky, this is Phil Kent—he is the one who found the body. Phil, this is Celip Locksmithe. He is the local coroner; everyone knows him as Locky."

Locky held out his hand and said, "I've heard about you; you're the writer who's staying in the Lecherman's house." Glancing at the other man who was now bending over the body, he asked, "What have we got here?"

I repeated my story to him as he looked closer at the corpse. "Do you recognize him?" He included both the sheriff and me in the question.

"I don't know him," I said.

The sheriff echoed my reply. "I don't think he is from around here," Pfieffer said. "I've never seen him. What do you think killed him?"

"I don't see anything obvious. I'll have to get him to the morgue—give me this afternoon to see if I can find anything." Turning to the other man, he said, "Andre, get the gurney to the top of the steps and bring us a body bag."

While Andre went to get them, Locky continued to inspect the body while he removed the sand that had half covered him. "Been here awhile, it looks like. It has taken several days to pile this much sand on him."

"That's a puzzle. Kent here says the body was not here yesterday morning. He was down here and would have seen it. We think that he was dropped off by some people in a boat this morning and they tried to bury him." I was glad to see that Pfieffer had bought into my theory that the early-morning callers were involved in this. The sheriff explained to Locky about the pre-dawn visit by the darkened boat. "I'll drop by the marina to see if there have been any strangers there. Surely someone around here would have noticed a power boat messing around these waters. Our fishermen keep a close watch on their fishing grounds. They talk to each other about any visitors." He looked at me intently when he said that and I knew what he meant.

Andre approached us with the body bag. I watched as the M.E. and Andre moved to the dead man. As they carefully brushed sand off of the body, Locky continued to inspect him, looking for anything that may give him a hint about the cause of death. Finally, they had the man completely free. Locky scanned him over again and then they carefully placed him into the body bag and zipped it up.

"Can you give us a hand with this?" asked Locky. He looked at the sheriff as he spoke. "He'll be heavy getting up the hill."

"I'll be back in a couple of minutes; don't disturb the scene here." I've watched enough crime series on television to know what he meant. I moved down the beach while I waited for the sheriff to return.

I watched as they carried the man up the hill. Although they were at one end of the body, Locky and Andre were straining to reach the top; Pfieffer, however, was by himself and looked as though he was transporting a rag doll. Officer Roget just followed them, offering no help. Once they reached the top, they placed the body on the gurney and Locky and Andre took over. The sheriff retrieved a roll of crime scene tape from his car and made his way back to me.

Pfieffer and his assistant walked around the area searching for clues, then he stretched the tape off between some stakes he carried and spoke to me. "If you see that boat again, give me a ring. My mobile number's on this card; call me any time—day or night. When you come down to the station today, we'll talk some more about this. I want to get down to the marina to check it out. I'll see you after a while." He looked around once more and moved to the steps. I followed him and he waited while I went to the house to get one of my cards. He got into the car with Roget and I watched them pull quickly away and then went back into the house.

"Well, what did you find out?" asked Cyndi.

"Really, not much of anything." I told her about the sheriff and the medical examiner and what they had said. "I have to go down to the sheriff's office this afternoon and make a statement. If you feel like going with me, after that, we'll go eat at that seafood place we like."

"A lobster sounds good; I'm ready for another one of them." She smiled as she remembered how tasty they were. "What time do you need to be there?"

"He said anytime this afternoon; I thought maybe about three o'clock would be good. That will give him time to go by the marina and talk to some folks about the boat I saw. Then we can probably make the Lobster Shack by four and beat the crowd. It's usually packed by five." Remembering the body, I pulled my iPhone out of my windbreaker. "Here are some pictures I took," handing her the phone. "They had been burying him in the sand, but stopped for some reason."

"We need to leave a few minutes early so we can drop Chelsea off at the vet's," Cyndi said. In all the excitement, I had forgotten that the vet needed to see Chelsea for her skin condition—the *Cocker Crud* was what our vet at home called it. Cyndi scrolled through the pictures; after only a couple of minutes, she exclaimed, "You know what this looks like, don't you?" I bent over to see what she meant. "See how the body is buried; look at what is not under the sand."

I stared at the picture; she scrolled to another. Finally, it hit me. "Of course! I see it now. That should have been obvious to me!"

CHAPTER 2

"Look at the one arm stretching toward the sky—the partially-buried face and body. Do you think that that's a coincidence? What about the one knee bent and the other hand showing? He even has a beard! He's a live— well, dead—replica of the sculpture in Washington. What's it called? We've seen it a number of times." I looked at Cyndi as she waited for a response.

Finally, I replied, "*The Awakening*—it's called *The Awakening*! It used to be out at that Point in Washington, but I believe it has been moved now. If we are right, somebody has gone to a lot of trouble to copy the statue. Look it up to be sure we are remembering it correctly."

I watched as Cyndi pulled the information on the Internet. "See, we are right—it looks just like it! Print a copy of it; I'll take it with me when I go see the sheriff this afternoon. I'll be interested to see if he thinks the way we do about it."

"The Point was Hains Point in Washington. The sculpture has been relocated to National Harbor in Prince George's County, Maryland. There is just too much similarity to be an coincidence," she said. I heard the printer click on and went to retrieve the picture.

"This is really strange. There may be more to this than someone being murdered in Nova Scotia. What do you think can be the connection? See if you can find any more information on the Web; I'm going to go back down to the beach and nose around some more."

"Be careful. Are the sheriff and deputy still there?"

"No; they looked around a little and then left. The sheriff wanted to get to the marina to check on the boat." Chelsea met me at the door as I moved away from Cyndi. I closed her in the house and made my way back down to the shoreline to search for anything that could help us solve the mystery. The sun was bright and high in the sky now, so it had gotten warmer. I started searching the sand, looking for something out of the ordinary. After a few minutes, I decided that I would put some structure to the search and laid the sand out into a grid. I moved slowly over each section without finding anything of value, mostly just broken sea shells and debris that had washed on the shore. Finally, nearing the end of the pattern, I saw something glint in the sun. Reaching down, I picked up a dull, round disc. I looked at it briefly and continued my search. Finding nothing more, I slowly made my way back to the house, my mind in a whirl.

"Did you find anything?" Cyndi questioned me as I entered the office where she still sat at the computer; even though the owner had a desktop sitting on the desk in the office, we used nothing but our laptop—well, our laptop and iPad. I moved to her and handed her the disc. She held it under the lamp and looked closely at it. "It looks like it has a figure on one side and writing on the other," she said, "but it's so dirty I can't make it out. Let's see if we can get it cleaned up some."

We went to the kitchen sink where she poured some dish detergent on it and used a small brush to scrub it under the warm water. It gradually became clean enough for us to see what was on it. "Look, the figure looks a lot like the sculpture!" She was excited as she pointed out the resemblance to me. She turned it over and looked at the writing. "It definitely looks like some type of letters or symbols, but I have no idea what language it's in."

I took the medallion from her and squinted to see the small letters. "I have to get my glasses to see anything here. Make a copy of both sides of it while I'm gone." I went to our bedroom where I kept my reading glasses. When I came back, Cyndi had made a copy of the coin, enlarging it so that we could better see what was on it. "You're right—the picture is a rough outline of the sculpture, not exactly the same, but it has a reclining figure on it. Turning it over, I looked at the writing and then at the copy. "I certainly don't recognize this script." Continuing to study the object, I said, "This looks really old—I think it's made of gold."

"You think everything you find is made from gold." She laughed and took the coin out of my hand. "If it is, it's old and has been treated roughly. You probably need to hand it over to the sheriff since there seems to be a connection to the body." She glanced at her watch and said, "We need to get ready if we are going to be there by three o'clock. Go ahead and feed Chelsea; it may be late before we get back home."

I stepped into the shower and gradually increased the hot water until the small shower filled with steam. Finally, I stepped out and dried off, then put on jeans and a light sweatshirt; the air would get cool after the sun dropped down tonight. I put dog food out, filled the water bowl, and called to Chelsea. I heard her finishing the food as we got ready. "Let's go out, girl." She came running—well, running as much as her arthritic hip would let her—and we went out, walking around to the back of the house. As she did her business, I looked over the cove below. *I wonder what is going to happen,* I thought as I remembered the boat and the body.

We collected Chelsea and my computer case and went to the Jeep. As we drove into Lunenburg, Cyndi and I continued to discuss the day's events. Neither of us noticed the car that pulled onto the highway behind us. We dropped Chelsea off at the vet's and told them we would be back for her after we ate. I parked the car in front of the sheriff's office and Cyndi said to me, "I'll stay in the car and read." She opened her iPad and leaned back into the seat; I always kidded her about her iPad and said it was her American Express card—

because she did not leave home without it. I entered the building and stopped in front of the desk there.

"Can I help you?" The question came from the young woman entering the room from the back hallway.

I looked at her bright blue eyes and smiled. "Yes, I'm Phil Kent. I . . ."

She interrupted me. "You're the person who found the body this morning. Sheriff Pfieffer said you would be by. I'm supposed to call him as soon as you get here." She picked up the mic and pushed the button. "Sheriff, Dr. Kent is here."

I heard the response, "Tell him I'll be there in five!"

"I'm Lucinda," she said. "Can I get you something to drink—coffee or bottled water? He's on his way."

I like coffee, but normally I don't drink too much in the afternoon, but after the day we'd had, I needed the caffeine, so it was coffee I requested. She left and came back after a couple of minutes.

"You look like a black coffee kind of guy," she said. "If you need cream or sweetener, there is some just inside that door.

"No, this is fine," I replied. I'll just sit here and wait for the sheriff. Lucinda sat down behind her desk and started looking through papers. I glanced at her and saw the resemblance. "Hmm," I thought. Within another five minutes, the sheriff burst through the door.

I held out my hand and he shook it again as I stood up. "Glad you could make it, Kent. I see you've met my niece; she volunteers as my receptionist when she's not in school. Let's go in back and talk."

I followed Pfieffer into his office, looked around and was pleasantly surprised at what I saw; it was not the typical small-town sheriff's office with government-issued furniture. The room was expertly decorated with an antique oak desk, old oak bookshelves, and a really old-looking oak filing cabinet. Opposed to the old classic look, there were a computer, a scanner, and a printer on the desk; there was even an interactive whiteboard on one wall. The room was painted in warm browns and had a nicely finished wainscoting of rich panels. The desk chair could have come from any fortune-five-hundred boardroom; the visitor's chairs were like those from the U.S. congressional offices. The floor was a polished hardwood. On the other walls were beautiful outdoor scenes captured by Ansel Adams. There was not one piece of paper out of place in the room. I am sure that the shock showed on my face as I stood and gaped at what I saw.

Pfieffer smiled at me. "You seem surprised at my office," he said as I tried to cover up my astonishment.

"It's beautiful," I replied. "I wasn't expecting this."

"You mean out here in the boondocks." He laughed heartily as he said it, showing that my reaction had not offended him. "I get that from most people who come into the office. My niece helped me decorate it; even I like fine things. Have a seat. Let's go over again what you know about finding the body this morning; don't leave out anything—even if you think it has nothing to do with the crime scene. And it is a crime scene! Locky said that there was evidence that the man was murdered. I'll tell you what he found out after we go over your story. I'll record what you say, print it out, and have you sign it."

I started again at the beginning, repeating everything that I could remember. He was especially interested in my account of the boat and asked several questions about it. I concluded with the story of the medallion. As I described finding it, I pulled it from my pocket and handed it to him.

"What are these markings on it?" he asked as he looked at the writing on the back of it. "Do you know what language this is?"

"No, I don't have any idea. I made a copy of it and Cyndi and I will try to determine that. I have a friend back in the States that may be able to help me with it. I think the coin is a really old gold piece. See the engraving on the other side. It is a rough sketch of the same pose of the body." I pulled the prints from my shirt pocket. "Look at these; this is a printout of a sculpture that is located close to Washington, D.C.; it is called *The Awakening*. I don't know the connection— if there is one—but the body seems a rough copy of the statue." I handed him the print. He looked at the picture of the body, the medallion, and the printouts.

"This gets stranger and stranger," said Pfieffer. "You're right, these all could be the same pose. As for the man, he was definitely murdered. There was a small-caliber bullet hole in the back of the head; he was executed. Locky estimated that the time of death was in the early hours this morning, which indicates that he was shot a short time before he was dropped off on your shore. There were no papers at all on him, nothing to identify him. Locky thinks he looks maybe Native American. The lab took tooth x-rays and sent them to the Canadian RCMP lab; the lab at Halifax was recently shut down and we have to now send them to Ottawa. If we don't get a hit there, we'll send them to the F.B.I. forensic lab and to Interpol."

"What about fingerprints?" I asked. "Did the lab send them also?"

"No, Locky could get no viable fingerprints? It seems like the ends of his fingers had been sanded smooth." As he spoke, he clicked the mouse a couple of times on his desk and the printer began to hum. Standing up, he retrieved the printouts and handed them to me. "Look at these, initial each page, then sign and date the last page. You won't be leaving in the next few days, will you? I may need to follow up with you if I think of anything else."

"No, we are planning to stay here for another few weeks at least," I replied. "We'll try to see if we can come up with anything else that can help you, especially translating the language on the coin. My friend may be able to help there. He's a language expert and teaches history at one of the colleges. He'll be interested in seeing this."

"Speaking of the coin, be careful. If the people on the boat realize that they lost it, they may come back looking for it. Of course, it could have come out of the pocket of the victim, but, since there was nothing else in his pockets, it doesn't seem likely they would have overlooked it. Do you have a weapon with you?" He reached for the signed statement and indicated that the meeting was over.

"I'll keep a lookout for them," I replied as I stood up. "And, yes, I have a handgun." I quickly added that I did have a carry permit issued in the States and that I was told that I could carry it legally if I filled out and had the form to bring in a restricted weapon here. I don't go anywhere without my Glock Nineteen. After years of not having a weapon of any kind in the house, I had bought it a couple of years ago and had completed the carry class before we went on our trip out west. "Could I get a copy of the statement?"

"Yes, of course." He moved to the all-in-one printer and placed the pages on the machine. In a matter of seconds, he handed me the copies.

"I'll let you know if I discover anything new. I'd like to be kept in the loop for what you find," I said, as we moved to the door. Passing through the front office, I caught the eye of Lucinda. "You did a great job decorating his office," I said. "You need to go into business."

"I'm majoring in interior decorating," she replied. "Thanks for the compliment."

I closed the door and joined Cyndi in our car. "Let's go eat," I said, as I closed the door and started the engine. As we went to the restaurant, I filled Cyndi in on the meeting.

Ye Olde Lobster Shack was reputed to be the best seafood restaurant in the Peggy's Cove area and was filled to capacity almost every day; even the locals dined there. When we arrived, there was already a waiting time of about thirty minutes. I gave them our name and Cyndi and I walked down to the shore. With temperatures in the upper seventies, it was a beautiful afternoon. We stood and watched the gulls follow the fishing boats as they began to return from the day's fishing. "I could get used to this really fast," I said, as we looked out at the tranquil scene. "We just need to retire here."

We heard our name called and walked back to the restaurant. I ordered giant crab legs and Cyndi ordered a lobster tail, both with a baked potato—loaded with bacon bits, butter, and chives. After getting our meal, we went out on the deck where we sat at a table overlooking the bay. I looked around at the people— there was not an empty chair in the place. The conversations were a mix of French and English and I thought that there were as many locals as tourists eating there. Tasting the food, I licked my lips and again said, "I could get used to this; we need to retire here." Cyndi just smiled, and, although I knew in her heart that she agreed with me, I also knew that we could never leave our small town in Tennessee. "Oh, well, we need to think about it," I sighed.

After eating, we walked around a bit, even going into a couple of the small stores located adjacent to the restaurant. Finally, moving back toward our car, I heard it first. Following the sound of the deep-throated engine, I looked to the bay to find the source. There was a thirty-five-foot cruiser idling along the same direction we were walking. As I looked at the boat, my eyes locked with those of the sinister-looking man standing on the bow; he was intently watching us and seemed interested in what we were doing. "Uh oh," I said to Cyndi. "Don't look now, but that is the boat; I'm sure of it." I looked at the lettering for the name on the boat and saw דיאָוואַקקענינג. "Look at the markings; is that the same type of letters on the medallion?" I moved behind a corner of a building and pulled my iPhone out. Accessing the camera, I zoomed to where I could get a good picture of the markings; I also snapped a couple of pictures of the boat. However, the man I had seen had disappeared.

I stepped back onto the walkway and looked around. Thirty yards away, a man quickly entered an open doorway and quietly watched them from the window as he talked on his phone. As they quickly walked to their car, he followed.

CHAPTER 3

"**A**re you sure he saw you?" asked Adar.

"Yes, I know he did," said Ahmud. "Hurry up and let's get to his house before he returns. It'll take him at least a half hour longer in his car." The boat cleared the speed-restricted area and began to accelerate. There were four men on board besides the driver and they huddled together and, even though no one could have heard them had they yelled, they talked in whispers—in a language most North Americans could not understand. As the boat entered the cove, the men pulled out the inflatable raft and triggered the pump. By the time the boat stopped a short distance from the shore, the inflatable was ready and was lowered quickly to the water. The men went single file down the steel ladder and within ten minutes had beached the craft on the shore and hurried up the steps to the house.

Adar pulled the tools from his pouch and within thirty seconds had the door open. As they entered the house, the men went different directions. "We have to hurry, so don't be concerned about getting everything back in its place. Just do your job and meet back here in fifteen minutes."

Adar looked around and spied the computer at the desk. Even though it was password protected, within three minutes after it had completed its boot sequence, he was examining the hard drive. "There's nothing here that I see," he said to no one in particular. He next looked at the history of Web searches and saw nothing that indicated the Kents had even accessed the Web. He turned the computer off and went to the bedroom where Ahmud and Juhall were going through drawers. They looked up and Juhall said, "Nothing. They must have it with them."

"Or they turned it over to the sheriff," spoke up Ahmud. "If he has it, that may be a problem."

Adar's phone vibrated and he answered it. "How long do we have?" He listened to the answer and ended the call.

He keyed the mic on his radio. "They left the restaurant and went to see the sheriff; I'm sure they told him about the boat. They should be here in about twenty-five minutes. Go back over every room—be sure that it is not here. We have another fifteen minutes."

Fifteen minutes later, they met back at the front door, all shaking their heads. Adar said, "We need to go; it must not be here. Everyone to the raft." They quickly exited the house and pulled the door closed behind them.

CHAPTER 4

"**I am sure that was the boat,**" I said to Pfieffer. After seeing the boat, we had immediately gone back to the sheriff's office. "The man definitely saw me looking at him. Before I could get a picture of him, he had disappeared. But I do have some pictures of the boat." As I spoke, I pulled my iPhone out and accessed the pictures. As I handed my phone to Pfieffer, Roget entered the room.

"What's going on?" the deputy asked, looking directly at me. "Has something else happened?"

"The Kents just saw the boat we've been looking for. In fact, he got some pictures of it and saw one of the men on board." Pfieffer dropped his eyes to the pictures. As he looked at them, he said, "Send these pictures to me. Some of the locals were talking about this boat. They seem to believe it is up to no good. It has been in and out of the dock area a few times in the last month—mostly late at night. No one has gotten off the boat to talk to anyone here; they haven't even had to gas up as far as I can tell. I appreciate you bringing this back by. I'll let you know if I find out anything else. You be careful; it sounds like they may know who you are."

We picked Chelsea up and went back to the cottage. As we crossed the porch, Chelsea began sniffing and became agitated. "What's wrong, girl? You excited about being back home?"

I opened the door and let Cyndi go first. She crossed to the bedroom and I heard her gasp, "Someone's been here!" I pulled the Glock from the holster inside my jeans and hurriedly crossed the room.

"Stay right here while I look around! I want to make sure no one is still here. Don't touch anything. I'll call the sheriff." I quickly went through the house, looking through all the closets and other possible hiding places. My mind was whirling now. *Yes, they definitely know who we are,* I thought and then wondered, *Are we safe here now?*

Within thirty minutes, Pfieffer and Roget were at the door. "I couldn't find anything missing," I said. "Things are just messed up—I think they were looking for something specific." I did not know if Pfieffer had discussed the coin with Roget or not, so I didn't say anything about it.

Roget spoke up, "They were probably just kids looking for money. We sometimes have break-ins like this. I'm sure it had nothing to do with the body you found."

I caught Pfieffer's eye as Roget said this. There was something there that indicated he did not believe what his deputy was saying. I made a mental note to ask him about this when we were alone.

"You are probably right," I said. "Nothing seems to be torn up or missing." We continued to discuss the case, but Roget would not leave Pfieffer's side so I had no chance to talk confidentially to him. "I'll let you know if anything else happens," I said to Pfieffer as the two officers left the house.

The next two days went by without incident and I was gradually beginning to get back into my routine. I heard nothing more from Pfieffer and saw no indication of the mysterious boat. I had talked to my college language expert and he had promised to call me as soon as he could find anything. Even though nothing else had happened, I still kept on high alert. I kept a magazine in my handgun and a cartridge in the chamber and I slept with it under my pillow—ready to fire! When I went for my morning run, I insisted that Cyndi keep the Glock by her side. She did not like this, but humored me in my request. We continually discussed the mystery and I knew that Cyndi was spending a lot of time on the computer; she was a glutton for information and did much of my research for me. As we sat down to lunch, my cell phone rang. Glancing at the caller ID, I said, "It's Bill Lander from the university—I hope he's found out something."

"Hello, Lander." I answered the call and placed him on speaker so that Cyndi could hear him. We both have known him for several years and we liked him and his wife, Lisa.

"Hey, Kent. Has anything else happened up there?"

"No, nothing. It's been quiet here for the last couple of days—well, we did have someone break in the house a couple of days ago, but they took nothing. I think they were looking for the coin. Were you able to get me any information about it?"

"Boy, you gave me a doozie! Without actually seeing the coin, I can only guess about it from pictures you sent me. I printed the file on my 3D printer. The language is an old form of Yiddish, I think. The closest translation I can get is that it means 'The Awakened' or maybe 'The Awakening'." You said you saw the same lettering on the boat. Does that make any sense to you?"

"The Awakening! That fits in with the other information we have. We think that the symbol on the back of the coin is a rough outline of the statue called *The Awakening*. The dead body was arranged in a way that seems to suggest that statue, also. What about the coin? Any ideas there?"

"I sure would like to see the real thing. Without it, I can't tell as much just from the plastic rendering I printed. Do you think the sheriff there would let you send it to me?"

"No, probably not—I'll ask him though. If he won't let me send it to you, how about a road trip up here? Don't you need a reason to take a short vacation? You can let your GA take your classes a few days, can't you? You always have a good graduate assistant.

Besides, isn't it about time for fall break? We have room here in the house—for Lisa, too, if she wants to come. You would enjoy this area; it's beautiful and you could even use the trip as a research project for your class. I know you teach North American Studies and all the folklore and legends related to the countries of the U.S., Mexico, and Canada. If the coin is as old as I think it is, you may get some new material for your course." I grinned as I added, "I'm sure your students would like that."

He laughed heartily at that. "You think my class is boring, huh? Actually, the trip is not a bad idea, although Lisa would not be able to join me; she's got that annual homecoming event to organize. You're staying on Mahone Bay, aren't you? There are a lot of stories about pirates and their hidden loot in that area of Nova Scotia. My accountant would like another deduction for this year. The sheriff there wouldn't resent me coming in and offering to help, would he?"

"No, I'm sure that he would appreciate any help he can get. But I'll feel him out about it and call you back. I need to check in with him anyway. You still have your passport, don't you?" I looked over at Cyndi as I spoke, "Also, bring your gun just in case, but be sure you fill out the paperwork for it."

"Yes, my passport is still valid. And, you know that I never go anywhere without my weapon. Besides, every time you call me for help, you get me involved in some dangerous mission. Sometimes, I don't think you know the difference in the fiction you write and your real life. Let me know what the sheriff says and I'll get started on getting ready on this end. I may even be able to get away by tomorrow morning," he said.

"You know you enjoy these adventures," I started saying as I heard him disconnect the call. My last novel had been set in the Anasazi Cave Dwellings in Mesa Verde, and Lander was right. I had called him for help there and we found ourselves in the middle of a major international story. *That was fun,* I thought as I remembered the treasure that was finally traced back to the ancient Incas in Peru. The Anasazi were part of the Pueblo tribes that emerged in the Four Corners area of the Western United States and then disappeared without any real indication of why.

"I'm going to run into town and talk with the sheriff," I said to Cyndi. "Do you want to go?"

"I don't think so; I'll just stay here and read. You won't be gone long, will you? Why don't you stop and pick us up some dinner? I'd like one of those good salads from the deli."

"Okay, that sounds good. I'll be back in a couple of hours. Keep the door locked while I'm gone. I'll take Chelsea out before I go," I said, as I snapped my fingers and opened the door. She came running—Chelsea, not Cyndi—and we walked out and she began her normal pattern: walking, sniffing, and squatting. She did this in sequence about three times and then moved to go back into the house. I gave her a goodie and said to Cyndi, "I'll see you in a little while."

I took the short ride to town in my Jeep and parked in front of the office. What Lander had told me about the coin sealed the connection between the coin, the body, and statue in my mind. Sheriff Pfieffer was just leaving, but when he spotted my car, he turned around and came back. "Let's go in," he said and turned to lead the way to his office. As we entered the lobby, I smiled at Lucinda and asked her how she was doing.

"I'm doing great. I've decided to take this semester off and stay to help Uncle Shaun. He doesn't like that, but I did agree to take a couple of classes online so I can get some credits. You gave him a mystery, but I think he is enjoying it; he was getting bored with nothing going on."

"Humph, I don't enjoy anything when someone is killed!"

"Did you get any information from the labs?" I asked as he handed me a cup of coffee.

"They were not able to identify the man; his fingers have been sanded, so there are no viable fingerprints to check against the ones on file. One of the locals did say that he looked like a person who has been nosing around Oak Island. There's always someone doing that—looking for the treasure that's supposed to be buried there. I'm going to run over there tomorrow to see if I can discover anything else about him if you want to go with me."

I filled him in on what Professor Lander had found out about the coin and told him that I had invited him to come up here. I had no doubt that Lander would know a lot about Oak Island and would jump at the chance to go there. "He could be here late tomorrow; could we delay going to the island until the next day?

Also, if you don't mind, could I take the coin with me so that he can see the original when he gets here?"

"Sure, that will be okay. You all meet me at the dock at eight o'clock that morning and we'll go see if this guy has been there. Oh, be sure to wear comfortable clothes—especially shoes. We'll be hiking over some rough terrain. I haven't got any additional information from any of the local fishermen. They don't seem to know what that boat has been doing around here; it's not been seen again since you saw it that afternoon. I've alerted the Coast Guard to be on the lookout for it. Maybe it's gone away. I hope so."

"Yeah, me, too. I'll see you in a couple of days," I said, as I got up and moved to the door. As I left the building, I passed Jacque Roget coming in. Although he spoke to me, I got the feeling that he still didn't like or trust me. "Oh, well," I thought. "He may just be a little jealous that the sheriff is including me in his investigation."

CHAPTER 5

It was just before eight when Lander and I parked my Jeep in the lot of the marina. I had picked him up at the airport at Halifax the afternoon before about five o'clock. When I showed him the coin, he was definitely intrigued. We spent much of the night discussing the mystery and I went back over all the events. I could tell he was excited and really liked the idea of taking a trip to Oak Island. We walked toward the docks and spotted Shaun already there.

"Shaun, this is Bill Lander. He is the college professor I talked with you about. Bill, meet the local sheriff, Shaun Pfieffer." Lander stuck out his hand and grasped the hand of Shaun. Although Bill was a big man, his hand was lost in that of the sheriff.

"Glad to meet you, Sheriff. What has Kent here gotten you into?" He smiled as he asked the question. "I have to watch him; he's got a knack for causing problems."

"I wish you had told me that two weeks ago—I might have thought of a reason to run him out of town. We haven't had anything exciting to happen around here in years. But now, I guess the town will have a way to see if I am worth the big bucks they pay me to man their office." I could tell immediately that Lander and the sheriff were going to enjoy working together.

I looked around and was glad that Roget was not anywhere in sight. Pfieffer seemed to read my mind and said, "I invited Deputy Roget to come along, but when he found out where we were going, he said he had something else he needed to do."

"Well, let's get with it," he said, as he stepped into the boat. "Oak Island's not far from here and will take us only about a half hour to get there if it stays calm." He started the boat and, as he spoke, he expertly guided the boat through the sheltered marina and out into the open water of Lunenburg Bay. Once clear, he gave the engine gas and we increased to a speed of about forty knots. Pfieffer navigated around East Point Island and turned north, easing into Mahone Bay. Off to the right, he pointed out Little Duck Island, then Hackman's Island off the coast to our left. Once into Mahone Bay, the sheriff again increased the speed. "We're in Mahone Bay now; there are about three hundred fifty islands here, so we'll stay toward the middle of the bay so we can make better time."

As we settled into our trip, Shaun gave us a brief lesson on the history of Oak Island. "Oak Island is a small island sitting just off the coast of the community of Western Shore. It is supposed to have a money pit on the island and people think that a pirate—maybe Captain Kidd—hid his treasure there. The first discovery of a possible site was in the late 1700s. We have had a lot of people who have tried to find the hidden treasure during the last two hundred years, but so far, no luck. There's been at least six men that have died looking for the treasure. Even President Franklin D. Roosevelt was reputed to have an early interest in the search. Still now, every couple of years, someone comes here with new-found information and wants permission to dig there."

"I'm sure that people cannot just land on the island and start digging, can they?" asked Lander.

"No, they can't. A person—or company—must go through the Nova Scotia Department of Natural Resources in order to get a permit—actually the registrar at the Registry of Mineral and Petroleum Titles. It's called the Oak Island Treasure Act or locally known as the Treasure Trove Act; the license fee is over six hundred dollars, so it's not cheap. One of the officers is going to meet us today and answer questions and give us a tour." As he said this, Lander's face lit up in anticipation for the session to come. I could tell that just this brief tour today made his trip north worthwhile.

We continued to talk about the island as Pfieffer steered the boat around some of the numerous islands that dotted Mahone Bay. He slowed and pointed us to one of the docks. "This is Oak Island Marina, even though it's on the coast of Western Shore. This is where we are meeting our guide. The land over there is

Oak Island; you can't tell it from here, but from the air it's shaped like a peanut."

As we stepped to the landing, a refined-looking man got out of a car and began walking toward us. "Are you Sheriff Pfieffer?" he asked, as he moved across the dock.

Pfieffer stuck his hand out as he replied, "Yes, you must be Thomas Lively. This is Phil Kent and Bill Lander. We certainly do appreciate your taking time to meet with us today."

"Glad to do it; it gives me an excuse to get out into this great weather. Let me get the cart; I'll be back in a minute." He turned and headed back to the shore. Walking up to a small building, he pulled from his pocket a key, opened the door, and disappeared from sight. We heard a motor start and then saw Lively emerge, driving a four-wheeler.

"This will help us get around the island," Lively said, as he braked in front of us. "It will carry the four of us comfortably—well, as comfortable as an all-terrain vehicle can be." We climbed into the Polaris four-seater, Lander and I in the back and Pfieffer rode shotgun.

"Before we begin, let me show you a picture." The sheriff pulled a printout from his pocket. "This is the man that was murdered that I spoke to you about. Someone told me he looked like a man who had been nosing around Oak Island."

Lively took the picture from Pfieffer and looked closely at it. "I've not seen him, but Flubert over at the diner usually sees anyone who stays for any length of time. I would check with him when we get back," he said, as he handed the photo back to the sheriff.

Lively steered to a small rutted, dirt road. "This is the causeway that was built to connect Oak Island to the mainland, but it is closed to the public." He drove across the road and inched up to a locked gate; stopping there, he handed a key to Pfieffer. "Let us in, then lock the gate behind us."

After the sheriff had secured the gate behind us, we set off on the overgrown trail heading toward the interior of the island. "Does anyone mind if I record our comments?" Lander asked. "I won't actually use the recording, but I would like to go back when I have time and make myself notes about the island; this trip will help liven my classes. I've heard that I need help there." He looked at me and smiled as he said that. We all assured him that we were okay with the recording.

"But I don't want to see us on YouTube," I said as we stopped in front of a stone plaque. On it was engraved:

OAK ISLAND MEMORIAL
1795—1995
IN MEMORY OF THOSE
WHO LOST THEIR LIVES
WHILE PURSUING THE
OAK ISLAND QUEST

The stone also included a rough outline of Oak Island and the list of the six people who have been killed trying to find the treasure; the first was an unknown from 1861. The next was M. Kaiser in March of 1897. The last four were all killed in August of 1965. Using his iPhone, Lander snapped a picture of the memorial.

Lively said, "You can see the names of the men who have died trying to find the treasure. There are rumors that there were several more, but we don't have proof of that. Though permits are required, I know that pretty often, someone sneaks on the island to search for the treasure. A few times, we have found abandoned boats and could find no one that may have driven them here. That's just helps to boost the mystery surrounding the area. Legend has it that seven people must die before someone can find the treasure."

"I hope none of us becomes the seventh," I grimaced as I replied.

Lively released the brake and we continued southeast from where we were. Although the trail was still faint, the trees and undergrowth were encroaching on the little-used tracks and we had to watch carefully so that an overhanging branch did not slap us in the face. The road was rough, but the four-wheeler was able to handle the hills and lower muddy areas with ease. I was glad that we were not walking the island. I looked at Lander and he was using his phone to get picture after picture; his face was animated and I could tell his mind was already working on a new syllabus for his class. We went about fifty-five yards and stopped in front of a rusty drill.

"This was one of the old mobile drills used on the island," Lively said. I stepped off the Polaris with

Lander and went with him to get his photos; the sheriff and Lively stayed with the four-wheeler. After we had resumed out seats, we continued, going now northwest for about a tenth of a kilometer. As we toured the island, Lively kept up a running conversation—well, commentary—about the land.

"There are all kinds of rumors and folklore concerning the treasure. Most of them concern buried treasure from pirates. There are tales of various bandits, but the most believable are those revolving around Captain Kidd. As you may already be aware, he was known to have sailed in and around these waters during the last part of his life."

Lander jumped into the conversation then and I could tell he had already done his homework on the legends of Oak Island. "Some think Captain Kidd buried treasure here in the 1600s. They base that on the fact that he supposedly hid his loot on an island east of New York. Put that together with the belief that there is treasure on Oak Island and you can see where they can make that jump. Others think that Blackbeard was the pirate who hid his treasure here. I don't know if I believe either one, but it makes for interesting reading—and discussion in class," he said with a chuckle.

The four-wheeler came to a stop as Lively said, "Just ahead is the site for another interesting discovery. It is where the hidden wharf was found. You probably want to know about it," he said as he looked at Lander. "We could have gone straight to the shaft, but I thought you would want to see the whole island."

Lander smiled and replied, "Yes, give us the whole tour."

I was enjoying this, too, but I knew that Lander and Lively were the ones who really were into the history and folklore of the island. To keep us moving, I asked Lively, "What is the significance of the hidden wharf?"

"Follow me and you can read the sign that explains it." He led us a short distance and pointed. According to the sign, the wharf was uncovered by Triton Alliance in 1972.

"Triton Alliance was formed by two men in 1967 and they bought most of the island in 1971. It is thought that the company found the hidden wharf here about three feet underground. As you can see from the sign, they discovered iron spikes dating back to the early 1700s and the remains of two leather shoes." Lively continued, "But the real contribution by the Triton Corporation concerns the excavations they carried out at the treasure pit. I'll tell you more about that as we continue to the site."

We looked at the sign that read:

HIDDEN WHARF.
THIS HIDDEN WHARF WAS UNCOVERED IN
1972 BY TRITON
ALLIANCE LTD. IT WAS BURIED ABOUT 3 FT.
BELOW THE
EXISTING BEACH. SPIKES IN IT ARE
WROUGHT IRON AND

**TESTED AS BEING MADE PRYOR TO 1750.
ABOUT 8 FT. BELOW
WAS FOUND TWO LEATHER SHOES, ONE OF
THEM MEASURING
OVER 12 INCHES LONG.**

He continued, "Many think that this is the location where the treasure was brought ashore. It is closer to the alleged burial spot than the other landing areas on the island. The water is deep from the edge of the land here so a boat could conceivably get all the way to a docking area here. That would certainly have made it easier to offload heavy chests." As he spoke, I imagined what the land would have looked like a hundred or more years ago; it probably wouldn't have changed much because it was mostly protected from heavy winds and seas here in the bay.

"Do you know any more about Triton?" asked Lander.

Lively started to reply, but the sheriff beat him to it, "Triton Alliance did a lot of exploring and searching here."

"You're right, Sheriff," said Lively. "Daniel Blankenship and David Tobias formed Triton Alliance. They were supposed to have dug a shaft of over two hundred feet deep and lowered a camera to a cave at the bottom of the shaft. Reports were that they could see some chests and some human remains, but the shaft collapsed before they could ever verify that. They subsequently dug another shaft, but then ran out of funds and were never able to complete the excavation; they eventually dissolved the partnership."

"Are they the first ones who made a real effort to get to the treasure?" asked Lander.

"No, there were earlier attempts." I could tell Lively was enjoying sharing his knowledge of the island as he continued. "Let me go back to the beginning. Daniel McInnes' family lived in Chester over on the mainland. When he was sixteen, he paddled over to Oak Island to hunt for game. While walking over the southeastern end of the island, he found a depression in the ground; above the twelve-foot-diameter depression, he saw an old ship's tackle block hanging from a sawed-off limb of an oak tree. This got him excited, because he had heard tales of hidden pirate treasure. Not far away was the port of La Have; this was supposed to have been a hideaway for pirates preying on New England shipping. The next day, Daniel returned with two of his friends, Tony Vaughn and Jack Smith. They began to dig in the depression area. Supposedly about ten feet down, they hit a platform of old oak logs. Just knowing that they were about to hit the jackpot, they kept digging. At twenty feet and then at thirty feet, they again hit oak platforms."

"How in the world did the boys dig that deep?" asked the sheriff.

Lively continued. "I'm not sure how they did it, but I would guess that they used a rope and bucket to lift the dirt from the hole after it was too deep for them to just shovel it out; they may have used the block and tackle to help them. Anyway, it was becoming too hard for them, so they went back to their homes and tried to get others to help, but they would not do it. It seems everyone was afraid to go on Oak Island—it was supposed to be haunted by two fishermen who disappeared there in the 1720s. So, for a while, the boys gave up the search. Later, McInnes and Smith settled on the island." As he said this, he pointed toward a spot ahead. "That's good timing; this is the old McInnes homestead. There's not much here anymore, but this is where Daniel lived until his death. He never gave up looking for the treasure. The rest of the story was outlined in a *Readers' Digest* article. Shortly after he moved here, McInnes and Smith joined up with a wealthy man named Simeon Lynds from Nova Scotia and they formed a treasure company."

As he continued with the story, we moved past the McInnes homestead. "With the money for equipment, they began digging in earnest. Again, every ten yards deep, they discovered oaken platforms. At about ninety feet down, they discovered several objects that gave them hope. The most important of those was a stone slab with symbols etched into it. Some cryptologists have interpreted those symbols to mean 'Ten feet below, two million pounds are buried.' Others claim that the inscription said forty feet below was the treasure. At any rate, at the end of the day, using a crowbar, five feet farther down, they struck something solid. This really got them excited as they thought they had found the treasure chest. Standing guard during the night, they prepared to tackle the final digging the next morning. But when they entered the shaft the next morning, they were devastated to find that their pit had sixty feet of water in it. For weeks, they tried bailing the water out, but it was fruitless; no matter how much water they took out, the water level remained the same."

"Was the water salt water?" asked Lander.

"Yes, it was," replied Lively.

"Then it may have been a "trap conduit" set so that when the digger got to a certain level, it would divert flood water from the sea and keep him from getting to the treasure," I spoke up. "I've read stories of these type of tactics devised to keep treasure hunters from getting to the hidden prize. What did they do?"

We began moving again, down an overgrown trail. Lively said, "This is thought to be the original road to the excavation site. Now, where was I in the story of the island?"

"You had just told us about the flooding of the shaft," Lander replied as he looked at Lively.

"Oh, that's right. My memory is not as good as it once was." Lively grinned as he said those words—but, looking at his face, I could tell he was in complete control of the story. "Different accounts give us contrasting stories about what has happened here, but they all come to the same conclusion. One story has McInnes and Lynds digging another shaft parallel to the first. Once they reached about the same depth, they began to dig connecting tunnels to the flooded shaft. About two feet away, the walls gave way and this tunnel was also flooded to the same level as the money pit. Out of funds now, they abandoned their search.

McInnes lived out the rest of his life on the island, a defeated man."

As the four-wheeler bounced along the rutted path and we dodged overhanging limbs, we reflected on the tale that Lively was spinning. Finally, Lander spoke up. "What's the rest of the story? I know that it didn't end with McInnes and Lynds."

"You are right," Lively continued. "There were different groups that attempted to salvage the operations during the last two hundred years. Even Franklin Roosevelt was said to have joined one of the groups—the Old Gold Salvage group—during the early 1900s. As I told you earlier, at least six men have died trying to locate the treasure, although I personally think there have been many more than that. The fact of the matter is that several people have gone missing in the area, but are not included in the death count simply because their bodies have not been found. Some believe that the flood waters were set up as booby traps for those who attempt to retrieve the buried riches. One of the groups supposedly inserted red dye into the shaft and found at least three outlets to the ocean around the island. That discovery lends support to the idea that a complex tunnel system was devised to get the treasure into the burial place and also gave an escape path if needed. Here we are at Smith's Cove," said Lively, stopping the all-terrain vehicle.

"What happened at Smith's Cove?" asked Lander. "Is this where one of the outlets to the sea was found?"

Pfieffer entered the conversation. "Isn't this one of the death sites?" he asked. "I seem to remember reading about some men who were killed here."

"Yes, you are both right," said Lively. Looking at the sheriff, he added, "A group was pumping water from a shaft here. One of them fell in when the edge he was standing on gave way. Others tried to pull him free, but they also perished in the attempt. The general feeling was that their deaths were caused by a combination of carbon monoxide, methane gas, and drowning. You can see the names and details on the sign just ahead." He alighted from the Polaris and we followed him to the wooden sign.

"Is this the main excavation area?" I asked, looking around.

"No, that will be our next stop," answered Lively. "It is about one-half kilometer inland from here. I suppose it is time to visit the main attraction. All this other is just to give you background information about the real quest on the island."

We all hurriedly returned to our seats in the all-terrain vehicle and Lively turned the vehicle around and we headed away from the sea. After a bumpy five minutes, he slowed and said, "I lied to you. There is one more place we need to stop before we get to the excavation site."

He drove up to a sign and stopped. We looked at the message on the sign. It gave some additional history about some of the excavation attempts. We read the sign, discussed its meaning, and again took off for the final goal. By this point, we were all eager to see what we had come to find. Rounding a curve, we came to a clearing with a fenced area and another sign that announced that we were at the "Money Pit Area." A somewhat circular wired fence surrounded a depression in the ground. Lively stopped the vehicle and we all got out, moving toward the sign.

"Stop!" cried Lively. "Someone's been here!" He pointed at the new mound of dirt to one side of the pit. "This is all new since about two weeks ago. I've not been here since then. Somebody's sneaking in here and doing their own prospecting."

"Maybe someone's gotten a permit to explore the pit," said Pfieffer.

"No, no. They let me know if anyone has gotten permission to even come on the island. No, these people are here illegally." Lively was looking agitated as he spoke.

We grew quiet and listened for any noise that would indicate we were not alone. "If anyone had been here, I'm sure they heard our motor and cleared out before we got here. There are four of us, so how about we each take a direction and see if we can find anything?" I said this while at the same time wondering if this was all connected to the body I found.

The sheriff spoke up, "Good idea. Let's look around, but don't touch anything. If you find anything that doesn't look old and rusted, give us a shout."

As we moved off in our separate directions, Lander looked at me and said, "You've done it again, haven't you?" Someone who did not know him would think he was criticizing me, but I knew the statement was meant as a compliment. He enjoyed these little escapades more than he would admit. They were a good balancing complement to his rather tame academic life. I knew how he felt because I harbored those same feelings— that in some small measure we were characters in a Cussler novel.

"What about snakes?" I asked the sheriff.

"There are no native venomous snakes in Nova Scotia," he said. "But keep an eye out—even a non-poisonous snake bite can hurt."

The search grew quiet for several minutes. Suddenly, Lander cried out, "Over here!" He waved his arms so we could all see where he was. We hurried to his side and he pointed to a tarp lying on the ground. "Something's covered up with this canvas," he said as he gestured to the camouflaged-colored tarp.

"You would have to be right on this to even see it," said Pfieffer. "Good job finding it!" He moved to a corner of the covering and lifted it, pulling it away from the equipment underneath.

"That's an auger," said Lively. "They use those to drill holes. This one can be connected to a motor and would give them a way to move a lot of dirt in a short time. In fact, some of the new-four wheelers have connections that would work with them; that saves having to drag a large motor in to power the auger.

"I've seen them attached to four-wheelers for ice-fishing. I guess they would work for drilling in the dirt, also." The sheriff scratched his head as he thought about this.

"Down here are some extension bars," Lander said. Holding up the other end of the canvas, he was looking at heavy extensions, each about six feet long. "Whoever these belong to are certainly serious about getting deep."

"I'll have the local sheriff come out here and confiscate this equipment; I'll make that call as soon as we get back. We'll shut this operation down immediately," said Lively. "Let's finish our search and get back to the mainland." Even though everyone was on heightened alert now, nothing else was found that indicated the illegal search. They met back at the fenced area.

"As you can tell—and as the sign says—this is the money pit area." We paused to read the information presented on the sign. "This is the spot where most of the island action has taken place over the years." Lively was not nearly as animated now that he was concerned about the intruders. Lander moved around taking his pictures and making notes on his smart phone; he was still excited about the trip out here.

We were all subdued on our trip back, each of us lost in his own thoughts. Lively paused at the spot where our boat was tied, let us off, and said, "Wait for me—I'll be right back after I return the four-wheeler." He zoomed off and was back within five minutes. He looked at the sheriff and pointed toward the main road. "Stop at the diner there and show them the picture. If that guy has been around here, someone there has probably seen him. I'm off to see the local sheriff."

We all thanked him for giving us the tour of the island and the information he supplied, then began to walk toward the diner. Pfieffer said, "We'll grab a bite to eat here and see if someone can help us with our body."

CHAPTER 6

We entered the restaurant and I looked around the dining room. It was just like many others that we all have eaten in—tables and booths spaced over the black and white tile floor. The walls had pictures and small items hanging on them; even though the walls could use a new coat of paint, they were a cheery yellow. But the thing that caught my eye first was the large fireplace in the side wall; it went from floor to ceiling and the small fire burning there now gave a welcoming touch to the diner and felt good under the slowly-turning fans spaced across the ceiling. Although there were only a couple of tables taken, we made our way to one of the booths at the back of the room; we had a lot to discuss and did not want others listening in.

"Welcome to Flubert's Diner," said the waitress almost before we were seated. "What can I get you to drink?"

The sheriff ordered coffee—black—and Lander asked for sweet tea; I ordered water. As the waitress left to get our drinks, Pfieffer said, "I'll be back in a minute. I'm going to see if someone recognizes our man here." As he spoke, he pulled the picture from his vest. We watched as he made his way to each of the people in the restaurant. The owner came out from the kitchen area and spoke to the sheriff, who then made his way back to our booth.

"They don't know who he is, but he did eat here a few times a couple of weeks ago; he was always alone and they never even saw him talking on his phone. He told them that he was up here to get information but he seemed really secretive about what it was. Of course, everyone assumed it had to do with the treasure on Oak Island; that is what almost everyone that comes here is after. But, listen to this. We are the second group that has asked about him."

"Let me guess," said Lander. "The other group was from that mysterious boat."

"Yes," said Pfieffer. "According to witnesses, there were at least four men on the boat; they all seemed to be Middle Easterners and spoke very little English and no French. They were trying to find him a week ago. The boat docked only that one time that the men came to the restaurant inquiring about our unidentified corpse. The owner did say that he had heard the boat a few other times, but it was always out of sight."

The waitress approached our table and began to set down plates of food. "I don't think these are ours—

we've not ordered yet," I said, as she placed one in front of me.

She just smiled and said, "These are yours—this is what you want." And turned and left.

We all looked at each other. "Well, I guess we might as well eat," said Pfieffer. He tasted his meal and smiled. "She is right—this is what I want."

The table fell silent as we all dug into our meals. I agreed with Pfieffer—the meal was excellent. After a short time of eating, we began to talk about what we had learned during the day. I knew Lander's day was worth the trip up here. He had enough new information to excite his students. As we talked, I noticed a solitary man enter the restaurant and talk with Flubert, who was now manning the cash register. Flubert pointed to our booth and the man came our way.

"Hello, are you the sheriff from over at Lunenburg?"

Pfieffer replied, "Yes, I am Shaun Pfieffer." He pointed at me, then Lander, and introduced us.

"I'm Pierre Balaquet. I own the marina and take visitors on cruises around the bay here. I understand that you were asking about a stranger that was seen around here a while back." Although his English was laced with a strong French accent, I could understand him clearly.

Pfieffer pulled the picture from his vest and held it out to Pierre. "This is the man; did you see him?"

"Yes, he was here. In fact, he hired me to show him around the islands."

"Did he give you a name? What else can you tell us about him?" The sheriff was excited as he talked.

"The name he gave me was Liam Foster. He said he was from Fond du Lac, Minnesota and was going to meet some others here this week. He had me take him all around the bay and islands, but he really was interested in Oak Island. I showed him the shoreline all around the island and where the protected bays are. He asked a lot of questions about the history of the area, especially the Oak Island treasure. It seemed like he knew what was on the island and I got the feeling he had been there, but I may be wrong about that. He could have gotten all that information from that Google, I guess. I was supposed to take him out again three days ago, but he never showed. Cost me a half-day wages as I turned down someone else." Balaquet frowned as he said this.

"Have you seen a large motor cruiser around in the last week or so?" I asked.

"Yes, I've seen it a couple of times, once when Foster was with me. There must have been at least four men on board because we saw three and there had to someone else piloting the boat. Foreigners—they were. May have been from the Middle East somewhere. The boat had a name, but I couldn't read it—looked more like symbols or chicken scratch than a real language to me."

I pulled my iPhone out and accessed the picture of the boat that I had taken. "Is this the boat?"

"Yes! That's it. And the name is the same. Foster got all excited and seemed scared when it looked like the boat was following us. But, after a few minutes, they left and I haven't seen them since. Foster calmed down after that, but he kept looking over his shoulder to see if it returned. He used his phone to call someone, but I couldn't tell what he was saying; he turned away from me and whispered to them. Why are you interested in the boat?"

Pfieffer looked at him, studying him for a moment before he answered. "Foster here was found shot dead on the shore of Mahone Bay. We think the people on the boat may know something about that. Can you think of anything else about Foster or the boat that may help us?"

Balaquet thought a minute before answering. "No, not off the top of my head. Wait, he did ask about renting a boat. He said he wanted to take his friends camping on one of the islands when they got here. He indicated that he could pay whatever it cost to rent one for a week or so. He also asked about buying a gun to protect themselves against bears, but I told him he could not do that here."

The sheriff handed him a card and said, "If you think of anything at all, call me. Or, if you see the boat again, let me know. Anytime, day or night." He shook his hand and said, "Thanks, you've been a great help already."

"Okay, I will. I'll keep my eyes open and ask around. The fishermen . . . "

I interrupted him. "Yes, we know. The fishermen keep tabs on strangers."

As Balaquet walked away, Lander looked at me. "What have you gotten us into?"

CHAPTER 7

Tetik slowly backed his Jeep Cherokee into the brush under the trees. Although he had a real name, no one he worked with knew it; he had been known as Tetik for the past twenty years. Tetik had earned the Slovak name for Trigger and he was proud of it. He stepped from the car and looked around. This was an isolated spot and, as he expected, he saw no one. Working quickly, he pulled his drag bag from the back of the Jeep and laid it carefully on the ground and began to place fallen limbs over his truck. When he was satisfied that it was well-hidden, he pulled on his outer layer of clothes, picked up his bag, and began the trek up the hill, staying off the trail and being careful to leave no tracks. With his camouflage, he knew he could virtually disappear at the first sound that he was not alone. Even though the hill was steep, he walked up it as easily as most of us stroll down the sidewalk; he spent two hours a day working out and worked under the assumption that his obsession with fitness could be the difference in a critical situation.

The sudden sound came through his ear bud. "They have arrived back at the dock; I expect that they all will go to Lively's office. You need to be ready!"

"I'm almost in position now," Tetik replied. As he spoke, he made his way up the last section of the hill, clicked his phone off, and looked around. This was the highest spot around that had a sight line to the building. The sun was dropping and shadows were beginning to stretch while the coming night began to spread a chill. He looked around and moved to a spot on a large flat rock under a tree; he had been here the day before and knew this was the ideal spot. Although it was thirteen hundred meters away from the kill zone, he could place his bullet in a man's eye from here. He quickly laid his equipment bag on the rock and opened it. From the top, he took out his shooter's pad and spread it on the rock. He removed the special built THOR M408 rifle and carefully laid it on the covering, then reached back in the bag. For a hefty fee, he had obtained the equipment from a source in Moscow and knew it could never be traced to him. He removed the scope caps from his telescopic sight, then reached back into the bag for the ammunition. The subsonic rounds were specially manufactured match-grade military class; he liked the boat-tail ammo for its superior ballistic performance. He loaded the seven-round box magazine and clicked the bolt action to chamber his first round. Reaching to the front barrel, he unfolded and locked the adjustable bipod. He lay down and balanced the bipod on the shooting mat. Fingering the dials at the side of the Nightforce scope, he checked distance and wind velocity. His rifle was zeroed with his scope at a thousand meters; he checked his book to see what adjustments of MOA he would need at thirteen hundred meters. MOA is Minute of Angle and is an adjustment either up or down or right or left for the distance beyond the point where his rifle was zeroed in at. With no wind today, the only MOA adjustment was for distance to take care of the drop of the bullet caused by gravity. This would be an easy shot for him. The built-in rifle flash-hider and sound suppressor would keep anyone from spotting the quick flash or hearing the sudden blast. Although he would leave nothing at the site, he used gloves for the entire operation. Supple enough to handle small objects, their pattern matched the camouflage in his suit. He powered up his phone, accessed the photos and stared at the faces on them. Only then did he look through the scope at his target area.

He was like most trained snipers—he could lie motionless for hours at a time, waiting for his target to appear.

After about thirty minutes, there was movement in his scope. He focused closely on the man that appeared, then relaxed; it was not one of his targets. There was not a sound or motion for another hour. Suddenly, he smiled; one of the men entered his sight. He looked carefully at the area around the man for the others, then focused back on him. He was alone, but it was the primary one he was looking for; he felt no anxiety and would have killed them all had they been there. He knew exactly where he wanted his target to be. He looked around, making sure no one had come up the hill in the last few minutes. Seeing no one, he took three deep breaths, placed the cross hairs on his target, expelled his breath, and slowed his heart rate. He slowly squeezed the trigger. There was a slight sound and the rifle gave the kick he was expecting. The recoil was straight back to his shoulder through the butt plate and he kept the scope keyed on his target. Even after the shot broke, he sustained the squeeze to the rear; he knew the steady follow through was critical to a clean kill shot. He continued to look through the eyepiece and decided a second shot was not necessary.

The sniper easily moved to his feet and effortlessly broke down his equipment and stored it in his bag. Even though he knew he would find nothing, he looked around once more, then began the quick hike down the hillside to the spot where he had concealed his car. At the bottom of the hill, he stayed in the trees and completed a circle around the vehicle, looking for anyone who had trailed him here. He saw no one and approached the hiding place. Removing the limbs that had concealed his car, he opened the rear, stored the equipment bag, removed his top layer of camouflage, and placed it into the suitcase lying there. He closed the truck and got into the Jeep Cherokee. He felt no regret for his actions—it was just another day on the job for him, one like the many others that had come before. Half his fee had already been placed in his offshore account and he knew the rest would be there by the next day. By that time, he would have been secreted out of the country.

Easing through the rough fire trail, he punched the contact on his phone. "It is done! The primary target has been eliminated." He listened for a moment, then turned off the phone. The GPS had already been deactivated. When he went by the alpine lake, he tossed the throwaway phone into the water. Only then did he remove his gloves.

CHAPTER 8

We left the diner, full from the good meal—and even more full of thoughts of the mystery that seemed to be growing by the day. Making our way back to the boat, we were quiet as we reflected on what we had learned.

The sheriff spoke up as he steered the boat slowly through the docking area. "At least we have a name now. That should help us—if that is his real name and he is from Minnesota. What was the name of the city Balaquet said he was from?"

"He said Fonda Lake, I think," I replied.

Lander corrected me, "It was Fond du Lac. It is north of Minneapolis near Duluth if I remember my geography; that is an Indian reservation, a band of the Chippewa. The Ojibwa have an excellent community college there. I went there to help them open the new library they built with federal grants. The architecture is beautiful; most buildings are designed to represent a huge bear paw, with some in the shape of drums. They are really proactive in establishing leading-edge technology to help their community."

I stared at him. "How do you remember all these facts about places you hardly know?"

He just shrugged his shoulders and looked at me with that silly grin. "One of my classes focuses on Native Americans and their contributions to North American folklore. That is one of the places that my class has a video-conference with; we have a virtual tour of their reservation."

The sheriff spoke up. "Let's decide on our next steps. We need a plan going forward. Lander, continue to find out what you can about the coin and what the language is. That may help us if we can translate the words and symbols—or even decide where it's from. Kent, why don't you research the meaning behind the way the body was arranged, if we can agree that it did not happen randomly; there may be more there than meets the eye. I'll touch base with officials in Fond du Lac to see what I can find out about Foster. Lander, I may need your help there since you have contacts with people on the reservation. Check with them about Foster; who his friends are and what they may have been planning."

"Sounds like a plan to me," I said, as Pfieffer guided the boat around the next island.

CHAPTER 9

"**T**he target is approaching!" The voice **was** excited as Adar listened on his phone. "They should be around the island in about five minutes."

Adar turned to his companions and asked, "Is everything in place? Do you have the flashbang grenades?"

Ahmud answered, "Yes, we are ready for them. I will be happy to get them, how you say, taking care of?"

"Taken care of," corrected Adar. "Get to your assignments. Falad, keep the boat hidden until I give the word."

Shortly, they heard the sound of the motor. Adar looked at Falad. "Keep back until they round the island and have their back to us. I'll tell you when to go." As he spoke, Adar's face became animated as it always did when he was about to kill. He watched as Pfieffer's boat rounded the tip of the island, then accelerate as it entered the deeper waters of the bay.

"Now! But easy. Get behind them!" Adar's commands were instantly carried out. Their large cruiser began to ease up behind the target. The occupants of the other boat had not yet detected that they were now being followed. When they were about twenty yards behind the boat, Adar yelled, "Gun it, try to swamp them." As he spoke, he placed an M84 stun grenade in each hand. On the other side of the boat, Ahmud lifted his assault rifle.

With a great roar, the powerful cruiser began to close the distance quickly.

CHAPTER 10

Pfieffer kept a loose hand on the throttle of the boat as we continued to discuss plans. Though the boat could go faster, he kept it a speed that would allow us to hear each other.

"I will get Cyndi to help. . ." I stopped in mid-sentence. I turned as my mind registered the low roar from behind us. "Uh oh," I cried. "We have company!" I knew before I saw the big cruiser that it was the same one that we had been watching for.

"Can we outrun it?" asked Lander, as Pfieffer pushed the throttle forward. The little boat immediately responded with a burst of speed.

"No way," I said. "Get ready to get wet. Dive deep and try to keep our boat between us and them. We need to get to shore if we can." As I spoke, the cruiser aimed right for us. I saw one man lift the assault rifle and another raised his arm. Pfieffer was seeing the same thing I was and he suddenly jammed the throttle closed as he spun the boat.

"Now!" he yelled as Adar's arm began to move forward. We all hit the water just as the grenade landed in the boat. Even under water, the flashbang explosion felt like I had been kicked in both ear drums.

I forced myself even deeper as I heard the rat-tat-tat of the assault rifle. It was being shot in bursts of three rounds each. I stayed down as long as I could. With my lungs on fire, I had to get to the surface even though I could tell that our assassins were circling our boat. Looking up, I saw our overturned craft. "That may work," I thought. I saw Lander and Pfieffer and motioned for them to follow me. We surfaced underneath our boat and gulped for air.

"Are you all right?" I asked. "Did anyone get hit?"

Lander looked shaken, but he said, "No, I'm okay."

I looked at Pfieffer. He had been the last one out of the boat. I could see a trail of blood down his left arm. He looked at it and said, "I took a shot to my shoulder, but I think it only grazed it."

Lander pulled off his shirt, wrapped it around Pfieffer's shoulder, and pulled it tight. "That should stop the bleeding for now. How are we going to get out of this?"

"We have plenty of air for now—just stay put for a while. Maybe they will think we have drowned and leave. If you hear them approach, dive again. Those bullets will go right through the hull of this boat."

"Too bad we don't have a water-proof mobile phone," said Pfieffer.

"But I do!" I cried, as I pulled the iPhone from my pocket. "The new case is water- and shock-proof." I hit the button to activate it and handed it to the sheriff.

Lander looked at me and I read his mind, "Don't say it," I said.

The sheriff made his call, clicked the phone off, and handed it back to me. "Lucinda will call the Coast Guard. They have a search and rescue center close by here at Mahone Bay. She will let them know that there may be possible trouble as they approach. We'll stay here under the boat until they get here; as they approach, they will call your cell phone to identify themselves. Lucinda will give them your number."

"Sounds like a plan," Lander said. "Do you still hear the boat that attacked us?"

We all grew quiet as we listened for the deep-throated cruiser. "I think I may hear them—but off at a distance," I replied. "I'll surface on the far side of our boat and see if I can spot them."

I ducked under the water and came up outside the hull of the boat. Pulling myself toward the bow, I looked around it. I spotted the boat, still circling at a distance to our overturned craft. Quickly diving, I emerged under the boat again. "They are still here, looking for us," I said. "We need to stay hidden until the Coast Guard gets here."

Pfieffer said, "It shouldn't take them long. They have a crew always on call. It is made up of seasoned veterans, but also provides summer work for interns from local colleges who may want to make a career out of the CCG; Lucinda worked with them one summer before she decided to go into interior decorating. This branch of the Canadian Coast Guard is known as the Inshore Rescue Boat Service (IRB Service). There may or may not be an armed helicopter at the center. We don't have much occasion for armed conflict in this area of Canada."

We continued to float quietly underneath the boat for about fifteen minutes. We could hear our attackers as their boat continued to circle the nearby waters. Suddenly my phone rang and all of us jumped. I looked at the caller ID display and handed it back to the sheriff. He answered and brought the caller up to date on what had happened. He ended the call and handed the phone to me.

"They will be here in about seven minutes. We should be able to hear them as they approach. They will make sure the other boat is gone before they approach us."

After about five minutes, we heard the attack boat gun its engines and move off in the opposite direction. Gradually the sound of sirens grew louder and we ventured out of our hiding place. The cruiser was nowhere in sight. We waved our arms to get the attention of our rescuers. The red and white colors of the CCG approached, engines were set to idle, and the crew lowered a ladder so that we could get into the boat. One of them was waiting with a first-aid kit; he looked at the sheriff, and said, "I'm Bear. Lucinda said you were shot, but not serious. Let's take a look at that wound."

Pfieffer replied, "It's not bad—it just grazed me is all." He removed Lander's shirt and Bear explored the injured shoulder. Pfieffer flinched as Bear squeezed the deepest part of the gash.

"It looks pretty clean. Let's get some of the antibiotic on it and get you to a hospital." As he spoke, Bear looked at the pilot and told him to get us to shore as quickly as possible.

"I don't need to go to the hospital," said Pfieffer. "It's not too deep and has already stopped bleeding."

Bear replied, "Yes, you are going to the hospital. You have been floating in the water for some time now; no telling what's gotten into your wound. You'll need a shot and antibiotics. Tell us what happened—and start at the beginning."

As we bounced across the waves, we told the story from the point when I found the body. This was the first action they had seen for a long while now and they were completely absorbed in the tale. When we finished, Bear asked, "Can you describe the boat?"

"I can do better than that," I replied. I pulled my phone from my pocket and accessed the photos. Handing the phone to Bear, I said, "This is the boat. It seems to disappear almost at will." Bear got up and went to his radio. After a couple of minutes, he put the mic down and came back to us and handed me my phone. "I've called in a description of the boat and requested that we get a helicopter up here. We also need to get someone to tow your boat in. It looks pretty torn up. We'll get it to our station—we'll want to look it over anyway to see if we can tell anything from the gunshots or explosives that would help us ID the suspects."

As the boat pulled into the dock, a Jeep Grand Cherokee skidded to a stop close by. "Let's get you to the car," said Bear. "Seal is the driver and will get you all to the hospital. The helicopter should be here in another hour or so and we'll get started looking for that boat. I'll let you know if we find them."

We all shook Bear's hand and saluted the rest of the crew. "Thanks for the rescue. I think that the killers would have just waited us out if you had not shown up."

We introduced ourselves to Seal and got seated in the car. I looked at Seal and said, "Bear and Seal; does everyone have an animal name?"

Seal smiled and said, "No, not until they have proved themselves. At that point, they adopt the name of an animal or fish—preferably one that is known for its strength and cunning. Once a CG worker has earned that nickname, he or she becomes one of us. And, as Pfieffer knows, yes, we do have females in the CG."

The sheriff replied, "That's right; Lucinda earned hers—she was Dolphin. She wanted to be known as a friend and help to mankind."

We had been operating on adrenalin and as it began to wear off, I realized that I was tired. I lay my head back and before I knew it, Lander was shaking me and said, "Let's go; we're at the hospital."

We thanked Seal and slowly entered the hospital.

CHAPTER 11

Since our boat had been destroyed, Pfieffer had to call Roget to come get us. The sheriff had his wound taken care of; although the bullet had not gone deep, it had created a long gash as it grazed his shoulder and it took eighteen stitches to close it completely. We left the hospital and walked back to the shoreline. We sat down on a bench and discussed the case while we waited for the deputy to get there. As we talked, we saw Bear approaching the dock in his boat. He stepped ashore almost before the boat stopped and looked at us.

"I'm glad you are alright," he said. "Have you heard about Lively?"

We all looked at each other. "No, what happened?"

"He was shot after he left you. One shot to the head from a high-powered rifle; he was dead before he hit the ground," replied Bear.

"This has gotten serious, I think," said the sheriff. "Maybe you all need to leave for a while. I'm worried that they may come after you next."

Lander looked at me and said, "What have you gotten us into?"

But I could tell from his glance that he was not wanting to run back home. "I don't think we will be leaving soon," I said. "We want to help you close this down."

Although it was not the answer Pfieffer expected to hear, I could tell he was glad we were going to stay. "In that case, don't go anywhere without your weapons," he said.

Bear said, "I've requested extra help from the Coast Guard. In addition, we are getting assistance from the Canadian Security Intelligence Service; it is the closest organization to your FBI. The Atlantic Region has offices in Halifax and they are sending a task force down here. The CSIS mainly collects and analyzes internal threats. We are also getting assistance from RCMP; the Mounted Police Security Service will help with the physical investigation. This has become a major threat and we need to do what it takes to stop it now. The Lieutenant Governor has issued a statement to the media and he has let us know that we will have whatever resources we need to neutralize this threat. We are having a combined task force meeting tomorrow afternoon at the town hall building. I would like you all to join us if possible; the meeting is scheduled for three-thirty."

"I'll be here," said the sheriff, looking at us. Seeing us shake our heads, he corrected that, "We'll be here unless something else happens."

After Bear left, Pfieffer said, "We need to talk. You two are not normal college professors. Teachers don't go around looking for trouble. What is your background?"

I smiled as I replied. "We go back a long way. We were friends and played basketball together in college. After college, we kept in touch. Lander here joined the service and was in Special Forces. He retired ten years ago, moved back to my home town, and began teaching. For the last eight years, he has been training me in survival and assault tactics; we spend at least a week in the woods every year with all our weapons. He's taught me to use high-powered rifles, shotguns, handguns, and knives; we can survive for weeks in the woods. We even don disguises and walk around campus without being recognized. The background helps me in my writing—it's also fun getting out in the wilds. A couple of times, it has come in handy as we have gotten into some dangerous situations."

"Like last year in Colorado," Lander said. "That was fun!"

"Yeah, it was a ball—now that we can look back on it—especially when we were chased to the edge of the cliff. But that's a story for a different time," I said, as I looked at the sheriff.

Hearing a car approach, he recognized Roget and said, "Here's our ride."

CHAPTER 12

Falad steered the cruiser around the nearby island as they accelerated away from the sirens. "They must be dead," said Ahmud. "They could not stay underwater that long."

"I would still feel better about it if I had seen the bodies," replied Adar.

"Maybe the sharks got them," said Falad. "I have heard they like the meat of the Americans."

Adar just stared at him for several seconds and then said, "We need to get off the bay and to our hiding spot as quickly as we can. Tetik called and Lively has been eliminated. I need to check in." He moved away from the others and accessed his contact list.

Adar spoke quietly into the phone. "Lively has been taken care of. We swamped the boat with the sheriff and two Americans in it. We could not find the bodies, but they have to be dead. We circled the overturned boat for thirty minutes and they did not surface." He listened for a minute and then answered. "We were too far out into the bay for them to have gotten to one of the islands. Someone must have seen the attack because the Coast Guard showed up, so we had to get away. We are on the way back to our safe spot now. Everything is in place to begin moving the treasure."

He ended the call as the boat turned into an inlet on one of the small islands close to Oak Island. Falad expertly idled up to the shore line and cut the engine as Ahmud tied the boat off. Adar moved to the electronic pad, clicked a couple of buttons . . . and the boat disappeared.

CHAPTER 13

When Bill and I got home, Cyndi wanted to know everything that had happened; we had called her after we left the sheriff and she had coffee ready for us when we arrived. Our clothes were still wet and we looked like we had been in a shark fight. "The first thing we are going to do is get a shower and change clothes," I said. Bill went toward the guest bathroom and I moved to ours. I let the hot water pull the soreness out of my muscles and stayed there until it began to get cool. I dried off and put on fresh clothes and felt almost human again. Moving back to the den, I met Bill. We all sat down and discussed the day's events with Cyndi. She became concerned when we told her Lively had been shot and we had been shot at, but this was not the first time she had heard of our dangerous exploits. Bill and I had agreed to meet Sheriff Pfieffer the next day for lunch; we would discuss our strategy and then take a car to the task force meeting at three-thirty in Chester. But we had a lot of research to do before that meeting tomorrow. Both Lander and I got our weapons and made sure that they were loaded.

I looked at Cyndi and asked her to continue to explore *The Awakening* statue angle. She was good at looking at a lot of information on the Internet and quickly discriminating among the many linked pathways to curate the pertinent information we would need. We then got to work, each of us concentrating our energies on a piece of the puzzle. Lander said he would continue to look for the origin and meaning of the mysterious coin. He also agreed that he would talk with his contacts in Fond du Lac; we both felt like there was a connection there that could help us.

"Speak up if you find anything interesting," I said to both of them. I took my laptop and sat down in my chair overlooking the bay. Since Cyndi was investigating the body-position clue, I decided to focus on the history of Oak Island and the possible treasures located there. Although I had already done a lot of it, I wanted to see if there could be further connections to the Middle Eastern men that were here.

But, as usual, when I opened my laptop and turned it on, Chelsea came to me and began scratching at my legs. "Okay, Chelsea . . . I'm taking the dog out," I announced to Cyndi and Bill, as I stood up and went to retrieve her leash. After I opened the door, I looked all around before leading Chelsea out to do her business. I was back in the house in about five minutes, grabbed my coffee, and placed it in the microwave to reheat it. I again sat down to begin my work.

It got quiet as we all were concentrating on our tasks. I found nothing that connected the Nova Scotia treasure to the Middle East. After about forty-five minutes, Cyndi said, "Hey, guys, come look at this."

Bill and I moved over to the chair where Cyndi was working. "What did you find?" asked Bill.

Cyndi replied, "This may not mean anything, but it sure is interesting. It may just be a coincidence." But we all felt the same way: most coincidences were not coincidences.

"Did you see a connection with the body arrangement?" I asked.

"No, but I did find out that it has happened other places besides here in Nova Scotia."

"What do you mean?" I said, as I looked at her.

Cyndi got up and moved to the wireless printer that was now churning out some pages of ink. She collected them and came back to us. "Look at these news reports," she said as she handed some pages to each of us.

We got quiet as Bill and I scanned the articles. Bill looked up and replied, "This can't be just coincidental. They are too much alike to be random. There was a body found in Washington, another one in Jerusalem, and another in Montreal. They were all found on the same day as the one Phil discovered here; the descriptions of the bodies could all have been describing the man Phil found here."

"My other reports are the same; only the bodies found were from other places: the coast of Southern England and Paris," she said. "I'm printing these others also."

I continued staring at the pages while my mind was trying to make sense of the whole thing. "Cyndi, see if you can find us a name we can talk to about these murders."

"I've already sent inquiries," she smiled as she replied. As usual, she was one step ahead of me. I could read her mind—she didn't have to say it this time.

While we were together, I told them I had not found anything new. Bill was still trying to get information about the coin. He did say, "I've sent messages to my contacts at Fond du Lac to see if they can tell me anything about Foster. I will probably hear from them after classes there are over for the day."

We went back to our respective searches. I began reading again. There were seemingly thousands of links to hidden treasure on Oak Island and I saved the ones to my Favorites that were most likely to help. Occasionally, I would see one that seemed more interesting and I stopped to read it; however, like most Internet searches, I had to keep my focus on the main topic or I would get off on multiple rabbit trails that led off on unrelated tangents. That is both the strength and the weakness of a Google search. Although I saw some links to alleged treasure being buried there by other groups, I kept my search to those that pointed to buried pirate treasure. Most of the articles repeated information about the history of Oak Island and the events with which we were already aware.

It was getting late and we were becoming tired. Just as I was shutting down my laptop, I heard a phone ring. I looked up as Bill put his phone to his ear. Watching him, I could tell he was excited about what he was hearing. After a minute, he tapped his phone and put it back in his pocket.

"That was a call from Jack Lauftis, a friend at Fond du Lac. He is a professor at the college. It seems as if there have been some developments there that may play into our case here. He said that there are several locals that I need to talk with, but that they probably would not talk to a stranger over the phone. I think I am going to take a quick trip to see them. We have the meeting tomorrow over at Chester, so I could catch a flight after the meeting. Would you want to go with me?" he asked as he looked at me. "We can get a flight out of Halifax tomorrow night, be in Fond du Lac by morning, get our information hopefully in one day, and fly back either that night or the next morning. Jack can shake loose to pick us up in Duluth and drive us to talk to those that he said we need to meet with. Just another day at the job!"

"I can probably do that," I said as I looked to Cyndi.

She replied, "Go ahead and go. Maybe I can get something done here without you all around." I looked for a smile with that statement, but she held it in.

Bill said, "I'll call him back and tell him it's a go. We need to get on the Internet and make reservations. That shouldn't be a problem in the middle of the week." As he spoke, he pulled out his phone and began tapping keys.

CHAPTER 14

The next morning dawned bright and pretty, with just a little fog hanging over the bay. Bill and I went for our morning workout; Chelsea took the day off. At the end of the five miles, we both had worked up a good sweat and walked for a distance to cool down. Then we climbed the steps to the house and took our showers—in separate bathrooms. We selected our Keurig coffees and waited while our mugs were filled, then sat down to a breakfast of bacon, eggs, and toast. We let Cyndi join us for the meal. Actually, she cooked it, so I guess I should say she let us join her for breakfast.

We were going to meet Sheriff Pfieffer at twelve o'clock for lunch and then go to the meeting with him. We had reservations for our flight at eleven-forty tonight; the redeye would get us to Duluth at five-fifty their time tomorrow morning.

After breakfast, we sat down to our computers and continued our search for answers. Cyndi had gotten two responses from the authorities at the sites around the world that seemed like they may have connections to our murder here. That information seemed to confirm that it was a widespread operation. I think she may have been the first to connect the dots.

I continued to find a lot of information on the Internet about Oak Island. Most of the articles connected the alleged treasure to pirates, but occasionally I found a possible trail to other groups. Although I kept my focus on a pirate origin, I did print out some of the more interesting ones from other sources.

Bill spoke up. "I wonder if Sheriff Pfieffer would let us take the coin with us. One of my friends there could analyze it and let us know its composition and how old it is. Without knowing those facts, it will be difficult to trace its origin."

"He may let us take it. I think he trusts us now and is really glad we are trying to help him. We'll ask him when we meet him in a while." I looked over at him as I responded. "I'm beginning to think this is an international mystery and not just a local incident."

At eleven-fifty, we pulled into a parking spot at the diner. I looked around and spied the sheriff's car. "He's already here."

We walked into the restaurant and the person at the cash register made eye contact. "Are you meeting with the sheriff?"

"Yes, we are," I replied.

"He is in the back room. He asked to be seated where you all could talk." She pointed toward a door at the rear of the dining room. "I'll get someone back there to take your orders. Do you both want coffee?"

We nodded our heads. "Yes, please."

We entered the room and moved to seats across from Pfieffer. "How are you today, Sheriff?" I said, as we shook hands with him. "Any new developments?"

He started to speak, but paused as the door opened and the server entered. She put our coffees down on the table and said, "Creamer and sweeteners are on the table if you want them. What can I get you to eat?" She looked at Bill and me.

The sheriff spoke up, "I've already ordered. The fall special is really good here."

"That sounds good to me," I replied.

"Make that two," Bill said.

"I'll get that to you in just a few minutes." She turned and exited the room.

We doctored our coffees and then looked back at Pfieffer.

"They still have not located the boat. When we were rescued, you may have seen the helicopter from IRB that came onto the scene. After they were sure that we were picked up safely, they began their search for the boat. At one time, they thought they saw it turn into a secluded cove on one of the islands, but when they flew over the inlet, they were unable to find it. They searched the area for a couple of hours, but they said it was if the boat had just disappeared. Maybe they will have something new for us at the meeting."

"That falls in line with what all the fishermen have said. It suddenly appears for a short time and then simply vanishes. A boat that size ought to be hard to hide." I scratched my chin as we all reflected on my words.

We told the sheriff about following up our leads at Fond du Lac. "Lander has some connections there at the Indian Reservation and one of them has some expertise in analyzing artifacts for their age and origin. Do you think you could let us take the coin to show him? We'll bring it back with us."

"Pfieffer thought a minute and replied, "I guess that would be okay. We need to get some more information about it. Remind me to give it to you when the meeting is over; I have it with me to show the others."

I looked at the sheriff and said, "I have one more request. Under the circumstances, I don't like leaving Cyndi by herself. Is there any way that you could post someone outside the house to be sure she has no visitors while we are gone?"

Pfieffer scratched his head and I am sure he was comparing the cost of a deputy to the value he thought we were providing his district. "I think I could do that," he replied.

"Could it be someone besides Roget?" I asked. I expected that he would question that and I really did not want to have to explain it to him.

He looked at me a moment, then slowly nodded his head. "I can arrange that. I have a retired man who I call on occasionally to help us. He will do a good job and be glad to get the time in. In fact, Roget will not even know that you all are going."

My estimation of the sheriff went up a note then as I understood that his thoughts were in sync with mine. "I really appreciate that," I said.

We looked at the food as it was set in front of us. I took a deep whiff and smiled as I reached for the bread. "Time out for the important things," I said as I bit into the French loaf. "We'll continue this conversation as we drive to the meeting." I got no argument from either of them as they dug in.

Twenty minutes later, we were finishing the last of the meal. The waitress placed our check down on the table and asked, "Coffees to go? They will be at the register as you leave."

We left the diner and walked to Pfieffer's car. As we opened doors and sat down, he said, "You can leave your Jeep here; it will be okay. I would like to get there early and look at the spot where Lively was shot. We should have a couple of hours to kill before the meeting."

On the trip over to Western Shore, we discussed the highlights of the new information we had uncovered and talked about the upcoming meeting. The sheriff indicated that he wanted us to present our information to the taskforce and we readily agreed. With our background, neither Bill nor I had a problem with speaking in front of groups. As we finished our planning for the meeting, Pfieffer pulled into a parking spot. "Here is where Lively was shot," he said.

We left the car and moved to the sidewalk and stopped at the chalked outline where Lively fell. "Which way was he walking and where did the bullet enter his head?" Lander asked.

The sheriff replied. "He parked over there and was walking this way to his office. The entry wound was above his right ear."

"What about the exit wound?"

"It was in his neck." The sheriff thought a minute and continued, "That means that the killer was above Lively and shot down at him."

Lander just nodded, moved to the spot, and looked all around. His eyes gradually shifted to the hill overlooking this area of the town. "Can we get to that summit?" he asked, pointing to the top of the rise.

Pfieffer followed his finger and scratched his head. "Do you think someone could have made the kill from that far away?"

Bill replied, "This was a professional job; a real sniper could have done it. It looks about twelve hundred yards from here. That's well within the range of a trained shooter. I would like to see it from that spot."

About fifteen minutes later, we found the road that took us to the bottom of the hill. We pulled to the side and parked under a copse of trees. Lander was out of the car before the sheriff shut down the engine. I followed him and watched as he began moving in expanding circles over the area. He stopped and pointed. "This is where the shooter parked. He backed in here where his car could not be seen from the road.

He used all these limbs to cover his car in case someone came around. He probably climbed the hill staying away from the path to the top. We can take the easiest way up." As he spoke, he led the way up the hill.

By the time we reached the top, we were all sweating. Lander walked all around the area, then paused. "This is the spot. You have a clear line of sight to Lively." He carefully looked around and bent down to look carefully at the large flat rock. "I think he had a shooter's pad and laid it out here. You can see this section on the rock has been cleared of the debris that is prevalent on the rest of it. I don't see a shell casing, but a trained sniper would have picked it up. We won't find anything else up here."

By the time we retrieved our car and made our way back to town, it was almost time for the meeting. Pfieffer parked beside other marked cars and we went into the town center. Bear was waiting for us in the lobby. He greeted us and said, "Follow me; we're meeting in the conference room upstairs."

Bear led the way, followed by Pfieffer. Lander and I trailed them as they entered the conference room. We moved to the empty chairs at the table. The man at the end of the table stood and said, "I think everyone is here now. Let me begin the introductions. I am Cedric Baudré and am the local sheriff here in Halifax County."

Even though he had a slight French accent, Baudré was easy to understand. He was average size with dark, sundried skin and dark hair that was shading toward gray around his temples and ears. But his eyes were his distinguishing feature. Although his face was animated, his eyes were intense—the kind that could see to your very soul.

He pointed at the man beside him. "This is Antoine Armand; he is the Director working out of the Halifax Regional Office." Armand had on the uniform of the Canadian Coast Guard. His Navy-Blue Jacket was decorated with the bars of his rank; he had a chest full of medals displayed on his right side. The matching pants above his black, polished shoes were spotless with a military crease. He nodded to us and touched the official cap worn on his salt and pepper hair.

"The next man is Captain Lucian Billarand. He flies our helicopter; it is used primarily as a rescue vehicle but is also armed and he and his crew have battle experience." Billarand looked to be a shade over six feet and stressed his clothes; I could imagine that the uniform hid well-developed muscles. He looked our way and lifted his hand in greeting.

He next introduced a man dressed in a dark suit; his name was Ashton Bonteur and he was an official with the CSIS. Although the Coast Guard would work most closely with us, the final responsibility lay with the Canadian Security Intelligence Service.

I moved my eyes to the next man in line as Baudré spoke. "You all have met Bear, I think." Bear smiled at us as Baudré paused. "I will let Sheriff Pfieffer introduce the rest of the group."

Pfieffer stood and introduced himself, then Lander and me. "I will ask that Dr. Kent begin the meeting with giving you the background of the problem. It was his discovery that began the mystery."

I stood and looked around the table. Beginning with why I was in Nova Scotia, I outlined the story. There were no questions as I stuck to the facts explaining the finding of the body. When I talked about the coin I found, I pointed to the sheriff. "Sheriff Pfieffer has it and will pass it around to let you see it. I also have pictures of it that I will give you to take with you. Bill and I are going to Minnesota to let an expert artifact analyst look at it." I went on to explain what we had found out about Foster and that we may get some information related to the case from his friends there on the Fond du Lac Indian Reservation. When I told them what Cyndi had discovered from around the world, they began to ask additional questions.

"What makes you think that these other incidents are related to ours?" asked Armand.

"There were just too many similarities that points to that. It could be coincidence, but I really don't believe too much in coincidence. They were all dressed alike and all were bearded men who were killed close to the same time on the same day."

Bear spoke up. "So, this may be more than someone just coming here to look for buried treasure?"

Lander replied, "I think the buried treasure is a major consideration of the story, but I agree—it is more than another treasure hunt."

For the next hour, we discussed what we knew—and what we knew was not much. At this point, we had many more questions than we had answers. We outlined the topics and established a timeline as we knew it. We had first the murder in my cove and then several more worldwide, all with similar characteristics. There was the powerboat, which seemed to appear and disappear at will. Billarand told us about his search with the helicopter. He showed us a long-range photo of the boat that he took before it darted into the cove. He could not explain why he could not locate it once he flew over the inlet where it had entered. "It was like it just disappeared. One minute it was there and the next minute there was no sign of it. There was no other exit from the cove and I could find no covered areas where it could hide. It was really strange—I've never seen anything like it."

Pfieffer replied, "That seems to be the standard message we are getting about this boat. Our fishermen have spotted it, but then it just goes away. They are calling it the ghost boat."

We had the mystery with the treasure on Oak Island and then the connection of the murdered Foster with Fond du Lac. There were the rough positions of all the corpses that seemed to link with a unique statue in the U.S. The name on the boat, although in an almost forgotten language, seemed to echo what seemed to me to be the theme of the whole operation.

Then there was the shooting of Lively. Had he somehow gotten too close to the perpetrators? If so, then we were all in danger. Speaking of our danger, I had almost forgotten the break-in at our house. I told them about the break-in; that brought the concern level up another notch.

We agreed that we would meet again in two days after Lander and I returned from our trip. In the meantime, all available resources will be called into play. We exchanged contact information and filed out of the building.

When we started for the car, Armand yelled for Pfieffer to wait for him. Lander and I went on to the car while they stood still and talked. I saw Pfieffer nod his head and say something to Armand, who shook his head like he was saying no. After a couple of minutes, they shook hands and Pfieffer joined us at his car.

"Problem?" I asked.

"Not now," he replied. "Armand wasn't too happy about you and Lander being included in this investigation. But he's fine with it now after I vouched for both of you; I had to provide some background—I hope you don't mind. I think he was worried about civilians getting hurt in an explosive case."

"That's okay," said Lander, as I nodded in the affirmative.

The sheriff unzipped a pocket on his coat. "Here's the coin, before I forget it."

He handed me a ziplock bag with the artifact in it. "Thanks, I'll take care of it," I said, as I rolled it up around the coin and placed it in my front pocket with my keys.

"What time's your flight?" asked Pfieffer.

"We leave at eleven-forty tonight. It's about a nine-hour trip, but we'll gain a couple of hours going. We are meeting Bill's friend at five-thirty in Duluth; he's taking the whole day off to be with us."

"How can you expect to work after flying all night?"

Bill grinned at him and replied, "We've been on enough planes that we can sleep fine on them. We'll get our coffee and be ready to go, unless Phil here is getting too old for adventure."

I just laughed at him. "I can keep up with you. If I'm getting old, then you are staying almost a year ahead of me."

The trip back to Lunenburg was uneventful. We filled Pfieffer in on what we had planned for Fond du Lac.

"I sure hope you can get some information about what Foster was up to and how he got connected to this other group. We need to corral them before somebody else gets hurt . . . or killed. And I'll have my man to stand guard at your house the next two nights. You did say you all would be back in a couple of days?"

"Yeah, that's our plan. We'll come in to see you as soon as we get back."

The sheriff left us at our car. Thirty minutes later, we entered my house and there was an excited female to see us—and I loved it! Chelsea always greeted me like that—Cyndi also said she was happy we were there, but she wasn't going to squeal and shake her tail like Chelsea does. Oh, well!

We had told Bill we would take him to eat seafood, so we got ready to go pretty quickly. I took Chelsea out and fed her. Bill checked all the locks while I pulled the Jeep out of the garage. We did a quick survey around the house and looked out over the cove. Everything seemed to be clear, so we took our places in the car and headed for the restaurant. Although we had to stay alert, it was time for a little down time.

"This was the best lobster I have had in ages!" Bill leaned back with a smile on his face. "I could get used to this." He paused, then said, "On second thought, if I ate like this much, I would have to double my workouts."

I agreed with him on all fronts as I looked at what was left of my giant crab legs. I really liked them better than I did lobster—although both items were on my treat list. Cyndi had eaten clam chowder and a seafood salad and I knew she would love to get any of this good food back in Tennessee.

After the meal, we walked around a little, then started back home. By the time we got there, it was almost time for Bill and me to leave for the airport. I told Cyndi that there would be an officer outside our house during the night. Of course, she said that wasn't necessary, but I told her it was already taken care of.

Chapter 15

We took Highway 3 out of Lunenburg and then merged onto 103 North. We stayed on 103 through Halifax and up toward Enfield. This highway took us to 102; the Bell Road exit took us over to the airport. It was dark when I stopped the car at the Parkade, the daily parking lot at Halifax Stanfield International Airport. We locked the car and walked to the concourse. Neither of us had a bag; our smart phones and clothes on our back were all we were taking with us. Although the airport was modern and clean, there was not much traffic this late at night. We found our gate, checked the schedule to be sure our flight was running on time, and sat down to wait.

We were interrupted with the announcement that our plane was now loading, so we stood up and walked back to the gate. The girl checked our tickets and we entered the jet. We were flying coach, but not many others were loading for this trip. We found our seats and listened to the directions for emergency procedures. Within fifteen minutes, the jet was sitting at the end of the runway, ready to go. We listened to the whine of the engines and the plane began to move, slowly at first, but then quickly accelerated. The wheels left the runway and we heard them retract into their slots and we were airborne. Once we had leveled off, Bill told me he was moving to the next row where he could stretch out. The trip was about a nine-hour flight and within twenty minutes, we were both sound asleep. The flight must have been smooth, because I woke up about seven hours later. I stretched and glanced at Bill, who was looking at me.

"Good morning; I thought you were just going to sleep until we were on the ground."

I replied, "Just getting my rest. We've got a long day coming up. How long have you been awake?"

"About an hour, I guess. I slept well, too—but not as good as you. Cyndi ever tell you how loudly you snore?"

"She says I snore pretty good at times. Where is your friend meeting us?"

"Jack will meet us at the front gate. He is probably already there."

"Where did you meet him? At one of those conventions you are always going to?"

Bill, replied, "No, I met him in the service. We were in Special Forces together. When we left the scrvice, we both started teaching and just kept in touch all these years. He is from the Ojibwa reservation there and returned to help his tribe. As I told you, every semester, I connect my class with him. You'll like him."

They felt the plane touch down and heard the engines reverse their thrust as the jet began to slow. It made a left-hand turn and slowly taxied to its gate. We heard the steps connect and the door opened. We made our way past the flight attendant who looked at us and said, "Have a great day—thanks for flying with us."

We went out into a bright blue sky with temperatures in the fifties. My jacket felt good. I heard someone yell, "Hey, Bill!"

We followed the sound and saw Bill's friend waving to us. "Let's go," he said. "We've got a lot of ground to cover."

As we moved to his car, I looked at Jack. He was a shade over six feet and looked as if he were in great shape. His dark hair was long and was pulled to a pony tail in the back. His sharp eyes looked out of a well-tanned face. He was in jeans and had a light Columbia jacket on; his boots were the rugged hiking type. He was dressed for action. We crossed the street and met him by his truck, a black, four-wheel drive Toyota crew-cab Tacoma.

Bill grabbed him and gave him a bear hug, then backed up and pointed to me. "Jack, this is Phil Kent. You've heard me talk about him. Phil, Jack Lauftis."

I shook his hand, then said, "I hope he hasn't told you all the bad things he got me into."

Jack grinned and said, "He told me he had to threaten you to get you to pass the basketball to him in college. He said sometimes you forgot you were a point guard and not a shooting guard."

"Not true," I replied. "At that time, I would rather get an assist than my shot. I looked for the pass before I ever tried to set myself up—except on fast breaks; Bill could never get down the court fast enough."

"That's true," said Bill. Two of our four years, we averaged over a hundred points a game; we were a running team . . . That was fun, wasn't it?"

"Yes, it was," I said. "But enough about the past. What are our plans for today?" We got into the truck—me in the back seat and Bill and Jack up front.

Jack said, "I've got at least three people I want you to talk with; they may lead us to more. The first is a tribe member who lives on the Reservation. We've got an appointment with him in a couple of hours. We'll stop for breakfast up the road here first. I know they didn't feed you much in coach."

Jack took Grinden Drive away from the airport and made three turns to head toward I-35 South toward Fond du Lac. I noticed that he kept looking in his mirror as we left the airport. There were restaurants at the entrance to the freeway and Jack pulled into the parking lot for a pancake house. "They have good breakfasts here, but they have great coffee," he said as he shut the engine off.

After a meal of pancakes and eggs—and, yes, we had coffee and it was as good as Jack said—we drove around several blocks before we circled back and entered I-35 toward Fond du Lac. There was very little traffic, so we made excellent time and, within an hour, we took the exit to Fond du Lac and the Reservation. Jack drove through the reservation and took an unmarked road north. It gradually became just a hardscrabble path and he finally stopped in front of what could be best described as a fancy lean-to. Although it looked much sturdier than the typical lean-to, it was built on the same principles. It had a slanted roof covered with natural habitation and had side walls built out of the same type limbs. At the back of it was a rocky cliff that towered above it. The door was closed as we exited the car and I saw a man watching us from the small window to the left of the door. Jack led the way to the door, which was opened before we got to it. Standing there with a rifle in his hands was a big man with a serious look on his face. He looked at Jack and said, "These the men you talked to me about?"

"Yes," replied Jack. "This is Phil Kent and Bill Lander. They would like to ask you some questions. Phil, Bill, this is Magisi."

"Magisi, we are pleased to meet you and thank you for agreeing to talk with us," I said.

Magisi replied, "It is an honor. If Sakima is your friend, then I, also, am your friend."

I looked at Jack. "Sakima?"

Magisi replied, "Sakima is honorary name for Jack; it means Chief or one of high rank. Jack is most educated and highest accomplished of our tribe. He is hero to our people. Come in and sit down."

Jack bowed his head and said, "I am not sure about the hero status. Magisi means Eagle; he stays up here so he can watch over the valley."

Magisi showed us into his small home and had us to sit at a rough-hewn table; the chairs were smooth-cut logs stood on end. Only then did I look around. The inside of the house was nothing like I expected from the outside. The front and side walls were solid hardwood logs fitted together so closely I could hardly even see the seams; the back wall was the solid stone cliff rising behind his home; the stone wall was polished straight and smooth. The floors were hardwood and polished to a high sheen. There was a small gas stove against the back wall. I did not see a bed in the room. The left wall had a fireplace built into it with charred logs from the previous fire. On a desk in the corner sat a computer and printer. Another monitor showed six different views from outside; I had not even noticed the cameras mounted in the ragged walls. Magisi sat so that he could see the feeds from the camera. He placed his rifle next to him. I noticed that Bill was also taking it all in.

"I heated some water before you got here. I hope you like tea." As he spoke, Magisi poured tea from a metal pot into mugs. I saw the steam rise and, although I would have preferred coffee, I looked forward to the hot drink.

When Magisi joined us at the table, Jack spoke up. "I didn't go into detail with Magisi about your search. I will let you explain your visit to him. He used to live in the town. We felt like we needed a private place to speak so he asked that we come here."

Magisi replied, "I have moved out here full time now. There has been too much happening to take a chance on someone finding this location."

I looked at Bill and he pointed to me and said, "Go ahead; I'll fill in any spots I need to."

I began the story with the happenings in Nova Scotia and gave Magisi just a little background of why I—and then Bill—was there. As we talked, Magisi pointed out that Jack had been in Special Forces with Bill and that was the connection with the two of them.

I continued, "The first man who was killed was Liam Foster. He had hired a local there to act as his guide. The guide said that Foster had told him he was from Fond du Lac. It just so happened that Bill knew Jack here and called him for information. Jack recommended that we come here to talk with a few people who may have some knowledge of what Foster was doing in Nova Scotia and what may have gotten him killed. You are the first person we have met here." I looked at Magisi as I paused.

Magisi looked at me and asked, "What do you know about Foster?"

"Almost nothing. We talked with a couple of people with whom he had contact in Nova Scotia. The guide was showing him around the islands there; he was especially interested in Oak Island."

When I said Oak Island, Magisi's eyes lifted just a fraction. He looked at Jack and then asked me, "What is significant about that island?"

"Oak Island is reputed to have hidden treasure on it. Every so often someone shows up there and thinks he has new information to find it. Have you heard about the island or do you know if Foster said anything about it to anyone here?"

I watched Magisi's face as he considered how to answer that question. Finally, he said, "I would ask that you and Bill step outside a minute while I talk with Jack." He looked at me as he spoke and stood to his feet.

Bill and I got up and moved outside. "What's this about?" I asked.

"Magisi is trying to determine if he can trust us; he knows a lot more than he has told us so far. Jack will reassure him." With the door closed, we could hear none of the conversation.

After about ten minutes, the door opened and Jack motioned us back in. Magisi was standing near the table where we had sat earlier.

Magisi looked at us and spoke: "I hope you understand that asking you to go outside while we talked was nothing personal. Foster went to Nova Scotia to try to find the treasure. We need to talk to Mokuk. He is aware of some of what has happened. Follow me." He stood and moved to the back of the dwelling and pushed a hanging hide to one side. He then reached above his head and pushed on one of the stones. A door-sized section of the wall opened. Magisi picked up a lantern, lit it, and entered the cave; he motioned us to follow him. We walked single-file through the opening and up a gradual slope for about ten yards, where it looked like the path ended. Magisi moved to his right, ducked low, and eased through a cleft almost out of sight in the wall. The rest of us followed; we had to squeeze through the tight crevice. On the other side of the wall was a circular room large enough for us to all stand. On the far side of it was a series of steps chiseled into the wall. Magisi moved to them and begin to climb. There was no talking as we made our way up the makeshift ladder. Bill followed Magisi, Jack was next, and I brought up the rear. We climbed for what seemed like ten minutes and, by the time I had reached the top, I was glad that I was in decent shape. At the top, Magisi waited for all of us. I looked around and saw a number of tunnels branching off this room. Magisi chose one on the left and led us through the path. This tunnel had walls with some kind of writing and pictures on them. Every fifteen feet or so, a lighted torch was burning in a shelf carved into the wall. Magisi paused at the opening to another room, spoke to someone there, and we entered. I stopped and stared in amazement. We were in another circular room about twenty feet in diameter. The walls were as smooth as those in the best-finished house. Again, there were many pictures and strange writings on each wall. The warm lighting came from flickering torches spaced around the room. I looked up and could barely make out the ceiling some thirty feet above us. I finally realized that Magisi was speaking to us.

I gave him my attention as he pointed to the old man making his way to us. "This is Mokuk," he said. "He is the wise elder of our tribe and is the Truth-Keeper." He nodded to him reverently and spoke softly, "Mokuk, these are the men that I talked with you about. You know Jack. This is Bill Lander and Phil Kent." He pointed at Bill, then me.

I could not tell how old Mokuk was; he could have been anywhere between sixty-five and ninety-five. His face was pale and lined with deep lines around his eyes and mouth. His hair was completely white and hung to his shoulders in two braids. His hands were wrinkled and his fingers knobby with arthritis. In spite of this, his eyes were bright and when he moved toward us, his step was lively. He wore a white robe that fell to his knees and covered his arms. On his feet were leather moccasins.

"Come in and sit," Mokuk said. We followed him to the chairs spaced around a bearskin rug on the far side of the room and we all sat facing him.

Mokuk bowed his head for a minute, then began to talk. "This is the day which my people have been afraid of for years. We have always known that our secret would one day be in jeopardy." His voice was shaky and deep and he was straining to make us hear him. "Magisi says that Jack knows and trusts you, so I will talk to you."

Magisi spoke up. "Jack has been here before, but you two are the first from outside our tribe who have ever seen this room. Jack assures us that you will tell no one else about it."

Both Bill and I shook our heads. "Your secret is safe with us."

Mokuk said, "Please tell me what you know about our tribe's connection with your problem."

They all looked to me, so I began our tale again. I talked for thirty minutes without an interruption.

When I finished, Mokuk spoke, "What does this Foster look like?"

I pulled my iPhone out and accessed my photos. "This is him—or was him," I said, handing my phone to Mokuk.

Mokuk stared at the picture for a long minute. After a while, I began to think that he did not recognize him. Mokuk shook his head and said, "I know this man, but Foster is not his name; he is Ahmik. He is a member of our tribe who left our people, got into trouble, and spent some years in prison. He returned to our reservation about six months ago; he said that he had left his troubles behind and wanted to change his name so that men who he met in prison could not find him. About two months ago, some men came here looking for him. They finally caught up with him at the casino. Since that time, I have heard various stories about what he was involved in."

"Who were these men that came for him?" Bill asked.

"I have heard no names; I do not know." Mokuk looked at Magisi and Jack, who also shook their heads "No."

"Did you ever see them? What did they look like?"

Magisi looked at me as I asked and he replied, "They were not from around here—that was for sure. Those who saw them said they may have been Middle Eastern."

I followed up, "Have you heard why they wanted to find Foster—or Ahmik?"

"Here is the story as I have heard it," Mokuk said. "While Ahmik was in prison, he made friends with a man from Syria. Ahmik told him that our tribe had knowledge of a great treasure that has remained hidden for hundreds of years. They made a pact that when both were free, they would try to retrieve it. One of our people"—he looked at Jack when he said this—"checked with the prison system and discovered that Ahmik's friend was released about nine weeks ago. That checks with the time that Ahmik had his visitors here."

"Where is this great treasure supposed to be buried?" asked Lander.

Mokuk just looked at him, then said, "I think you know that."

"Nova Scotia . . . Oak Island!" I interjected. I thought a minute, then asked, "Why would a Native American tribe in Minnesota have treasure buried in Nova Scotia?"

Bill spoke up, "I could probably answer that question, but I will let Jack tell us."

We all looked at Jack, who thought a minute and then turned toward Mokuk. "May I speak freely?"

Mokuk slowly spread his hands toward the group and responded to Jack's question, "These men can help us. You trust them, so I trust them. Please share what you wish."

Jack stood to his feet, stretched, and began to walk around the circular room. We watched him pause every few seconds and touch the wall. When he returned, he sat down and smiled. "My people's history is told on these walls. The story is old and few know about its existence here under the mountain. Mokuk is the one that was chosen many years ago to protect this sacred place. He has selected Magisi to carry on that work when he passes. I discovered the rooms here by accident. As Bill knows, I like to explore and one day I found the cave behind Magisi's lean-to and entered it to escape a storm. While I waited for the weather to improve, I found the opening, then the ladder. When I climbed it and discovered this room, I thought Mokuk was going to shoot me. Instead, we sat and talked until he was satisfied that I could be trusted to keep his secret. After that day, Magisi moved into his dwelling here full time in order to keep anyone else from doing what I had done; that is when the interior was fortified; it can now survive a pretty intense attack. Most of our people will not even come to this mountain as they have been told from their youth that there are evil spirits here and their families will be killed if they enter.

"Many years ago, our people lived in Northeastern Canada, with many of them in Nova Scotia. It is said that in the thirteenth century men from Europe landed there and established a colony. We taught them how to hunt and use the animals for food and clothing; they gave to us new seeds for growing vegetables. For years it was a peaceful coexistence. Then, in the early 1300s, other boats arrived from France. Those boats carried knights escaping from the King's orders to have them executed; the men unloaded their boats and began new lives there. We know they had horses on the boats and also brought with them gifts for the natives living there. Gold coins were presented to the chief in exchange for the right to expand the colony. It is this chest that we still protect here.

I pulled the gold coin from my pocket and handed it to Mokuk. "This is the coin I found near Foster's body."

Mokuk took the piece from me and peered closely at both sides. "I think this is like the gold coins that were given to our ancestors. According to legend, there are many chests full of these buried on Oak Island. I am the one chosen to protect my tribe's history; you can see it documented on the walls. In addition, books are stored here that speak of our heritage. Another one of my duties is to protect the location of the coin chest that was given to our people."

"You still have those coins?" Bill asked excitedly.

"Wait here", Mokuk said. He got up and moved to the far side of the room. He pushed against one of the paintings and a section of the wall slowly opened up. He entered the opening, turned to his right, and disappeared from our sight. I heard a definite groan, then, as he reentered the room, he was moving noticeably slower; I could see he was carrying a wooden box. He sat it down in the center of us and spoke. "You are the first people outside of the tribe's Truth Keeper to see this item in the last four hundred years. What you see and hear must never be spoken about outside this room."

He went to another area of the room and turned his back to us. I saw him make several movements with his hand and a flat rock slid to the side. Mokuk bent down and removed a cloth before he came back to us. He opened the fabric and removed a key. He offered the key to Magisi and asked him to unlock the box. "First take this cloth and wipe the box clean before you open it."

Magisi took the material and wiped the box. Although the chest was hundreds of years old, it still looked solid and began to shine as Magisi rubbed it. It was about twelve inches long, about eight inches wide, and about eight inches tall at the highpoint of the curved lid. The hinges and lock looked to be made of brass. He carefully inserted the key into the lock as we all leaned in to see the contents. The hinges creaked as the top was lifted. I expected to see five or six coins, but the box was chock full of them; there was a small fortune sitting in the chest. He held the box out to Mokuk and Mokuk removed one coin.

"Compare the two coins," he said as he handed both to me.

I took them and looked at the sides with the etching on them. There was no doubt that they were the same. Turning them over, I looked at the writing; both were identical. "They came from the same source," I said.

"Is this real gold?" asked Bill.

"Yes," said Magisi. "We took one of the coins to have it analyzed some time ago. The man evaluated the coin, but it was stolen from him before he could return it to us. He said it was an eighteen-carat gold piece. When you consider the history of the treasure, just this small box is priceless. Large chests filled with these gold pieces would be worth a fortune."

"Who else knows about these coins here?" asked Bill. "Did Foster know that you have them?"

Magisi answered, "He may have had suspicions, but I always thought that he did not know, but now I am not so sure. I suspect he was the one who stole the coin from the jeweler."

"If he didn't get it from him, then he must have found a cache on Oak Island." I let everyone consider the implications of that after I spoke. "Did he speak to anyone here about searching for the treasure?"

Jack replied, "Yes, he did. I will take you to talk with a man that Foster tried to recruit to help him. Then we will talk with a lady who saw his foreign visitors."

Mokuk was obviously worn out and we got up to leave. He looked pleadingly at us as he handed me my coin. "When your investigation is over, you must return this coin to us. You have to stop this group. The future of my people may depend on you."

We thanked him and pledged to do what we could to help. Magisi walked with us to our car. He hugged Jack and shook our hands. "You must be careful. These people have already killed and won't hesitate to do it again. Watch your backs and keep your weapons close by."

Before we took our seats in the car, Jack opened the lockbox in the bed of his truck. He shuffled some things around in the box and pulled out some handguns. He handed a gun to Bill and said, "I guess you still like the H&K .45; Bill said your preference is a Glock 19." He handed the weapon to me and gave us both two loaded magazines. Bill and I checked our weapons and placed them in our waistbands." Jack chose a rifle—a high-powered Savage—and, after he checked it for load, he slid it into the rack at the rear window of his truck. Then Jack pointed the truck toward our next appointment.

After a rough ten minutes, Jack turned his truck into what could hardly be called a driveway. The house was run down and looked like it had been empty a long while; I could see no evidence that anyone lived there now. We got out of the truck and each of us looked all around before we moved away from the vehicle. Jack stepped up on the sagging porch, eased to the door, and knocked loudly; Bill and I hung back watching the windows and the sides of the house. Jack knocked again, even louder, and finally, we heard footsteps in the house. The door opened a crack and someone yelled, "What do you want?"

Jack answered, "Tom Wilson? We want to talk with you a minute. Can we come in?"

"No, go away. I don't know you!"

"We just want to talk. You know Liam Foster or Ahmik. I was told you were seen with him several times in the last couple of months. We need to ask you some questions."

"Ask him. I don't know nothing!"

Jack replied, "Ahmik is dead. We think you can help us find who killed him."

"He's dead? I tried to tell him to stay away from them." He slowly opened the door and we entered his house.

Jack introduced all of us. Tom jerked his head from one side to the other and kept looking out the shaded window as if he expected more company. He was clearly scared. He hadn't shaved in weeks and I'm sure it had been at least that long since he had a bath. There were empty beer bottles and candy wrappers thrown all over the room. The house was shut up tight and no light at all got in. He was surviving in the dark and was obviously afraid to go out.

"What are you afraid of?" I looked at his eyes as they darted from one to the other of us.

"I told Ahmik they were trouble, but he wouldn't listen to me. How did they kill him?"

"He was shot in the back of the head—executed," I replied. "Do you know why?"

"I grew up with Ahmik here on the reservation. We used to run together and talked about going away and getting rich; there had been rumors for years in our tribe that there was a fortune in gold on some island in Nova Scotia." He jumped up. "There's somebody out there!"

Bill moved to the window and looked out. "There's nobody there."

I spoke to Wilson as he sat back down. "You were telling us why Ahmik thought there was gold in Nova Scotia . . ."

Tom shook his head to clear his thoughts. "While we were growing up here on the reservation, all the boys heard the tales: how our people used to live in Canada and we left a treasure buried there. Most of us didn't believe it, but Ahmik was convinced it was true.

He told me he had talked to a man in Halifax that had seen a sample of a coin one of our elders had taken to him to see if it was really gold. Ahmik ran into him in a bar in Halifax. They talked over a beer and when the man heard Ahmik was from the Reservation here, he told him about the coin."

"Did the man say where the coin had come from?" asked Jack.

"He didn't know, but he told Ahmik there was something written on the coin in a really old language. That just made Ahmik more sure that there was truth to the old stories."

"Were there words on both sides of the gold piece? Did Ahmik tell you what was on the other side?" I looked at Jack as he continued to question Wilson.

"Ahmik said the writing was on only one side. According to the man who saw the coin, there was some picture of a man on the other side. Ahmik claimed it was some religious symbol—maybe Mahammia or someone."

"You mean Mohammed?" Bill corrected him.

"Yeah, that's the word. Anyway, I was ready to get out of here and it sounded interesting, so we were saving our money so we could go check it out. But that was all put on hold when Ahmik got caught with drugs and was sent away to prison. When he got out, he looked me up. I found out that he really had the coin; he had stolen it from the jewelry shop. We quickly made plans to go to Nova Scotia and were ready to leave when they showed up."

"Who is they?" Bill asked.

"One of them had been in prison with Ahmik; he was from Syria, I think. The other man was a friend of the Syrian's; he was from the Middle East somewhere. I don't know either of their names. I met with them once with Ahmik. When I found out that they were going to go to Nova Scotia with Ahmik, I told him I didn't want to join them. Ahmik did not like that but he said that since I didn't know their names, they would probably not insist. I was scared to back out but not nearly as scared as I would have been to go with them. I wouldn't turn my back on those two."

"Why would Ahmik tell someone in prison about the gold, someone he didn't know?" Jack asked.

"He told me he was afraid in prison—you know what they do to little men in for the first time. He was trying to make a friend that would keep the other prisoners away from him. He thought if he told the Syrian about the treasure he would protect him. But he didn't think the man would follow him here."

"When you met them, what did they talk about? Were they just interested in the treasure?" I thought I knew where Bill was going with this question.

"They definitely wanted the treasure, but I got the idea that they wanted it to help them pay for some other thing they wanted to do. They mentioned an upcoming event that they said would 'change the world.' They didn't know I heard them talking about that or I don't think I would be here today. That's all I know . . . I swear!"

Jack asked, "Did Ahmik tell you where in Nova Scotia he was looking?"

"He said the treasure was on an island there. A lot of people think it was buried by pirates, but Ahmik seemed to think it was brought there by a group that had escaped from France. He claimed that there were many chests that were filled with the same gold pieces. It would definitely be a fortune, but I wanted nothing to do with them Islams."

"Actually, the people are Muslims; the religion is Islam. What else can you tell us about the Muslims? How long were they here? Do you have any idea what special event they were planning—or when it was going to happen?" Bill was watching Wilson closely as I quizzed him.

"They were both average height and weight, I guess. Dark skin, black hair, medium cut. Pretty good English, but definitely had accents. Stood out here in Minnesota."

Bill took up the questioning: "How did they get here? Did they fly or drive? Where were they staying? Did you ever see any weapons?" He threw one question after another at Wilson.

"I don't know how they traveled. They had weapons; I never saw them, but I saw the bulge under their coats. It looked like they carried handguns in their waistbands. I don't know where they stayed, but it had to be somewhere; they were here for several days."

"We can find out where they stayed. Did you notice anything else about them? Nothing stands out—no scars, no tattoos, no limps?" I replied.

"Nothing."

"Do you have any idea why they would have killed Ahmik?"

"No, they seemed to get along fine when they were here. Maybe they shot him after he told them where the treasure was buried. I can't believe they killed him; I warned him about them. I could tell they were evil."

There was nothing else we could learn from Wilson. As we got up to leave, I gave him a card and told him if he thought of anything else to call me. It was early afternoon and Jack pointed the truck back toward town. As we turned from the driveway onto the highway, none of us saw the truck parked just off the road. The two men in the truck smiled as we passed within twenty feet of their vehicle. They watched until we were five hundred yards down the highway, then looked to be sure no one else was around. They saw no one, so the driver reached to the panel attached to the dash and pushed two buttons. There was a slight hum and the truck suddenly appeared in the cutoff. It pulled onto the roadway and moved slowly toward the rundown house. Thirty minutes later, they left the house; the driver reached under his seat. "Here, change the tag," he said. After his partner had put the new Tennessee tag on the back, they made their way to the highway heading northeast. They felt sure that they had gotten all the information that Wilson could provide; he would no longer be a threat and their time in Minnesota was over.

Jack parked in front of a Subway and said, "Let's get lunch—all this sleuthing makes me hungry." We exited the truck and looked around before we went into the restaurant. Jack ordered turkey, Bill asked for a pastrami, and I got my favorite, an Italian BMT. We all got chips and drinks and sat at a table where we could see our truck parked. We checked out the other diners, then, like hungry men everywhere, we spoke not a word while we ate.

Bill grinned and said, "That was good—I was ready for something to eat."

We all agreed. Jack said, "Our next stop will be to see a lady who saw the visitors talking with Ahmik. She lives with her two kids just outside town."

"How did you find out she had seen them?" asked Bill.

"She told me. She is an admissions clerk at the college. That is where we will meet her."

After a thirty-minute drive, Jack drove through the beautiful campus and pulled into a parking spot with his name on it. We followed him into the Administration Building. He greeted the ladies in the front office and led the way through a short hallway and knocked on the second door to the right. "Come on in," I heard the cheerful voice respond.

Jack introduced everyone, then asked how her family was doing. After chatting a few minutes, he posed the first question: "What can you tell us about Ahmik's visitors?"

She replied, "They were strange . . . and scary. I saw them with him a couple of times. The first time was at a fast-food place; they must have gone through the drive-through, then parked at the side of the lot to eat. The two Middle Easterners were in the front seat and Ahmik was sitting in the back."

"What kind of car was it?" I asked.

"It was a white Land Rover, not a new one but in good shape. The windows were tinted so I could barely see in the car; the back window was down and I saw Ahmik in the back seat and I got a glimpse of the two people in the front. After I'd gone through the drive-through to get dinner for my kids, I started home. A few minutes later, the Land Rover came up behind me and then passed me. I could see the license plate was from Maine. But then it got really strange. I saw them pull off to the side of the road and park maybe a quarter of mile in front of me, but when I got there, I couldn't see the truck. It was like it just disappeared! It was a four-wheel drive, but there was nowhere for it to go."

"When was the other time you saw them," I asked.

"I just passed them—or at least the car—a couple days later. I couldn't see in the car, but I was sure it was them. I'm really not sure Ahmik was with them this time, but they were coming back from the area where Ahmik had been staying."

We asked a few more questions, but she couldn't remember anything else. She assured Jack that if she remembered anything else she would contact him. We followed Jack to his office and the first thing I saw in the room was a Keurig. Jack saw me looking at it and said, "Help yourself; the coffee is in that drawer."

I opened the drawer and saw a variety of K-cups. I chose a half-caf and placed it in the Keurig and punched the button for the large cup. "We may not have answers, but we have coffee; anyone want to join me?"

Bill answered in the affirmative, as I knew he would. "I'll take a decaf, black," he said. Jack opened his refrigerator and pulled out a Propel.

After we all had our drinks, we sat down and began reflecting on what we had learned today. The more we discovered, the more I believed that what was happening was far-wider-reaching than Mahone Bay and went deeper than a search for buried treasure. After we ran out of topics to discuss about the mystery, Jack volunteered to show us around the college. Bill had told me the college was beautiful and our tour proved him right. Shortly before five, we returned to Jack's truck and left the campus. We stopped at a local restaurant for dinner, then Jack drove us back to the airport for our trip home. When we reached the airport, we returned his handguns and entered the concourse. While we were waiting to board, I called Cyndi. She assured me that everything was okay at home and that she could see the deputy's car our front. She asked me if the trip had been helpful and I told her I would fill her in when we got there in the morning. I gave her our flight number and the time we were supposed to arrive in Halifax. I was exhausted and felt like I was on auto-pilot already and we still had the long trip home. We waited an hour to board and shortly thereafter was in the air. Cyndi had always accused me of falling asleep quicker than anyone she had ever seen. She won't believe me, but I'll tell her Bill has me beat; he was asleep almost before I could even get seated. The next waking thought I had was when the pilot announced that we were descending toward Halifax.

CHAPTER 16

With no luggage to retrieve, we were in our car within twenty minutes after the pilot shut down the engines and the doors were opened. We stopped for breakfast at a pancake house and were back on the highway before seven o'clock. I was driving the maximum speed allowed, but suddenly swerved to an exit.

"What are you doing?" asked Bill.

"Just spotted a Starbucks. We need coffee, don't we? What do you want?"

"Strong and black. Grande."

I circled the drive to the back of the coffee shop and stopped under the weather canopy at the order point. I heard, "Welcome to Starbucks; this is Lisa. What can I get started for you?"

"Give me a Grande coffee, strong and black. Also, I want a Venti Hazelnut Latte, extra hot, and one Grande Vanilla Latte, half-caf, extra hot. Better give me a slice of Pumpkin Bread, too. That'll be all. Oh, and put a stopper in the Hazelnut latte."

Lisa repeated my order and said, "Please drive around; I'll have your total at the window."

I stopped the car at the pick-up window and waited while they prepared our drinks. The window opened and I held my iPhone out so the server could access my account. She handed me our coffees and we resumed our drive. "Tell Cyndi we brought these from Minnesota. If she knows I found a Starbucks here in Halifax, I will have to come up here every morning . . . I'm kidding—I think—but we do like our Starbucks."

We made the seventy-mile drive in less than an hour and a half. I parked in our drive and went over to the deputy's car that was still sitting in front of the house. We talked a minute, then I moved to the porch. Opening the door, I called out to Cyndi to tell her we were home, but Chelsea had already let her know. I went to the microwave and heated her coffee. After a minute, the oven chimed and I got the coffee and went to the front room where Cyndi was working. "I'm home," I said.

She looked up and exclaimed, "Yea . . . Starbucks!"

Bill followed me and laughed at her reaction to the coffee. "I know where you rank," he said. At least, Chelsea was excited and wagging her tail. Cyndi was already eating the pumpkin bread and drinking her coffee. She looked happy, so I knew she was glad I was back.

We sat down and began bringing everyone up to speed on what had happened in the last day. Cyndi suddenly looked up and said, "Oh, yeah. Jack called early this morning. He tried to call your cell, but I told him you probably had it turned off on the plane. He wants one of you to call him immediately."

I checked my recent call list and saw where Jack had tried to get me; I clicked the number and waited. After just two rings, he answered. After inquiring about our flight back, he got straight to the point. "I went back out to see Tom Wilson this morning. I found him dead in his living room."

"What happened to him? I asked.

"He was shot, execution style. But he was tortured first. It wasn't pretty. My guess is that whoever did it was trying to get information from him. We can't locate that Land Rover. The sheriff said that he would begin checking local hotels today to try to find our mystery men."

"Okay, thanks for letting me know. If anything else happens or you discover new information, call me. And I will do the same for you."

"Oh, yeah. The man in prison with Ahmik. His name was Juhall. I don't know the other one."

I ended the call and told Cyndi and Bill what Jack had said.

"Maybe Jack can follow up that thread there. Okay, Cyndi, did you get any more responses while we were gone?"

"I received three more emails yesterday. Even though the murders were in different countries, it sounded like they could have been all talking about the same one. Middle-aged white man; bearded; half-buried in sand with one arm extended like it was reaching for the sky. Just too much to be coincidental. I gave them all the contact numbers of the ones who have responded to me. In fact, I set up a Dropbox folder where they could share information."

I chuckled. "Like that's going to happen!"

Bill flexed his neck and said, "I don't know. There's a lot more collaboration now than there used to be. Especially if they think the problem may be terrorist-related. And I'm beginning to think that is the case here. I need to make a call to someone in Washington. I'll be back in a few minutes."

Cyndi and I continued to talk about the case while Bill was away. After about fifteen minutes, he returned. He looked serious and said. "We need to go see Sheriff Pfieffer immediately," he said.

CHAPTER 17

I called Pfieffer's office and Lucinda answered. The Sheriff was out checking a local complaint. I told Lucinda that we really needed to meet with him, the sooner the better. She said, "I'll call him on his radio. I'm sure he will want to get back here to talk with you. How soon can you be here?"

"We'll be there in thirty minutes. If he can't get loose right away, call me on my cell—the number's on my card. Oh, and I'd rather you call him on his mobile—others could hear your radio contact."

"Okay; will do. I have the numbers right here."

It was twenty-five minutes later when I parked my car in front of his office. I introduced Cyndi and Bill to Lucinda and she pointed at the sheriff's office door. "Go on in; he's expecting you. If coffee's okay with you, I'll bring it to you; it's ready now."

We entered the room and found chairs. "How are you? asked Pfieffer. "When did you all get back from Minnesota?"

I answered him. "We got back early this morning. This case is getting stranger and stranger."

"I sure hope you brought me some good news," Pfieffer said. "People are getting spooked around here."

"Did anything new happen here while . . ." The office door opening interrupted Bill's question.

Lucinda sat a tray on the desk. We all reached for a cup of coffee and then sat down. We thanked her and she smiled as she backed out, closing the door behind her.

Bill began again, "Did anything else happen while we were gone?"

The sheriff replied, "No, not really. We have been looking for the boat, but it is nowhere to be found. What did you find out about Foster?" He looked at me for an answer.

"Foster is not his real name; he was Ahmik and was a member of the Ojibwa tribe at the Fond du Lac Reservation. We met with Bill's friend and he took us to see a few people there. One of them was called the Truth-Keeper for the tribe. I can't tell you all he told us, but he did verify that the coin did come from the tribe. Ahmik had stolen it and was planning to come to Nova Scotia to look for treasure that many in the tribe thought had been buried on the island. He had recruited a local, Tom Wilson, to come here with him. That was several years ago. Unfortunately, before they left Minnesota, Ahmik was arrested and convicted of dealing in drugs. While in prison, he met a Syrian—Juhall was his name— and, to buy his protection, he told him about the treasure that he thought was on Oak Island; they agreed that when both of them were released, they would come to Canada to seek the gold. Ahmik was released about six months ago and returned to the reservation. He met back with Wilson and they again planned to come search for the treasure. Ahmik really did not expect that the Syrian would come looking for him but he decided to change his name just to be safe. That's when the name Liam Foster was born. About nine weeks ago, Juhall got out of prison and he and a buddy went to Minnesota to search for Ahmik. Since Ahmik apparently did nothing to change his appearance, it didn't take Juhall long to discover that Ahmik was now calling himself Foster. From there it was easy to track him to Tom Wilson's. But Wilson feared the men from the moment he met them and wanted only to distance himself as quickly and as far as possible. That's when it became only three: Foster, Juhall, and Juhall's friend.

The sheriff thought a minute, then said. "The guide that Foster hired said there were four men. Where did the other come from?"

I replied, "I've got an idea about that."

The sheriff asked, "Could Wilson identify the men if he saw them again?"

Bill picked up the story. "He probably could have, but he was killed while we were in Minnesota. We talked with him and he was really scared for his life.

Shortly after we met with him, he was tortured and then executed."

"They were there tying up loose ends, weren't they?" Cyndi could talk the talk, too.

"That's what we believe," I replied. "We also talked to a lady that works in the college there with Jack, Bill's friend, and she did see Ahmik with them, or at least in their car, a couple of times. They were driving a Land Rover, white, with Maine tags. She also said that one time she saw it and a moment later it had just gone, 'disappeared' she said."

"Just like the boat here," Pfieffer said. "But big things can't just *poof* and be gone. I appreciate you all following up on Foster, or Ahmik, for us. But, if he was working with the Middle Easterners, why would they have killed him?"

"I think that they got what information they could from Ahmik and then terminated him. It looks like there may be more to the story than just a treasure hunt and, if so, Ahmik would be in their way; they felt like they needed to silence him. While we were gone, Cyndi worked on trying to establish a connection to other murders around the world. There were several that were almost identical to the one here. She got information and then was able to set up an agreement for the associated organizations to work together on solving them."

Bill continued: "This morning, I called a friend I have in Washington. I wanted to know if there was any indication that something big is in the works. He confirmed that there had been a lot of chatter in the airways that something may be going to happen soon. I brought him up to speed on what has happened here and he is attempting to see if our problem is linked in any way to all the chatter. He will let me know what he discovers. In the meantime, Phil and I would like to go back to Oak Island this afternoon and look around some more." He looked at the sheriff and said, "If you can get away, we would be glad for you to go with us."

"I have a meeting at one o'clock; it should last about an hour. If you can wait until it is over, I would like to go with you. In fact, I probably need to go with you. No telling what will happen if I let you two go off by yourselves."

"What's the chance we could get a boat? I would like to look around the islands. We may even get lucky and find the mysterious boat."

"I'll have Lucinda get in touch with Bear. It may be possible that he could take us. Unless you hear otherwise from Lucinda or me, I will meet you at the marina at two o'clock."

CHAPTER 18

It was a quarter to two when we parked at the marina. Bear was already there, waiting on the dock. We greeted him on the boardwalk and shortly, we spotted Pfieffer's car pulling to a stop and he walked out to join us. We followed Bear up the ramp and immediately his crew readied the boat to pull away from the pier. The water was a little choppy today so I was glad we were in a sturdy vessel; the boat cut through the waves with very little rocking motion, which pleased me since a rocking boat was one of my least favorite sensations. We saw a few other crafts in the bay, mostly sailboats, but saw nothing that resembled the boat that had attacked us. After a slightly bumpy thirty-minute ride, Bear eased his boat to the dock where we had tied off a few days earlier and we jumped to the landing. One of the crew walked to the garage and reappeared in a couple minutes with the four-wheeler we had used before. Bear said, "After

Lively was shot, I got the key to the Polaris; I knew at some point we would want to revisit the island. My crew will wait for us here."

Pfieffer said, "What weapons do we have? There's no telling what, or who, we will find at the dig spot. I've got my service revolver.

"I've got my Glock," I replied.

Bill answered, "I have an H & K."

Bear had his handgun and also an over and under twelve-gauge shotgun, probably set for convergence at forty yards. I knew there were additional weapons on the boat that his crew could tap if needed. We felt pretty safe with our firepower and moved to the all-terrain vehicle.

Bill asked if everyone there had a smart phone and if we could stay in touch with text messages. We all had our phones and made sure everyone had each of our numbers stored in the contacts; we also set us up as a group text so that when we sent a message to one of us, all of us would get copies of it. Bill said to put our phones on vibrate, so if others were there, they would not hear our phones ring.

Bill said, "I want to circle the island first; stay as close to the shore as possible." As we made our way around the island, Bill stopped us a few times. He got out of the four-wheeler and walked down to the shore. We followed him each time, but he didn't tell us what he was looking for. A couple times, he bent down and moved some of the vegetation aside and looked closely at the ground. After we had circled the island, he said, "Let's go to the dig site."

Bear drove us to the pit. We all got out and stood at the edge of the shaft. Bill said, "Let's split up again and spread out in each direction about fifty yards. Look for any sign of intruders or for any tools that we did not see the last time. If you see anything, don't touch it; just use your phone to text me that you've found something. Also, be sure to keep alert; the last thing we want is to be surprised by somebody sneaking up on us."

We each took a direction and began our search, beginning at the fence surrounding the pit. There was little sound for the next ten minutes until I felt the vibration in my pocket. I checked the message; it had come from Pfieffer and said that he had found an area he wanted us to look at. I marked my spot with the GPS on my phone so I could resume my search and began to walk south, which is the direction I had seen Pfieffer go. As I passed the pit, I saw the others moving in the same direction. We met about fifteen feet from the pit and entered the copse of trees. We followed the slight path through the woods and after about twenty yards, came to a clearing; the sheriff was waiting for us at the edge.

"It looks like they have been camping here. The grass is all tromped down and there is a fire pit." He pointed toward the center of the clearing.

Bill moved to the fire site and looked carefully at and around it; then he started walking in a circle, gradually spiraling away from the fire pit. Every few minutes, he would pause and look at something from different angles. It took him about forty-five minutes to cover the clearing. Finally, he stopped and turned to face us; we had followed in his footsteps through the whole procedure. "There were three tents set up here," he said. The tents had one person who slept in each of them. They were Muslims."

Bear looked at Lander and asked, "How in the world can you tell that?"

Bill shrugged his shoulders and looked at us like we should be able to come to the same conclusions. "You can see the outline of the tents and the grass laying down flat; the tents were round and had the floors built into them, probably tents built for cold weather. Once you see where the tents were placed, you can see the outline of the bodies that had lain in them; I would guess sleeping bags. You can see over there where they placed their prayer mats in order to answer the call to prayer. They were careful not to leave anything laying around. From the looks of the ashes, I would say they were last here day before yesterday." He looked around at the rest of us, "Did anyone else find anything?"

We all replied in the negative. He scanned the area one last time and said, "Pick up where you were when the sheriff called us over here; maybe we'll get lucky and find something important."

I pulled my phone from my pocket, accessed the app and let it lead me back to the spot I had last been. I continued searching my quadrant without seeing anything of note. After about fifteen minutes, I felt the buzz from my phone and looked at the message. It was from Bill, "Let's all meet back at the pit."

I tapped *K* on my phone and hit send. Within ten seconds, acknowledgement had been sent from all the group. I made my way back to the pit area where Bill was staring into the shaft.

When we all had gotten there, he said, "I don't believe that anyone has been in this shaft, at least in the last couple of days; I don't see any fresh dig marks nor is there any fresh dirt around the shaft."

"Maybe they got scared off," said Bear, "and won't be back."

"I doubt that," I said. "They have too much invested in the project now to leave without knowing if there is treasure here. Too many bodies!"

Bill chimed in, "No, they're not gone; they are around here somewhere. We've found all we are going to here; let's head back to the boat. I want to check out some other places."

After a quick ride back to the boat, Bill took Bear aside and talked to him. I saw Bear shake his head in agreement and they separated, Bill coming back to us and Bear going to the captain's seat. He started the motor, Pfieffer freed the ropes holding us to the dock, and we slowly moved away. As we began to ease around the island, Bill went to stand beside Bear. I knew that he was going to give him directions about where he wanted to have a closer look. Bear called his crew together and told them, "Get your weapons and I want one of you watching from the bow and one from the stern. The other two guard us from each side of the boat. I don't want any surprises today." They saluted and rushed away. Within two minutes, someone was posted at each end and side of the boat.

I turned my attention back to Bill and asked him, "What are we looking for?"

He said, "I don't know, but I'll know it if I see it."

I understood him, but I really would have preferred a more direct answer, one that would let "*me* know it if *I* saw it."

Bear kept his eye on the depth finder and maneuvered the boat back and forth, keeping a safe distance from the shore. When it looked as if there might be a hidden cove on the island, Bill directed Bear to get closer. We discovered four such inlets, but only two of them offered any possibility of easy access to the island. Bear marked and saved each of them to his GPS, so I did the same with my phone; that would give us directions to the locations coming from the sea or the land. There was a variation in the shoreline as most of it was almost level with the water and had trees and vegetation growing close; however, there were a couple of sections where the shore was rocky and dropped off quickly. We could see the rock bluff continuing below the water line.

It took us an hour and a half to circle the island; when we got back to our starting point, Bill scratched his head and looked thoughtful. He looked at Bear and asked him about the tide levels. Bear answered him, "We are at high tide now."

Bill asked, "How much difference is there between high and low tide?"

"We have a new moon now; the tide varies the most when the moon is new or full. The difference for those moon phases would be somewhere about three to four feet."

I guess that surprised me a little as I knew that the tide levels at the Bay of Fundy—not too far away—can be as much as forty-eight feet. But I knew that was unusual; in fact, the tides at the Bay of Fundy are the highest in the world. The unique shape of the bay leads to the extreme tide differentiation. I remembered Cyndi and me watching that high tide come in; it was impressive.

The conversation between Bill and Bear brought me back to the present. Bill was asking, "Do you have a tent I could borrow? Phil and I want to spend the night here in case they are coming in the dark to look for the treasure."

I asked Bill, "When are we going to stay here?" I knew what he was going to say.

"Why, tonight, of course. You can call Cyndi and tell her we'll see her tomorrow, that is, if she will let you stay out all night."

"The fact that I am with you may give her some concern. But I think I can handle it. But we'll need someone to come back in the morning to get us."

Pfieffer spoke up, "I'll come get you; meet you here at eight o'clock?"

Bill answered, "Make it seven if that's okay with you. If they are working at night, they will be long gone before sunrise."

I guess that I had just had my night planned for me and knew now why Bill had instructed me to wear all black for this trip. He hadn't asked me, but he knew I would be in. That was one of the qualities I admired about Bill; he was decisive. I'm sure that was something he cultivated in the Special Forces. Indecision there could be fatal.

Bear answered Bill's earlier question, "Yes, we keep a couple tents on the boat; we never know when we may need to work remotely through the night; you can use one of them. Do you want to use the Polaris, too?"

"Yes, that would be great; save us a lot of walking. What about night vision? Do you have NVGs?"

"Yes, we have FLIR. The U.S. has shared some of their improvements in night vision with NATO partners and made some of the devices available to its northern partner."

"Great, that will help us."

"Yes, they should help you tonight. Just be sure to take care of them."

I looked at Bill and he could read the question in my eyes. "FLIR—Forward Looking Infrared. It's different than the image enhancement technology you see on television . . . the green-screen technology that amplifies starlight and ambient light. FLIR paints images that show up with different heat signatures; so a person with a body temperature of about ninety-eight degrees will stand out against the heat produced by trees or grass. You 'see' a person's heat outline and get a better image than the older green screen enhancement. But it's not just people you can see;

anything that has a different heat signature will show up."

Bear turned and motioned Seal to join them. "Get one of the tents and two sleeping bags. Also, throw in some water and food for them. Bring a couple of the new FLIR goggles; we'll let them test them for us." Then, he eased the boat back to the dock and his other crew member tied us off. He handed Bill the key to the four-wheeler and Bill and I stepped onto the deck.

I called Cyndi and gave her the plans. She wasn't happy about it, but understood. I knew Chelsea wouldn't be happy either, and she wouldn't understand.

Seal came over to the edge of the boat and said, "Here" He handed a tent to Bill and gave me a duffel bag which I assumed had everything else in it. He said, "I also put a couple of flashlights and flashbang shells in there along with a few other items you may need."

We thanked him and laid the supplies on the dock while Bill went to retrieve our ride.

Pfieffer said, "Be careful. If you see them tonight, call me; don't worry about waking me up. If I don't hear from you, I'll see you at seven in the morning. I may even bring you some coffee."

With that, Bear reversed the engine and they drove away.

I looked at Bill and said, "What have you gotten me into?"

CHAPTER 19

We locked our supplies and equipment in **the** box at the back of the Polaris. "Let's go over to the diner and eat. It'll be a long night and we still have a few hours before dark." He drove the four-wheeler across the road and parked it where we could see it from inside the restaurant.

We went in and sat down at a booth in front of the window. The waitress brought us menus and asked, "What can I get you to drink?"

We both ordered coffee and looked at the menu while she went to get our drinks. When she came back, I asked, "What's the day's special?"

"Hodgepodge; if you've never eaten it, I would recommend you try it. It is one of Nova Scotia's comfort foods . . . lots of vegetables and a really good pork sauce."

We both ordered hodgepodge and neither one of us regretted it. It was a good hot meal with plenty of carbs and protein to get us through the night; it was a different version of southern vegetable soup. Bill is like me; we can eat soup or chili almost any time. We finished the meal with a piece of blueberry cream cake. In Nova Scotia, fresh blueberries, of course.

We left the diner and wasted no time getting back to the pit. When we got close, Bill looked for a place to hide the Polaris. He drove to the least likely route to the site, backed it in underneath some trees, and cut the motor. "We'll hide the Polaris here, then find our spot for the night," he said, getting out of the four-wheeler. We set our stuff aside and I helped him pile branches and leaves over the four-wheeler. We stepped back about ten feet and looked—neither of us could see the vehicle.

Bill grabbed the tent and I picked up the duffel and followed him. I thought he would take some time to find a camp site, but I was wrong. He pulled his phone out and followed directions to a spot he had already marked that afternoon; it became evident that he had planned to stay before we even searched earlier. We stopped in the middle of some wild growth and I glanced at his phone and, yes, there was an 'X' in the middle of his screen.

"Let's get the tent set up here," he said. I wish I could tell you that I helped him, but before I could even decide what to do, he had our shelter standing ready. We stashed our supplies inside and sat down. "Let's check out what Bear gave us," Bill said.

Before I opened the bag, I released the shotgun attached to the side; it was a .410 pump shotgun. I opened the duffel and began pulling items out. On top was some food; we had beef jerky and protein bars, along with some peanut butter crackers individually wrapped. There was a six-pack of water and some Gatorade. "Good choices," I thought. Next were a couple of all-weather jackets. I read the labels: hard-shell, three-layer, wind- and water-proof, and breathable. I pulled out a round container and read the label: Black Face Paint. There were two Special Forces LED flashlights with belt clips. There were a box of shotgun shells and two packs of similar-looking shells. I picked one up and asked Bill what it was.

"Those are flash-bang shells for the shotgun: extremely bright and loud. They are used to stun or create a diversion. They work well and are like a grenade launched from a shotgun. I hope we don't need to use them, but I am glad they're here."

The last items in the duffel were the NVGs. I pulled the packages out and handed one to Bill. We opened them and lifted out the night vision goggles. Bill said, "This is the latest in FLIR technology and can be used in complete darkness. With the head mounts they are hands-free operation. I'll show you how to use them." He walked me through the adjustment for the head straps and showed me how to trip the release that would let me swing the goggles away from my eyes. There were controls for adjusting focus and the eyepiece. This particular model even had integrated video capture. Bill was really happy with these, so I was also happy. If we saw someone, we could capture the image and share the video with others. Impressive!

"Just be sure to get the goggles off your eyes if we decide we need to use the flash bang shells—or any other bright light." Bill made me repeat what he said to be sure I understood the consequences of not doing so. The sudden extreme brightness could blind someone looking through the NVGs.

Bill picked up the face paint, covered his face with the black cream, then handed it to me.

It was almost dark now. Bill said, "If someone comes, they will not show up before midnight. Let's get some sleep while we can. I'll wake you about eleven. Be sure your phone is on vibrate. Once we begin our watch, we'll need to have complete darkness and silence."

I'd heard him say many times that when there is an operation happening you need to sleep and eat when you can because you never know when you will get another chance for either. We checked our handguns to be sure they were ready to go, left them ready to fire, and lay down to sleep. Just like on the plane, Bill was almost immediately asleep; it took me almost twelve minutes to get there.

The next thing I knew was Bill shaking me and whispering in my ear, "Wake up; it's eleven-thirty. We need to be ready."

I sat up and he handed me a bottle of water and some beef jerky; he slid a pack of peanut butter crackers my way. "Remember, no light or loud noise." I gave him a thumbs up to confirm I heard him; I laughed at that when I realized he could not see my gesture in the darkness. "Okay," I whispered. We sat quietly and ate; then we finished our waters. We checked our equipment again. I would wear my goggles and carry my handgun; in addition, Bill would carry the shotgun, its ammunition, and the flash-bang shells. We both had two extra full clips for our weapons. "If we establish contact with anyone, do exactly what I tell you to do." He did not have to remind me of that, but I'm glad he did. It seemed to say to me that he felt confident in whatever might happen.

We sat there in the dark with nothing but the silence of the night; we heard nothing for the first forty minutes. We kept moving and stretching muscles so that we would not get too stiff. Suddenly, Bill leaned over and put his index finger over my lips. "Shhh" he said. "Something's out there. Let's go."

I stood up, pulled my goggles over my eyes, and turned on the optics. Bill's form quickly filled my vision; I couldn't believe how sharp the image was. He was already at the door and I followed him out. We stood just outside the tent and slowly turned a three sixty, looking for a heat signature from a person. Even though it was completely dark with a cloud cover, I could identify all kinds of shapes in front of me: trees and bushes stood out like it was daylight. Suddenly, we heard twigs cracking. I wasn't sure what direction it came from, but Bill immediately moved to our right. With my Glock leading the way, I followed him. He approached a large bush and raised his right hand to stop me; he squatted behind the bush, parted a couple of branches, and looked through them. I followed his example. The noise was coming toward us. It stopped, then started again; I almost pulled my trigger when a moose appeared ten yards away.

I took a deep breath. The false alarm had at least given us a chance to practice; I needed it, but I'm sure Bill didn't. We stood up and watched the moose move on down the trail. Bill turned to me and whispered, "Let's check out the pit. See if anything is happening there."

Bill led the way, moving slowly and cautiously. We walked with the idea that there would be someone who could be alerted by the slightest sound. It took us almost an hour to pick our way through the brush to the fence ringing the pit. We stopped there and listened for ten minutes. Bill motioned for me to stay put and he began crawling toward the shaft. He circled the pit and then carefully peered over the edge. He watched for a few minutes and then quietly made his way back to me. He leaned close to me and whispered, "I think there are some men in the pit, but there are no indications that they accessed it from here. There must be another way down there. Follow me, but be quiet."

I pulled my sleeve up and looked at the luminous dial of my watch; it was almost two thirty. Bill led the way, staying away from paths. It was tough going. I thought about the Polaris sitting back at camp and how nice it would be to be in it now. Then I thought about the men that we were stalking and how they had already killed multiple times. I changed my mind and thought it was nice that the loud four-wheeler was sitting quietly hidden away.

It took us an hour and forty minutes to reach the edge of the island. Bill had led us to one of the rocky cliffs, I'm sure, on purpose. We sat down with our backs against trees. Bill said, "They will leave before sunrise. We'll wait here."

"What makes you think we will see them? There are no boats anchored here." As I spoke, I lifted my arm and pointed out to the bay."

"If you think about it, that's the only thing that makes sense," he replied.

I considered his statement and thought about what we knew and where we were. "You think there is an underwater cave that connects to the pit, don't you?"

"All those action books you read may be paying off," he replied. "There has to be another way to the shaft, either by water or by land. If there were another land tunnel, someone would surely have discovered it by now. I'll put my money on an underwater route."

We sat there until the sky began to lighten and saw no one. Once we thought we heard the whine of an electric engine, but could never locate it. At dawn, Bill stood and said, "Let's get back to the pit. I know whoever was down there has gone, but I want to confirm that." This time, he took the game trail inland and the going was much easier.

We paused at the edge of the clearing and listened. We saw no one nor did we hear any noise at all. I followed Bill to the pit and looked down into the darkness. It was quiet as a tomb this time. "Let's go get our stuff and meet Pfieffer."

It took us almost an hour to pack our equipment and drive the Polaris back to the shed. Bill locked the four-wheeler in the garage; Pfieffer was arriving when Bill rejoined me. We stuffed the tent and duffel in the back of his truck and got in. True to his word, the sheriff had brought us coffee. On the way back, we discussed the night's activities. Pfieffer got a kick out of the moose tale. In the daylight now, I, too, thought it was funny—but last night in the dark, not so much.

"So, you didn't find out anything to help us, did you?" said Pfieffer.

"That depends on how you look at it," replied Bill. "We now know that someone is going in the pit, but that they have to have another way in. I heard men talking down there, but they didn't use the shaft there at the money pit to get there."

"What's our next plan for action then?" I asked.

Bill thought a minute and looked at the sheriff. "I would like to do a couple of things, but they call on Bear's being able to help us again. I would like to search the shorelines again by water, but this time at low tide. I also would like to borrow dive gear if he has some available. I need to give Phil another lesson anyway," he said, looking at me and smiling. Bill, of course, honed his diving skills while he was in special ops and earned his certification; every so often, he serves as an instructor at the Y. This past summer's retreat for us had included an introduction to diving and I had passed my certification. It had even included instruction in cave diving, which can seriously compound the dangers of diving.

Pfieffer answered, "We'll talk to Bear when we get back to the office. I'm sure he can work something out for you."

When we pulled into the sheriff's parking spot, there was another car sitting in the next lane. "A rental," said Bill. "I think you have company."

Lucinda met us at the door. "There are two men in your office waiting. All they would tell me was that it was urgent that they talk with you. Since I knew you were almost here, I didn't call. They didn't give me their names, but they are arrogant like Americans." She blushed and looked at me after she said that. "I'm sorry. I didn't mean all Americans are arrogant. You act like one of us." She tried to make me feel better . . . and she did.

"No offense taken. I know what you mean."

The two men stood to their feet as soon as we opened the office door. Their eyes quickly moved from one to the other of us. One of them paused as he looked carefully at Bill.

"You," he said. "I might have known. It would take someone with your background to make the brass move as quickly as they have on this."

Bill said, "Hello, Marian. Good to see you, too. When Lucinda out there said there was an arrogant American in here, I should have known it was you. This is Sheriff Pfieffer and this is Phil Kent." We pushed out our arms to shake their hands.

"I'm Marian Johnson and this is A.J. Billings. I know Bill from our service days together."

"I thought my call to Washington would get some action," Bill said. "I think we have stumbled onto a major operation, one that could lead to quite a catastrophic end if it is not checked. You all have been flying most of the night; have you eaten this morning?"

"No, we haven't, but we're okay; you all have probably had breakfast."

"Actually, we haven't. Phil and I spent the night on a stakeout and the sheriff just picked us up. Let's go eat before we get too engaged. What about you, sheriff? Can you go with us? Then we'll come back here and continue our discussion. We'll call Cyndi and she can meet us here."

Johnson asked, "Who is Cyndi?"

Bill answered, "Cyndi is Phil's wife."

Billings said, "This discussion should be among Marian, Bill, maybe the sheriff, and me." He looked at me as he spoke.

Bill quickly answered him. "No, this discussion will be among all of us, including Phil and Cyndi. They know more about what is going on than anyone here."

The sheriff agreed. "They are privy to any information we have about what is going on here."

Billings looked at Johnson, who finally nodded his head. "Okay, we'll start out with everyone involved, then play it by ear."

Pfieffer replied, "Then that settles it. I didn't eat before I picked you up, so breakfast sounds good to me."

On the way out, Pfieffer said to Lucinda. "Call Cyndi and ask her to meet us here as quick as she can.

Tell her we have visitors from Washington and we are going over the case. You will need to go get her because Phil has their car here. We are going to get something to eat and will be back here shortly."

"Do you want me to send Deputy Roget? He's out on patrol."

Pfieffer looked at me and shook his head, "No, you do it and don't tell Roget what is going on."

"Yes, Sir. I'll do it immediately."

Although we could have all fit in the sheriff's car, he motioned to Billings and Johnson. "Follow us; the diner is just a couple of blocks from here." I think he agreed with Lucinda; they were arrogant Americans. In this case, I concurred with him.

We entered the restaurant and went to a large table at the back of the dining room. Do I need to tell you we got coffee? I ordered eggs, pancakes, and bacon. Bill and Shaun got eggs and sausage. The two from Washington ordered bagels and cream cheese. Bagels and cream cheese! What kind of men order that? I looked at Bill and he just raised his eyebrows and grinned.

After the order came, Billings spoke. "Tell us what has been going on in Nova Scotia and why is it connected to us?"

Pfieffer answered him. "We'll wait until we get back to the office to discuss it; we don't have everyone here yet and we don't want to be overheard in the restaurant."

Johnson looked at Bill. "You must still have some clout. We are here on orders from the CIA chief. It's unusual for him to get involved this quickly in a matter."

Lander replied, "I talked with Director Frazier yesterday. He expressed some concern that this could be a major threat."

We continued to exchange small talk and steered away from the main topic while we ate. As soon as we finished, we paid, got into our cars, and made our way back to the office. Lucinda arrived just as we opened the door; Cyndi entered the front room and looked at me. I nodded and she moved into the conference room with us. We all sat around the table and looked at each other; Pfieffer introduced the new men to Cyndi.

Billings spoke. "Now, if you can, tell us what has been going on in Nova Scotia and why is it connected to the CIA?"

Bill brought them up to date, beginning with the finding of Ahmik's body and ending with our stakeout of the island last night. They were smart enough to listen and didn't interrupt him at all. When he finished, Johnson asked, "Go over why you think this is a threat to the U.S."

Bill replied, "Not just the U.S. It could have worldwide ramifications. I'll let Cyndi explain the connections to other places and what information she has collected. She is the one who connected the dots."

Cyndi outlined what she had done, and covered it so clearly and carefully that everyone understood it from the beginning. There seemed no doubt that the same people were behind at least five other incidents around the world. As she talked, I sensed a subtle change in the attitude of both Billings and Johnson; arrogance was being replaced by a sense of concern. The proof of the change came with Johnson's question. "What do we need to do to help?"

Bill asked about the chatter on the social media. "What are you hearing? The Director indicated that there have been some hints about upcoming terrorist activity. Anything related to plans for a major incident, maybe being labeled as an awakening? The link to the statue has to be more than coincidental."

Johnson paused as he glanced at Cyndi and me, then shook his head. "We think the connection to the statue may be symbolic, a signal that perhaps set implementation plans in motion. There is talk that something big is being planned in all the areas where Cyndi discovered that similar murders had taken place. We are not sure how possible treasure here in Nova Scotia fits in the picture.

"I can answer that, I think. Tom Wilson overheard a conversation that indicated that the Muslims wanted the treasure to bankroll their activities. If they have several major incidents planned, they will need a lot of funds to finance them."

That thought hung in the air for a few minutes while everyone considered it. Finally, Billings spoke. "That's probably right. One of our inserts told us that the terrorist cells were trying to purchase bio-weapons. They might be able to find them, but they won't be cheap."

Cyndi spoke up, "Then it's important we stop them from getting the treasure here. If they don't have funds, maybe they can't carry out the devastation."

I agreed with her and reminded Pfieffer he was going to contact Bear. He went to the door and asked Lucinda to tell Bear we needed to talk with him ASAP. I saw her reach for her cell and thumb-type a text. In about forty seconds, the phone in the office rang. She answered it and said, "It's Bear. Who wants to talk with him?"

Bill moved to the phone and explained what we needed. He nodded and ended the call. He looked at me and said, "Bear will meet us in an hour and a half."

Billings asked the question that should have been asked early. "Do you know the names of any of the Muslims working here?"

"The one that was in prison with Ahmik is called Juhall. I don't know any of the others."

Johnson looked up. "Juhall? I've heard that name. He is one of the associates of a man called Adar. Adar has been on our radar for some time now and is being mentioned in all the chatter around the Internet. It is said that he is in Canada, so we'll assume that Adar is the one running the operation here."

"So, what's the plan moving forward?" asked Billings.

I looked at Bill for an answer. "We'll continue to work up here to terminate the treasure hunt. You all see what you can discover about the terrorist plots. Try to identify the targets, get some idea of timelines. Keep us in the loop and we'll share anything we get."

Cyndi broke in, "I'll send both of you access rights to my Dropbox files. I've gotten some good information from other sites. That will give you some contacts."

"Thanks. We appreciate that. And I apologize for the way we came on to Lucinda this morning. We assumed that we were on another dead-end pursuit, but I think this represents a credible threat." Johnson looked sincere as he spoke.

They got up and exited the room. I saw Johnson bend down and say something to Lucinda on the way out. She smiled and I read her lips, "No problem."

We sat around for about ten minutes and reviewed the facts. All of us were glad that we were going to get help from the U.S., but we couldn't leave it to them. Bill said, "Well, we've got work to do. We need to go to your house to change clothes." He looked at me as he spoke.

"Okay, we'll drop Cyndi off there and get what we need. We'll have to hurry if we meet Bear when we're supposed to. You ready, Cyndi?"

"No, I'm not going with you. I'm staying for a while with Lucinda and then she'll drop me back at home." I looked at Lucinda and she smiled. I think she smiles a lot.

CHAPTER 20

We ran by the house to change clothes and were at the marina ten minutes before we had told Bear we would meet him; he was already there. Walking across the deck of the boat to meet us were Bear and Seal. We boarded and greeted them. Bear said, "Sheriff Pfieffer called and said he could not go; something happened and he needs to stay here and take care of it. I told him we would get back to him when we returned." As soon as we were safely aboard, the boat backed from its berth and slowly turned to head out of the harbor. Within five minutes we were skimming across the waves in Mahone Bay. Bear looked at Bill and said, "Point me where you want to go."

"When is low tide?"

"Low tide will be about twenty minutes after we get to Oak Island . . . assuming that is where we are going first."

"Do we have dive equipment?"

Seal answered Lander. "Yes, we have it all. You all may want to go below and pick out dive suits. We have both wet and dry, but I suspect you will want the dry suits. The water temperature is close to the warmest it gets all year, but it is still cold."

"Yes, we want the dry suits. I would like to get all the gear ready before we get there. Can you show us where to go?"

Bear said, "Seal, go with them to help them get ready. I'll stay here and watch our backs on the way to the island."

Seal led us down the stairs and pointed to a room on the left. "Everything is there. Get what you need. Tanks are stored on the far wall; suits are in the trunk to the left; masks and fins are in the trunk on the right."

Bill said, "Thanks. What about other stuff like lights and weights?

"All those items are in the bins under the tanks."

I followed Bill into the room and he went directly to the tanks. He picked two of the one hundred cubic feet models and closely inspected them, checking for leaks in both the tanks and the valves; he opened the valves briefly to check the pressure and then set the tanks at the door. We moved next to the trunk holding the dive suits. He looked through them, picked two, and handed me an XL. "This should fit you, if you suck in your gut."

I laughed and said, "You have a double XL and it's not all because you are taller than me."

"Touché. Let's get them on."

We put the inner layer of undergarments on and dressed in our dry suits and selected the rest of our dive equipment: masks, weights, fins, and then dive knives that we would secure at our ankles. We carried everything to the deck and laid it out in order. We were just rounding the last island before Oak Island. I asked Bear, "Have you seen anything on the way over?"

By 'anything' he knew I meant the other boat and he replied, "All clear. Not a sign of it."

We carefully lofted our suits; from my earlier training with Bill, I knew it was critical that we get the right amount of air pressure in them. After all, it was this layer of air that would keep us comfortable in the chilly water. We adjusted the rest of the equipment and Bear double-checked all our hoses and valves; we verified that our communications were working. Seal reminded us that the suits had the typical air release vent at the left arm and told us that these suits also had self-activating foot vents as a safety measure; without the foot vent, a diver that gets upside down could find himself in a critical situation in which he would possibly not be able to right himself in the water. It can be done, but requires that the diver be skilled in executing an emergency tuck and roll, a difficult maneuver under water for someone not specifically trained for it. Seal also said, "You have about an hour of oxygen in your tanks—but that can be more or less depending on your depth and your breathing rate. Watch the dial and don't let it fall below twenty to twenty-five percent. If you need to stay longer, come back to the boat and I'll give you another tank."

Bill had Bear to steer the boat north until we were about even with where one of the rock bluffs began. "Anchor here; I want to check this bluff out," Bill said.

We moved to the ramp, Bear lowered it to almost water level, and we flopped backward into the water. We held ourselves at the surface a minute and checked our buoyancy compensators and when we were satisfied all was right, we slowly sank. When I had gone through my ocean training, I had been surprised at how much better vision I had in salt water compared to fresh water and the water here was really clear. We leveled off at about ten feet and Bill began moving toward the rock wall; he swam slowly so he could take in everything and, I suspected, so I could keep up.

Bill led us to the rock wall and slowly began moving to his left. Bill's voice came through my audio buds. "We know there are reports that there are flood tunnels from the sea to the treasure shaft; it is believed that those are booby traps for anyone that got to a depth of a hundred feet or so in the mine. But what we are looking for here is another way that someone could get to the treasure. Many of the groups that buried treasure years ago created back doors to the site. I think this one must have another entry because there were people in the pit the other night and they did not go past us to get there."

We remained at a depth of ten feet as we carefully inspected the underwater cliff. After about twenty minutes, we surfaced; we were almost to the southern end of the bluff. Bill descended to twenty feet and began moving back toward our starting point. We saw plenty of holes in the rocks, but nothing that would provide another path to the treasure pit. Suddenly I heard, "Bingo!" and Bill kicked downward to this right.

I followed him as he paused at an opening about twelve feet in diameter. "Stay out here while I check it out," he said. He shined his light into the cave, then flicked his fins and entered it. After a couple of minutes, I heard him say, "Come on in; it seems safe." I swam through the opening and followed the tunnel, which gradually narrowed until it was only about six feet in diameter and stayed that size until it ended at about fifteen feet into the bluff. We looked at the rock wall that blocked us; we could see no way around it. In the darkness, neither of us saw the cable that was snaked behind the rough rocks running the length of the tunnel. We turned and swam back out into the cove. "I thought we had found something," Bill said.

"So did I," I said. "Oh, well, that would have been too easy, I guess." We continued our search, but found nothing else that caught our attention. At the end of the bluff, Bill immediately kicked upward and I followed. Surfacing, we looked for our boat; it was still anchored, about twenty yards from us. Bill said, "Bear, bring the boat south to where we are." He pulled a red signal flag Velcro-attached to the leg of his dive suit and extended the handle and waved it above the water.

Bear said, "I see you. We'll be there in a couple of minutes." The boat accelerated toward us and within five minutes, we were standing on the deck with Bear and Seal.

"Nothing," said Bill. "But there has to be another way in there."

"Maybe we just overlooked something," I said.

"We may come back for another look," Bill said. I would have bet the farm that we would see something." He looked at Bear and said, "I guess we are ready to head back."

Seal looked at his partner standing at the helm and gave him a thumbs up. The boat immediately kicked into gear and leveled out at about forty knots.

CHAPTER 21

"**D**o you think they found it?" asked Ahmud. They were all on deck watching the Canadian Coast Guard boat sprint toward the open water. Although they were less than a hundred yards from the other boat, they knew that they were invisible to it.

Adar looked at him. "I don't think so, but we need to escalate the timeline; we need to get as much out right now as we can." He motioned to Juhall. "Get the boat in place, quickly. We'll get the subs ready." His use of subs, though not technically correct, communicated the idea. "Get your dive suit on," he said to Ahmud. He led the rest to the back of the boat. "Get them ready to go; we'll be in place in about three minutes." He jogged back to the front of the boat, where Ahmud was dressed and standing.

"What are you waiting on? Get the cable attached!" Ahmud heard the stress in his captain's voice; he used his gloves to grasp the cable attached to the winch and jumped overboard as soon as the boat had drifted to a stop. He descended quickly and attached the snap hook to the loop in the underwater cable and finned back to the surface. He bobbed up and down in the rough water; when a swell took him high enough to be seen from the boat, he gave a thumbs up to Adar.

Adar flipped a switch and the winch began to wind the cable; he watched it for thirty-three seconds and shut it down. "Trapdoor should be open," he yelled to Ahmud. He moved to the left of the boat and spotted his men already in the water and gave them the "Go" sign.

Three personal underwater vehicles sank beneath the surface and accelerated toward the rocky bluff. The fourth cruised to Ahmud and he grasped a ring on the PUV which then quickly dove and followed the others. They turned their spotlights on and slowed as they approached the open tunnel where Lander and Phil had just been. Ahmud moved past them to the front of the line and led the way into the opening, quickly getting to the wall that had blocked Lander and Phil; they entered the section that was now standing open. The water was moving a lot today and they had to continuously adjust their angles and direction to stay away from the sharp rocks along the passageway; the tunnel constantly angled down and had three lazy turns in it. After thirteen minutes, they spilled out into an open cavern. The room was a good twenty by thirty feet around; the ceiling was twelve feet above them. On one side had been an opening to the ground three hundred feet above; a cave-in had piled rocks in the crevice so that the room was not reachable from the shaft. They had the only access to the money pit.

The men motored to the side opposite the access shaft, dismounted, and tied their PUVs to rocky outcroppings. They turned their spotlights to the wall and stared at what they had come after. A shelf had been chiseled out of the fragile shale wall and on the shelf sat thirteen wooden chests; the rounded top boxes were water-logged but still as solid as when they were deposited here. On a second ledge was another group of square wooden chests. These boxes had been waterproofed and still were sealed with some type of rubber-like bead around the openings. Each one of the chests was secured to the rock wall with a heavy chain and lock. They had lost the first one that they had tried to get before they realized that the locks had a puzzle that would release them from the wall; they had thought they could just rip or pry the box loose, but had triggered a trap set by whoever had deposited the boxes there. The built-in booby trap had stolen that one from them when it fell into a deeper pit at the rear of the shelf; since then, they became more cautious and meticulous in trying to get the treasure. Ahmik had warned them that there were traps set to keep scavengers from stealing the treasure, but they had not believed him at first . . . and that proved to be an expensive oversight. Ahmik had also warned them that once they found a clue and used it, it must be placed exactly like it was found; otherwise, the subsequent clues would not work as designed. They arranged everything they would need and waited on Adar to join them.

On the boat, Adar felt his phone vibrate and looked at the screen. He grimaced and clicked 'talk'. "This is Adar."

"Have you secured the treasure?"

"My men are in the pit now to try to get them out."

"Why do you not have all of them on your boat by now? The deadline is coming up quickly."

Adar took a deep breath and blew it out slowly before answering: "Each chest is safeguarded and secured to the shelf by a locked chain, which if pulled on without being unlocked will cause the chest to slide away into a much deeper shaft and the treasure will be lost. We have to be careful that we do not trigger the trap." He did not volunteer that they had lost one chest already by rushing it.

"You have four days to get the treasure on board."

"That's too quick! Two days ago, you said we would have a week and a half to get it."

"That was before everyone else got involved trying to find us. Did you know that two agents from the C.I.A. were in town?"

"C.I.A. . . . as from the United States? What are they doing up here?"

"I don't know. I hope they haven't realized a connection between Oak Island and our bigger objective. Nevertheless, you must complete your task within four days; we have to have that treasure to fund our other projects."

"What if I can't do it by then?"

"You will." He didn't say "or else" but Adar clearly understood the threat. The man ended the call without saying anything else. He looked at his contact list and made the first of five more calls around the world.

CHAPTER 22

Bear dropped us at the marina and Bill and I went immediately to see Pfieffer. Cyndi was still there, working at a computer at Lucinda's desk. Lucinda looked up and said, "The sheriff is waiting for you; go on in. Cyndi, you need to join them, also."

I looked at Lucinda and started to speak, but she beat me to the punch. "I'll bring you some coffee."

"Great. Lucinda, let me ask you a question. I haven't seen Deputy Roget around lately; what's happened to him?"

"He got mad because he wasn't included in the meeting with the men from Washington; he tried to get me to tell him what all was said." She looked a little embarrassed but continued, "He made a phone call and then quit. I think he was jealous of the sheriff letting you and Cyndi work with him on this case. I really don't think my uncle was sad to see him go."

We went in and all sat down again at the conference table. Sheriff Pfieffer looked up and I could see the worry etched in his face. There was the beginning of bags under his eyes; his normal bright eyes did not have their usual twinkle; and his clothes looked like he hadn't changed them . . . right after he hadn't shaved. Something was definitely lying heavy on his mind. I asked him, "What's wrong. Has anything else happened today?"

"No, nothing's happened. I started with investigating a local murder and now have the feeling that we are in the middle of some worldwide terrorist plot. The C.I.A. wouldn't have sent two agents up here unless something big was going on. Johnson and Billings know more than what they told us."

I looked at Bill, waiting for a comment from him. Finally, he spoke. "I agree with you, Sheriff. I believe you are right. I think the men trying to steal the treasure on Oak Island are a part of a super cell that is planning a major attack. Johnson admitted to me that the C.I.A. also thinks that. If I know how the U.S. military works—and I do—then they have already activated covert operations to stop the upcoming event." He looked at Cyndi and continued, "I suspect that a team has been sent to each of the sites that you have discovered. Billings told me that, even though they had heard some chatter about something in the planning stages, they had not connected the dots until you told them what you had found."

"So, what do we need to do now?" asked Pfieffer.

"The other organizations, CSIS, C.I.A., Canadian Coast Guard, will pursue the terrorist angle. I think we need to concentrate our efforts on stopping the treasure hunt here. Except Cyndi. You should continue to collect what you can; you've already made some contacts in those other potential targets. Understand that the C.I.A. won't share all their information with you—or us—but you are ahead of them right now."

I spoke up. "I agree with Bill. We need to stop them here. Who knows? If they can't get the treasure, then maybe they won't have the funding to carry out their planned destruction. That needs to be goal one for the rest of us. Cyndi will continue to curate information for the larger picture."

"How do we stop this group here? We've not even seen their boat lately. The locals are calling it the ghost ship. If someone sees it, it quickly disappears in thin air." The sheriff was completely puzzled.

Bill answered, "I may have an idea about that, but I need to do some more research first."

Cyndi looked at him and asked, "I'll be glad to do that while you are out chasing the bad guys."

"Maybe. Let me think about it and I'll talk to you tonight at home. I need to straighten some of the ideas out in my head first."

Pfieffer got our attention again. "What are our plans for tomorrow? We've got to make some progress here. We don't know what the terrorists' timeline is, so we have to assume it's not far off. Bear and his crew are at our disposal until we get this cleared up. He will be here at eight o'clock in the morning."

"Good. Let's meet here at eight. I want to dive again tomorrow, but we may need to look for the boat in the morning first. If we can find it, we can stop this in its tracks. I don't think there is anything else we can do here tonight, so let's all go get a good night's sleep and be ready to go early tomorrow."

"I agree with you, Bill," I said.

CHAPTER 23
C.I.A. HEADQUARTERS: LANGLEY, VIRGINIA

"What did you think?" asked the director. "How much do they know?"

Billings spoke first, "They don't know much; they think it deals mostly with the treasure hunt there."

Johnson disagreed with him. "I don't agree, Mr. Director. Most of them don't have the background to understand the worldwide implications, but Lander certainly does."

"What makes you think so?" asked Frazier.

"I've reviewed Lander's file, of which you know most is classified, but we have special access. He was in Special Forces and participated in black ops around the world; in most of those he was the leader. He has three medals for his eight years of service. You obviously know him or you would not have reacted the way you did from his contact with you."

"Yes, I know him. In fact, I served with him on some of those excursions across enemy borders. Lander was a great analyst and one of the best field operatives we have ever had and could have been sitting in my seat if we had been successful in getting him to remain active. You don't think he knows much about the terrorist link?" Frazier asked.

Billings looked at Johnson, who finally responded. "I think he is aware of all the implications and knows much more that he let on to us."

"Will he share information with us?" asked Johnson.

Frazier replied, "Yes, I think so, but not if he thinks we are holding out on him. What about the rest of them there? Can we trust them?"

Johnson answered, "I think we can trust them, but you know that no one other than Lander has security clearance."

The Director spun around in his chair and gazed out the window while he thought. After thirty seconds, he turned back to face his visitors. "Meet me back here in an hour. I want to run this by Director Pollock." He was referring to the Director of National Intelligence. He immediately got to his feet and left the room, turning right in the hallway. He had an open invitation from Pollock to his office anytime, day or night. If Pollock was not there and Frazier deemed it important, Pollock would be in his office within fifteen minutes if he were in town. After a short walk, he paused in front of an unmarked door, knocked, and entered without waiting for an invitation. The Director was sitting behind his desk, talking on his landline, his choice of communication devices since it could be encrypted and was not subject to the same security threats that cell devices were. He looked up, saw Frazier, pointed at a chair, and held up his index finger, signaling "just a minute."

He placed his receiver on his phone and fixed his gaze on Frazier. "Bring me up to date; how did the visit to Canada go?"

"Pretty well. It now seems obvious that the events in Nova Scotia are tied with the threats we have been following. The Islamic group is trying to recover the buried treasure in order to fund their terrorist activities."

"Have they made any progress in locating the treasure?"

"It seems as they have. The Muslim group has reportedly found an access route to the underground vault and may have already gotten some of the coins out; they have assuredly located them."

"Can we send in a team to take them out?"

"We could and they would be successful. However, remember that this is in Nova Scotia and the Canadians like to handle their own problems."

Pollock replied, "This is a problem that may affect the world. It's not just about Canada or even Canada and the U.S. What do you recommend?"

"I would like to go there myself to meet with the local authorities. Remember that one of our best operatives ever is there now and is involved. Bill Lander is still capable of doing anything that a covert team could do and he already has the cooperation of the Canadian officials. According to Johnson, the group working with Lander there is impressive. In addition to Lander, there is a professor, Phil Kent, and his wife Cyndi. They have been friends with Lander for years. Phil played college basketball with Lander and they have remained in contact. For the past few years, Kent has gone with Lander each year for personal training similar to that Lander got in special ops. Kent is also an author and uses the training for background for his novels. The sheriff there seems more than capable and they also have the local office of the Coast Guard working with them. I think they make an effective team to work with us. We can assist them in the background."

"Do they have any idea how widespread the implications are or do they think it's just a local treasure hunt gone bad?"

"They know. In fact, the woman, Cyndi, was the first to connect the dots and brought it to others' attention. When she told Lander about it, he called me. It was not until that call that our department realized the connection."

"Will Lander still work with us?"

"Yes, he broached the idea that we could work together on this. However, he insists that the others be in the loop also. They can be trusted, but they don't have security clearance. But that may be the only way to keep Lander involved."

"I thought Lander was teaching somewhere in Tennessee. How did he end up in Canada?"

"It seems that Kent and his wife are staying in Nova Scotia for a time while he finishes the current novel he is working on. It just so happened that the first homicide victim was deposited on the shore below the rented house they are staying in. Besides discovering the body, Kent found one of the old coins from the treasure and called Lander, who took some time off and joined Kent in Canada."

Pollock took a deep breath. "We don't have the luxury of having a lot of time. Go meet with them and keep things moving. We can give them whatever they need while we stay in the background there. We do already have teams deployed to the other locations around the world, don't we?"

Frazier nodded. "Yes, they are all in positions and active."

Pollock replied, "Then, let's move on it! Keep me briefed of any new development or activity."

Frazier quickly exited the room, leaving Pollock deep in thought.

CHAPTER 24

It was six-thirty when we parked the car and went into the house. We had stopped on the way and bought a large pizza to take home. While I took Chelsea out and fed her, Cyndi got out plates and glasses; Lander raided the fridge. "What do you all want to drink?" he asked as he picked up a beer for himself.

"I want water," Cyndi said.

"I'll take a coke," I answered.

Cyndi looked at Bill. "Okay, tell me about my research. What do I look for?"

Bill explained to Cyndi what he was thinking. Both Cyndi and I looked at him like he was kidding. "Believe me, this stuff is real—as impossible as it may seem!" said Bill.

"I'll get right on it," said Cyndi. "I've got to see it myself before I believe it."

When Lander and I got up the next morning, Cyndi was stretched out in the recliner with her laptop and iPad with her. She looked up when we entered the room. "This stuff is unbelievable!" she said.

Lander asked, "Have you been up all night?"

She replied, "I guess so. I didn't realize it. Talk about your science fiction—except it's not!"

I spoke up. "Try to get some sleep today while we're gone. We're going back to Oak Island. We'll meet this afternoon and discuss it all. We've got to hit the road; we're meeting Bear and Pfieffer at eight."

"What about breakfast? Do you want me to make you something?" Cyndi started to lay aside her computer.

"No, we don't have time. We'll have coffee and a breakfast bar on the way." I opened the drawer and picked out two K-cups, inserted one of them in the Keurig, and pushed the button. The sound told me when the cup had been filled; I picked it up and handed it to Bill. I waited about thirty seconds and mine was finished. We grabbed two protein bars and a couple of bananas, left the house, and as the door was closing, I called out to Cyndi, "Keep the door locked. See you this afternoon."

CHAPTER 25

Adar **swam through the opening and came to a** stop in front of his men; they were looking at the treasure, waiting for further directions. He had left the boat sitting close by, but did not worry about it being seen. He pushed aside a piece of rock and stared at the clue. This clue had led him to the third step. He remembered the warning he had taken from Ahmik before he had killed him, "Five steps must be carried out in proper sequence or the treasure would be lost for all time." Ahmik had reported that the warning had been found in an old history of the Ojibwa tribe; he had snuck into Mokuk's lair while he and Magisi had gone to Halifax one day and discovered the old native writings. Ahmik had almost been caught in the cave, but had escaped with one page with minutes to go before Magisi and Mokuk returned. That page provided the clues to not only the location of the treasure but the first steps to retrieve it.

Adar knew that the primary directions had not been followed. At one time, the treasure was secured in this room without it being flooded. Because treasure hunters had tried to access the fortune through the money pit and shaft, they had triggered the first of the traps and had flooded the room. A subsequent attempt had keyed the second trap and the shaft from the surface had caved in. But he thought that if the rest of the steps were carried out correctly, he could still claim the prize for his own.

He had successfully moved through the first two steps. The first had been to locate the access tunnel from the shoreline bluff. The clues he started with was on the piece of paper that he had taken from Ahmik. It showed a map of a coastline with two sets of numbers: 4431 was the first and the second was 6418 with an "X" at a spot on the shoreline. Ahmik had directed him here and it did not take him long to confirm that those numbers were the latitude and longitude coordinates for Oak Island. After that, it had been relatively easy to find the room. He remembered with regret what had then happened . . .

# # #

When he looked around the flooded chamber, he could see two shelves with boxes sitting on them. *The treasure!* he thought. *I've found the treasure!* He swam quickly over to the shelves, where he was joined by his men. They could see all the chests, and a couple of the men moved to grab one of them. When they tugged on the first chest, the shelf beneath it suddenly disintegrated and the chest sank out of sight.

"Wait, don't touch any more of them!" Adar cried. The warning by Ahmik jolted his memory: he had to successfully move through each of five steps before he tried to remove the treasure; attempts to remove a chest before all steps had been completed would cause the treasure to be lost forever. That had proven to be true when the first chest sank out of sight.

He looked again at the old document; he found a faint reference to the number two, which Adar took to mean was step two. The numeral two had a faded symbol following it. Thus, clue two had been to find an Order symbol related somehow to the number two. It had taken him two days to determine that the Order referred to here was probably that of the Knights Templar. He had finally found an obscure reference that suggested that the Knights had escaped here back in the 1300s when the King of France mandated that they be terminated. That excited him because it meant that the value of the treasure would in all likelihood be much more than if it had been pirate's booty as most people believed. Treasure seekers had for years been looking for the lost wealth of the Knights Templar; it was reputed to be worth an untold fortune. After that insight, it had been relatively easy to find the symbol; it was in the exact middle of the cave they were now in and had been an image with two men mounted on a single horse; it was a recognized symbol of the Knights Templar. It had taken him some time to understand what he had to do with the clue.

"We've got to discover the other clues before we can remove the chests," he told his men. He was looking for clue three, but what did it look like? He swam all around the room, searching, but saw nothing obvious. He went back to the clue he had just found and studied it. This was the second step and the most noticeable aspect of the symbol itself was the fact that there were two men on a single horse. "Maybe that's it," he thought. "Clue three will have a relationship with the number three. Perhaps three men or three animals."

He explained to his followers what to look for: either an authentic symbol or one illustrated some way on the rocks, having something to do with the number three. "If you see something, do not touch it; alert me at once," he said. They began their search with each man assigned to one wall. Adar himself would search the ceiling and the floor. They were occupied with the quest for the next forty minutes, but no one saw anything that could even be stretched to look like a symbol. Adar was becoming frustrated and it showed in his jerky movements.

"You told me to remind you when we had only ten minutes' air left," said Juhall.

Adar glared at him and Juhall was glad they were down here in the water. "Okay, everybody, let's go," Adar growled. They quickly exited the way they had entered. Adar was the first to the boat and triggered the winch to lower the rock slab back over the entrance to the tunnel. Ahmud had remained at the rock and released the cable. He then followed the others to the boat. As soon as everyone was safe on board, Juhall steered them away toward their hiding spot. Adar went below and entered his room. He began pacing back and forth, talking to himself. "What have I done?" he thought. "I've got to get that treasure or I am history."

CHAPTER 26

We parked at the marina and found the sheriff and the Coast Guard crew already there. As soon as we boarded, the boat pulled from the dock. "Where to first?" Seal asked Bill.

"Let's just cruise around the islands close to Oak Island. I want to see if we can spot that speed boat. Do you have binoculars on board?"

"Yes, we do. "Shark," he called. "Go grab us some binoculars from below." The other crew member moved to get them.

We cruised around almost every island in the vicinity of Oak Island without seeing the boat. Bill said, "I know that they are around here close and they are probably watching us look for them."

Bear looked doubtful. "We've checked all the hiding places. I don't believe they're here now."

"If the treasure is still here, then they are still here," I said. "They've got too much invested in this to just run off and leave it."

"Maybe they decided it was getting too hot here now and have left for a while and plan to come back after the search cools," said Seal.

"That's a good idea, but I don't buy it," said Lander. "I think they are close by."

"Then, where are they? Even when a turtle pulls its shell over its head to protect it, you can still see the shell. And a big boat can't even do that." Bear was looking frustrated.

"Maybe it can do that," Lander said. "You remember what Sherlock Holmes said, don't you?"

I waited for the others to answer, then said, "He said the best hiding place was out in the open, in plain sight. *The Purloined Letter?*"

"*The Purloined Letter* was a Poe story, but it illustrates the same principle. Bill enjoyed correcting me.

"Are we going to dive again?" I asked.

Bill replied, "Yes, let's go over to the other bluff area and check it out."

In five minutes, we were anchored off shore and going below to get the dive gear; Bear was planning to accompany us this time. Although Pfieffer was not going in the water with us, he followed us to watch us get the gear. Suddenly, his phone rang. He answered and listened for a few seconds, then said, "When?" After five more seconds, he ended the call.

"Hold up, guys. That was Lucinda. We need to get back to my office. Somebody else from Washington will be there in an hour." He looked at me and said, "Lucinda is calling Cyndi now and will go get her. She needs to be in this meeting, also."

We stowed all the gear and went back topside. Bear gave Seal instructions and shortly, we were on our way back to Lunenburg.

CHAPTER 27

In forty minutes, we were filing through the door into Pfieffer's office. The sheriff had asked Bear and Seal to sit in on the meeting, so, in addition to them, we had the sheriff, Lander, and me. Lucinda had gotten back with Cyndi and they were in the kitchen area making coffee. As soon as it was finished, they brought it to the conference room along with cups. Cyndi took a chair next to me.

About ten minutes later, Lucinda opened the door and showed our visitor in. I saw Bill raise his head in surprise as he saw who entered the room. Lucinda announced to us, "This is C.I.A. Director Jarrod Frazier." The Director moved around to each of us, called our names, and shook our hands. The only one he did not recognize was Seal; he asked for his full name when he was introduced to him. Frazier had been briefed on who would be here and obviously had seen photographs of the rest of us. Lucinda took him a coffee and then left the room. Frazier pulled his phone out of his pocket, quickly sent a text to someone, then raised his eyes to us.

"You have an excellent receptionist there," Frazier said to the sheriff. "If she ever wants to leave you, I can find a spot for her."

"I think I'll keep her," Pfieffer said. "We're glad to have you visit us here in Lunenburg, Mr. Director, although I wish it were in different circumstances. How can we help you—do you have new information for us?"

"In this setting, I am Jarrod. There's no need to be formal in this meeting. This is an information-sharing session. First of all, I want to assure you that the C.I.A. does not normally collaborate with local law enforcement and meet with people outside the formal intelligence community." He looked at Cyndi and me when he said this. "In fact, this is a first and will not become common practice. As most of you do not know, Bill Lander and I worked with each other for several years and still stay in touch; he still helps us at times as a consultant and the reason I am here is because he alerted me to what is going on."

Bill smiled and said, "As an unpaid consultant, I might add."

We all laughed and Frazier continued. "I want to be sure that we all are on the same page here. As I think you are aware, we are pretty sure that what is happening on Oak Island is connected to a larger terrorist operation that may have world-wide implications. I want to thank Cyndi for making that connection—even before all our intelligence systems had done so." He looked at Cyndi and nodded to her. "We now have teams in those other sites to work on this problem. I was advised to send a group here, but when I found out Lander was here, I decided to visit you first to see if you need or want additional help. I don't want separate groups getting in each other's way. Lander knows what to look for and what action to take. I want to know if you all are comfortable in continuing to work on it yourselves. It was reported to me that you had a good, collaborative team and I wanted to be assured that was the case; that is why I am here. By the way, this trip is off the books for me. This meeting does not officially exist."

I spoke up: "Will we have two-way communication with you? In other words, will you share critical information with us if we keep you informed?"

"That was a sticking point with my advisors," Frazier said. "They recommended that we not give you information that you don't already have. However, that would not be right, even though it goes against past practice of our organization. Bill still has his security clearance, so I will feed information through him. He can make the decision to how much of it you need to know. I would ask that any intel that you get that it come to me from him. We've got a legitimate threat and we need to get in front of it. There will be no record of any communications between us—the collaboration will also not exist. I will leave an encrypted satellite phone with Lander; that will be the only way to get in touch with us."

Pfieffer said, "That all sounds fair to me. As long as you don't hold out potentially dangerous information from us—giving it to Lander will work for me—then I am on board with our continuing to work this case." I looked around and Bear and Seal nodded their approval.

"What do you need us to concentrate on?" I asked. "I assume our goal will be to stop the theft of the buried treasure, if, in fact, it is still there. Do you agree that the group wants the treasure to fund terrorist activity?"

"You are right; we desperately need to keep them from getting the treasure. What they are wanting to do will require a major infusion of cash to their operating expense."

Lander said, "Can you share with them what you think the terrorists want to do with that money?"

"Of course, but understand that anything shared with this group stays in this group. We have run extensive background checks on each of you and the consensus is that you can be trusted." He looked at his smart phone and read the text that had come in seconds ago. "Actually, before I came up here, we did those checks on you with the exception of Seal. That was just now completed. If anyone is not comfortable with holding that information to just this group, I would respectfully ask that you dismiss yourself from this meeting immediately."

He paused for almost a minute; no one made a move to leave, so he then continued. "Our sources tell us that there is a probability that this terrorist cell plans to use the money to purchase weapons of mass destruction and trigger them simultaneously around the world. If they accomplish this, it could potentially mean the deaths of millions."

"What type of WMDs are you thinking?" asked Pfieffer.

"Either chemical or bio-weapons," we think. "They can be created to be small enough to easily transport from one location to another."

"Where can they get those type weapons? They are not readily available, are they?"

"Good question, Bear. No, fortunately they are not commonly available—yet. Our informants tell us that for the right price, they will get them from the Russians. Former KGB operatives supposedly have access to them and they need the money more than they need the weapons now. Of course, Russia is denying even having chemical or bio-weapons, but we know that they do—and have had for the last twenty years. It is well known that there are terrorist groups operating close to the borders of Russia; some think that Russia may also be serving as a safe harbor for the insurgents. We'll continue to work on that front to try to stop the black-market sale of these weapons—or any weapons of mass destruction."

Seal asked, "What exactly is the KGB? I've always heard that term and know it is the secret police in Russia but that's all I know about it."

Frazier looked at Lander. "Do you want to answer that question?"

"You're right, Seal, it's Russia's secret police organization. The initials stand for *Komitet*

Gosudarstvennoy Bezopasnosti – or the Committee of State Security. It really became prominent in the nineteen fifties; it evolved into an autonomous organization that protected Russia from threats, both internal and external, and united almost twenty agencies in Russia under one umbrella. The KGB also became synonymous with being a premier world spy organization—they would say *the* premier spy agency. It was disbanded in nineteen ninety-one with the collapse of the Soviet Union. However, many believe that it still exists today and is going to reemerge as a force, especially since Vladimir Putin is the Prime Minister of Russia; he was a former KGB officer during the Cold War. Expect to hear more about the new KGB in the next five years."

Frazier smiled, "You've kept up with them, haven't you?" He looked at the rest of us and said, "At one time, Bill Lander knew more about the KGB than their agents did."

"Do we have a timeline for their planned destruction?" I asked.

"The intelligence suggests that they want to purchase the weapons before Thanksgiving and set the attack during the Christmas season. They feel like this is an important time of the year for Christians and it would really make a statement during a time of hope and celebration."

"Do we know who is heading up the terrorist cell?" asked Bill.

"We believe it's a new group, calling themselves the Islamic Revolutionary Jihad. It's patterned after most of the rest operating in the Western countries. They're looking for a huge event to give them creds. The one calling the shots is somewhere in Pakistan; we don't know who he is, but we think his second-in-command is Azeem Faisal, almost certainly not his true name. He is probably one of the two or three lieutenants of the top man, who stays in the background; even his lieutenants won't know his real identity. "

"That makes sense; Pakistan or Afghanistan is where many of the Islamic rebels are hiding, and will continue to do so until their governments decide to get tough with them. If they are able to implement their plan, it would give them instant recognition on the world stage. We've got to stop them." I could see the fire in Bill's eyes as he spoke.

Frazier said, "I agree; we have to eliminate this threat. Now, what about the treasure hunt? Where are you with dealing with it?"

I said, "We know that Adar has found the site, but we don't think he has been able to get the treasure out yet. We have seen, and heard, where they have been down in the pit in the last couple of days, but we don't know yet where their access point is. It is not land-based, at least not at the money pit shaft. Bill thinks that there is a tunnel to the site from the shore somewhere. If it is water-based, then it makes sense that the doorway is located somewhere on one of the bluffs overlooking the bay. We looked pretty closely at one of the two possible sites yesterday and were about to check the other one out today when we were called back here."

"Are they on just a treasure hunt, hoping to find some source for their funding? I know I have heard tales that Captain Kidd may have buried his stolen booty in these islands, but is this chasing after the golden pot under the rainbow? What makes you think that there really is some wealth buried up here?"

"We got most of our information from Jack over at Fond du Lac, Minnesota. He . . ."

"Jack? You don't mean Jack Lauftis, do you?" asked Frazier.

"Yes, you remember Jack. He is back working on his reservation after he retired. The first man who was shot here was from the reservation. Phil and I visited Jack and he facilitated a meeting with a couple of people. One of them is the wise elder of the tribe named Mokuk; he is called the 'Truth-Keeper.' It seems that their ancestors are from this area and were here when Europeans settled here with several boatloads of wealth smuggled out of France. To show their friendship, the Europeans gave the tribe a chest full of gold coins. Mokuk still has those and they are a perfect match to the coin that was discovered with the dead body here. He says that the new settlers buried many chests full of treasure on Oak Island. It is this treasure that Adar seeks. Jack is working with us to try to get additional information. One of the men who spoke with us there was shot the night we left Minnesota. The suspects are Middle Easterners that have been seen in the area. "

Frazier said, "You said wealth smuggled out of Europe. Are you then talking about the knights who fled France in the 1300s?"

"Yes, we are talking about the Knights Templar. According to Mokuk, they came to Nova Scotia and brought their treasure with them." Bear and Seal had not heard this and looked at me somewhat incredulously.

"Maybe you can recruit Lauftis to join your team here in Nova Scotia. I know he could be a help." Frazier looked at the rest of us. "Jack Lauftis was an exceptional agent with us when we were together in . . ." he looked at Bill, who nodded, and finished, "Special Forces."

Lander replied, "I need to check back in with him anyway. Maybe I'll run that by him if it's okay with the rest of you."

"If you can vouch for him, I would welcome any help we can get—as long as he will work with us and under the direction of Canadian forces." Bear seemed to speak the sentiment of us all, so Lander said he would contact Lauftis again.

Frazier spoke up again, "Before I go, is there anything else we can help you with? Anything giving you problems?"

Seal replied, "Not unless you can tell us how to locate a ghost ship."

"What do you mean? Why do you call it a ghost ship?"

"Someone spots it, but it then it seems to disappear at will. And, actually, the car in Minnesota is reputed to be able to do the same thing. We can't find the boat if we can't see it."

Frazier sat deep in thought, looking as if he wanted to say something, but holding it back. He finally spoke, "What do you think is happening? Any ideas?" He looked around the group. I could tell he knew what we were talking about.

Lander spoke up, "I might have an answer for you, or Cyndi may have it. She has been researching an idea that I had about the disappearing vehicles." He looked at Cyndi and asked, "Were you able to find anything else?"

"Bill and I talked about this last night. He told me about a new type camouflage called digital interactive camouflage. It is so new that there is not much public documentation about it. It seems that it is used to digitally blend an object into its background, so that when the background changes, the camouflage changes to match it in real time."

Bill looked at Frazier. "What does the C.I.A. know about this new technology?"

Frazier answered, "Before I respond, tell me what all you—and Cyndi—know about it."

"How does it digitally match the background so that it hides the object?" asked Bear.

Lander looked at Cyndi. "Go on," he said. "You're doing fine."

"I think how it works is this. Take the boat, for example. It would have tiny digital video cameras mounted on every side of the boat. If we were looking at the boat's side, then the cameras that were active on that opposite side of the boat would be pointed at the background we would see if the boat were not there.

That same video image would then be shown on the side of the boat we were looking at, so that we see the unbroken background. This same scenario would be replicated regardless of the angle of the viewer. It's amazing technology!"

Bear replied, "But what about the boat disappearing when we were in the helicopter. Shouldn't we have been able to see it from the air?"

Lander replied, "Not if the top of the boat also had that technology."

"Wouldn't there have to be some sort of screen or monitor mounted on the boat in order for it to show the image digitally?" Bear was having a hard time grasping the possibilities.

I spoke up, "Yes, but not necessarily the type of screen we are used to seeing. If you think about it, there are already flexible screens and peripherals; for example, we have keyboards that will roll up when we don't use them and work when unrolled. What if there were a way to cover an object with a flexible coating that could stay invisible when not charged, but become a digital image when the cameras were activated?"

"Would the image be bright and sharp enough to match the background? It would have to have a much stronger processor than we see today." Bear was thinking of his webcam technology.

"That sounds like science fiction," replied Seal.

Bill looked at Director Frazier. "What about it? Is this possible explanation science fiction?"

Frazier dropped his head for a moment, then looked up with resignation on his face. "No, this is not science fiction. That very well may be the real answer and there are advanced technologies that would duplicate the color and brightness in any condition, indoors or outside. There is the capability already for individual digital interactive camouflage. Using nanotechnology and the latest materials, interactive camouflage can change from setting to setting to truly mask the object by making it blend so well with the background that it becomes invisible."

Seal asked, "Used how? By hunters?"

Bill answered, "Yes, hunters . . . or by soldiers."

"What about for larger objects, such as for a boat? How advanced are we in that technology?" Bill asked. "I know at one time the military was exploring that possibility."

"How do you know that? Never mind; I don't want to know. We were almost there. Prototypes had been developed that would revolutionize the camouflage technology, but it was brought to a stop almost a year ago. The scientist that led that project was killed in an accident. We have found no one yet that could expand on his work."

Bill replied, "How did he die? Was it really an accident?"

Frazier answered him. "Dr. Bronson was being taken to a remote lab in a helicopter when it went down. He and the pilot both died in the crash."

"Were they positively identified and the bodies recovered?" asked Bill.

"No, the helicopter went down over the ocean and sank before anyone could get there. Neither the copter nor the men were ever found; they were in water too deep to go after them. The pilot sent out a distress warning and an explosion was heard over the radio. That was the last contact we had with them."

I asked, "Could the scientist have been kidnapped and the crash staged?"

"We never received any kind of ransom communication. Usually, a terrorist group will ask for a million dollars for a high-ranking target. Of course, it is our policy not to pay ransom payments, but that doesn't stop them from asking."

"Maybe they thought his knowledge was worth more than any possible ransom. Just something to think about." Bill was leaning the same way I was.

Frazier sat deep in thought. "We'll look again at that possibility. Your 'invisible boat' would certainly fit into the scenarios he was working on. However, this man was a true patriot; I don't think he would help terrorists."

"That may very well be true, but it brings us to the next question. Does he have family?"

Frazier answered me, "Yes, he had a wife and two young daughters. They have been devastated by his death."

"What if his family were threatened? Would Dr. Bronson help the terrorists if doing so would save his family?"

"He might, or I guess he probably would; he was devoted to them and had turned down a promotion because they would have had to move to a less-desirable location."

Bear spoke up, "Even if the boat is invisible because of this digital interactive camouflage, it would still show up on radar, wouldn't it?"

Frazier hesitated before answering, "It may or may not. That was another idea Dr. Bronson was working on when he disappeared. He thought he had developed a method to use the digital capabilities to hide the object from radar. If the terrorist group does have Dr. Bronson, he may have provided that technology to them, also."

Bill concluded the meeting with a task for the Director. "Go back and trace the last flight of that helicopter. See if it made an unscheduled landing somewhere; if so, the terrorists may have switched Dr. Bronson with another person before they staged the crash over the ocean. He may very well be alive and be the architect of the new camouflage technology the terrorists seem to be using."

CHAPTER 28

MOUNTAIN CAVE IN PAKISTAN

It was still dark outside when the man stretched in his bedroll and stood up. He was already dressed because he slept in his robe and sandals; he had to be ready to flee at a moment's notice. He moved to the opening of the remote cave and looked out. He stood tall, just a shade over six feet and four inches, but weighed under one hundred seventy pounds. Living on the run in the mountains and eating when he could did not allow for excess pounds to accumulate on his body. His dark hair was straight and fell limply over his shoulders. His scruffy beard hung from his chin and was turning gray. His hair and beard were so dirty that it was difficult to tell what color they really were. His robe, once white, was now covered in the colors of the earth where he walked. His sandals, although old, were in good shape. He had discovered long ago that he had to have good shoes on his feet in order to traverse the mountain trails. From his vantage point, he could spot his followers; they were placed around his lair so that anyone approaching would be seen before they got close to the hideout.

Faisal looked out over the mountains. It was only a few miles to the Afghan border, but it would take him two days to walk up and down the mountainous terrain to get there. But that was nothing to him; as long as he was safe and fed, the passage of time meant little. He had a meeting with his active cells in three days close to the Pakistani/Afghan border and he would need to leave his home soon in order to make it.

He moved back into the cave. Although he had personal riches and could live in a modern home in any city he wanted, he chose to lead this ascetic lifestyle, at least while he was hiding; he felt he had been chosen by Muhammad to lead his people. Well, Muhammad and his superior. Although he didn't know his name, he had been tabbed to carry out a great task, one that would set the world on its ear. Beside his sleeping bag sat the only piece of modern equipment he had with him. He picked up his sat phone, moved to the cave entrance, and sat down. As good as satellite communication was, it would not work under ground. The phone was still a marvel to him. When it was brought to him, he resisted using it, and thought a simple cell phone was all he needed. But his lieutenant had chosen well; now he realized that he could not operate without it. He opened the carrying case and removed the phone; its label marked it as the newest on the market. It had global coverage, even in the polar regions, and had built-in GPS capabilities. It was built to military specifications and was dust, shock, and water proof. He turned the encryption on and his GPS tracking enabler off. Faisal keyed his contacts and tapped the first one.

"Yes?"

"Are you getting ready?" asked Faisal. Although the communications were encrypted, he had instructed his subordinates to never use names when they were on any device.

"Yes. We've got coverage in the local media; our hibernants are making contact now and putting the plan in place. I have a meeting with them in two days' time." He used the term for people who move into a community and become part of it, then at a prearranged signal, emerge as a threat. Although he spoke with a French accent, Faisal had no trouble understanding him. Faisal had attended MIT and could speak five languages fluently.

Faisal ended the call without any warning. He believed any superfluous words took valuable time and extended the time that a trace could be effected.

He looked at the next contact and initiated the call. Again, he got confirmation that the dormant cell had activated, this time in London. He smiled to himself as he thought of the code name for the plan. *The Awakening* fit the project to a tee and he was proud of his choice. The copying of the statue was a fitting symbol for his upcoming activities; his lieutenants in the five major cities assured him that they could get pictures in the various media outlets. It was the pose of the body that was the trigger for setting the plan in motion. And they were so spread out over the globe that he felt like no one would connect them. After making his five calls, he felt secure that his plan was being successfully initiated.

Except in Nova Scotia.

That was a problem.

Adar had assured him that he could retrieve the treasure. When Adar had approached Faisal with Juhall, they tried to convince him that there was buried treasure on Oak Island and that Adar knew how to get to it. Faisal didn't believe him until he revealed the old coin. After that, Faisal had traveled to Moscow and sat down at a computer. After days of research, he began to accept Adar's claim that the treasure had been buried there by the Knights Templar. Faisal learned of the tale of the escape from France of the Order and thought Nova Scotia might be where they relocated. If he could find the buried wealth of the Knights Templar, he had no doubt that it would be enough to fund their ambitious plan. He would be instantly recognized as a leader of the jihad and he would eliminate millions of the infidels.

He remembered his first contact with Arkady there in Moscow . . .

# # #

CHAPTER 29

Faisal **was cold. Moscow was covered in a major** snowfall that had come in from the north. Although Faisal had attended university in Boston, he had been back in the Middle East for five weeks and he was acclimated to the desert climate. He found the cyber café on one of the main streets of Moscow and paid cash for the use of the computer located in the back of the room where no one could see what he was doing. He spent four days running down any link to treasure in the Nova Scotia area. Most of the sites attributed any treasure there to pirate theft; especially compelling was the connection to Captain Kidd, who was known to frequent the waters of the northeast coast of the U.S. and reportedly buried some of his loot on an island off the New England coast. Finally, he found an obscure reference to the Knights Templar, who were known to have escaped France in the fourteenth century with boatloads of the wealth they had accumulated in Europe. Few historians thought they landed at Nova Scotia and set up a colony there. But what Faisal read about them didn't rule out that possibility. Add that to what that idiot Ahmik, or Foster as he liked to call himself, told us about the early history of the band of Native Americans and he was ready to believe that the treasure just might be there—waiting for him, of course.

After he accepted that premise, he set out to accomplish what he had really come to Moscow for. He could have gone to any major city in the world for his research, but Moscow was the place he needed to be in order to get his plan started. Moscow had gone through some difficult times after the break-up of the Soviet Union. Most Russian people did not know how to thrive—or even survive—in a capitalist economy. The climate was perfect for the proliferation of organized gangs and mobsters and they did know how to take advantage of the free market. Many of the former KGB operatives navigated to the underworld and they became some of the most successful and wealthiest of the nouveau riche in Russia. They had contacts and, because of their former activities, had no qualms about using force to further their causes. Some of them had even retained their possession of deadly weapons of mass destruction and it was known that they were available to the highest bidder. It was just that type person Faisal had come to the cold city to find.

He knew that he would have to get off the beaten paths where the true workers and the wealthy tourists congregated. It took him just a few questions and a fistful of rubles to get a map where he could perhaps contact a former agent. Faisal knew enough about the gangster world that he understood he would not be able to find his target. He would have to put out bait to make them come to him. And, even though it might not be wise, he decided to walk the dangerous neighborhoods. But he also knew he was not the typical tourist; he could take care of himself in most situations.

Since he was staying at the Courtyard Moscow City Center, he started in the surrounding neighborhoods. He knew the City Centre area was an ideal location for muggers and pickpockets because many of the wealthy foreign tourists stayed in this part of Moscow. It was possible that one of the minor criminals may be able to help him find a person like he was looking for. He went for dinner at an upscale restaurant around the corner from his hotel. After eating, he returned to his room, lay on his bed, and relaxed while he watched the local news channel on television.

When his watch showed nine-thirty, he showered and dressed for his night out. He was experienced enough in cold weather to know to dress in layers. Faisal first put on some long underwear, synthetic with good wicking action. He wore black wool pants; he put on a thick gray sweater over a black long-sleeved pullover shirt. Black rubber-soled Gore-Tex boots over thick, woolen socks completed his dress. He separated a wad of rubles into three stacks and placed each stack in a different pocket. He slipped a six-inch switchblade into his coat pocket and another fixed-fighting blade in an ankle sheath. He picked up his Visa and put it in an inside coat pocket; he knew that the Moscow police could stop a person at any time and demand to see his travel documents. On his way out, he grabbed a heavy, long pea jacket, gloves, and a woolen knit cap. He had a face mask in his pocket and he donned it before he put on his gloves and hat. He didn't like the Russian winter, but he could at least stave off the bitter cold.

Faisal carefully picked his way down the icy steps of the hotel, looked both ways at the sidewalk, and chose the left. He walked three blocks down Voznesenskiy to the first major intersection and turned left again; he was now on Eliseevskiy. He kept a lookout for the Gopniki. The Gopniki traveled in groups and considered themselves the young original gangsters. He was approached once by a gansta wannabe and asked for money, but when he grabbed the youngster by his throat, he shook loose and ran. He went into a dark club and ordered a drink while he watched and listened to a loud, obnoxious band. After an hour, he had all he could stand and left. He wandered around the City Centre, choosing streets at random to venture down. He had no more contacts and decided to go back to his hotel and get some sleep.

The next day was even colder. Faisal had looked at his maps when he returned to the hotel last night and had three districts marked to visit. He randomly chose to go first to the Golyanovo District. Golyanovo is the most populous district in its Okrug and is located in the northeastern edge of the Eastern Administrative Okrug in Moscow. He walked four blocks to the Metro and looked at the schedule. He bought a ticket and when the train arrived for Golyanovo, he entered and selected a seat to himself. The train stopped, the doors opened with a whoosh, and he exited the train. Walking from street to street, he was looking first for somewhere to eat. He spied a coffee shop, entered, and ordered an open-faced breakfast sandwich made from rye bread, butter, and sliced sausage. Although the morning drink of choice in Russia is black tea, he asked for coffee. By the time he had finished, he had warmed up and felt better when he left the café. He strolled along the streets and turned left into a dark alleyway. When he was about halfway down the alley, he saw a couple of men fall in behind him. Almost immediately, two more men entered the passage in front of him; he was now boxed in. One of the secrets to survival is to show no fear, so he continued walking forward. Though he could feel the men behind him moving closer, he refused to turn and acknowledge them. When he was within ten feet of the men coming at him from the front, he stopped and turned his back to the brick wall on his right. His hand went to his pocket where he gripped his switchblade. Then he waited for them to make their move. They closed to within three feet of him and stationed themselves in a semicircle around him, cutting off escape routes in every direction. He took them for the members of the Gopniki.

One of the men spoke, "What are you doing in our district?"

Faisal answered, "I am looking for a man." He identified this man as the leader, as the leader of a group is usually the one who speaks first. If he had to fight, he would go after him first.

The same man said, "What man are you looking for? You may have found more than you bargained for." The men took a step forward.

"I have money. I want to buy some weapons."

"You can't buy weapons in Russia. What's to stop us from just taking your money?"

"You could probably get it, but at least two of you would not live to enjoy it. I want to buy a handgun and then I want to meet with a man who can sell me a great weapon. I have a little money with me now, but I have a lot back at my hotel."

"Why do you want these weapons?"

"I want the handgun for protection while I am in Russia. I want the great weapon to use against our common enemy. Can you introduce me to such a man?" Faisal pulled his hand from his pocket and offered it to the leader of the group.

The man reached his hand out and took the proffered money, a stack of rubles worth about one hundred American dollars. "I am Faisal. There is more if you can help me."

"How do we know you are not a member of the politsiya?"

"Look at me. Do I look like a Russian policeman?" He removed his head coverings.

The men looked at him and, finally, the leader spoke, "Call me Ivan. Give me your cell number and I will get back to you." Faisal had anticipated such a request and had already written it down and he gave him the paper with the number of a throw-down phone.

"Call me by tonight or I will find someone else to give my money to," Faisal said and pushed his way through the men and walked out of the alley and went back to his hotel. He knew he would receive a call before the evening was over.

At seven thirty, Faisal's phone vibrated. He keyed the talk button and said, "Yes, go ahead."

"I have the first part of your order. I will meet you in an hour."

Faisal asked, "Where can we meet?"

"We'll meet where we talked earlier today. Can you find it?"

"Of course; I'll be there."

"And bring American dollars; I don't want rubles."

He quickly dressed and went to the lobby. He exchanged some rubles for American currency and left the hotel, retracing his steps. It was dark when he entered the alley, and, though he was leery of the spot, he didn't hesitate to move to the circle of men already standing there.

One of them greeted him, "Man, you are one brave dude . . . or else you are one stupid man. Which is it?"

"I'm just smart enough to know I have something you want; most of it is not on me so you will work with me to get more of it. You have something I want, also, don't you?"

The leader of the group handed a bag to Faisal. Faisal reached in and pulled out a small handgun. He used the flashlight app on his phone to look closely at it. It was an old Smith & Wesson Military and Police model. He pressed the thumb catch and the cylinder swung out. There was no ammo in it. He locked the cylinder back in and pulled the trigger. It dry-fired and everything seemed to work okay. He would have preferred a semiautomatic, but the revolver would do.

"What about ammo? Do you have some with you?"

"Of course. If you want the gun, it will cost you six hundred American dollars. Thirty rounds will be one hundred dollars extra."

Faisal counted out the money and handed it over. The second man gave Faisal a container and Faisal stuck it into his coat without opening it. He did not want to offend the men by showing them distrust. "Can you help me with the other request?"

"We can take you to a man. He said he would meet with you, but if he suspects anything at all, you will not walk away from him."

"When do we meet him?" Faisal asked.

"Right now, if you are ready. Follow me. But, first, give me the handgun. You will get it back when we return." He accepted the revolver and the bullets, turned, and began walking to the end of the alley. One of his men walked beside him and the other two fell in behind Faisal. When they reached the road, a large black Mercedes slid to a stop. Ivan quickly opened the back door and told Faisal to get in. Faisal slid across the seat to the other side and Ivan sat down beside him. The front seat held two men.

Ivan pulled a long piece of black fabric and leaned over to Faisal. "I will now blindfold you. Leave it on until I tell you to take it off."

Faisal had expected something like this, so it neither surprised nor bothered him. He would have operated the same way if it were reversed. They rode about thirty minutes, making turn after turn; there was no way Faisal could have memorized the route taken. The car screeched to a stop and Ivan told Faisal to keep his blindfold on and to follow him. Faisal slid across the seat and stood in the cold. He could feel snowflakes hitting him in the face.

Ivan said, "Here, hold onto my sleeve and follow me." They moved through the snow. Faisal could tell they were walking in an isolated spot; each step fell onto a high fluffy snowfall with no previous footprints worn down into the snow. "Up three steps," said Ivan. Faisal heard a door open and he followed Ivan into a building. After the door closed, Ivan said, "You can remove your blindfold, but keep it in your pocket; you'll need it when you go back—if you go back." The man laughed at his own attempt at being funny. Faisal did not laugh.

He looked around. They were in some type of commercial cinder-block building, maybe an abandoned warehouse. All walls were painted a dull gray and with the dim lights glowing, the building looked depressed. There was no furniture or equipment at all in this large room. He followed Ivan to the far side and entered another smaller room through a steel door. The only item in it was a steel desk; the gloss had long ago worn away and the dull finish was marked with scratches and dents. Behind the desk sat one of the largest men Faisal had ever seen. He was dressed in all black. The man had a chest that would have impressed any NFL coach; his neck stretched the oversized sweater he wore. But it was his head that caught Faisal's attention. He wore a Fu Manchu mustache that surrounded full lips that turned down at the corners. His nose was large, bulbous, and had obviously been broken, probably more than once. His bushy eyebrows shadowed the darkest, meanest eyes Faisal had ever seen. His head was shaved clean. When he spoke, he sounded like a tuba hitting the lowest notes in its range.

"What weapon are you looking for? And don't bullshit me if you want to walk out of here."

Faisal knew that this man was not the top dog. He would be the screener and only if he were satisfied would Faisal get to the man in charge. "I am looking to purchase some WMDs. I will need at least five and I will pay a fair price for them."

"You will pay the price we charge if we do business. Where will you use these weapons?"

"I will discuss that with the man in charge. That is not you."

The man growled at Faisal's insolence. "What makes you think you can get to him?"

Faisal smiled and replied, "Because I have the money! Now, go tell him I will speak with him."

The man laughed, this time as a show of respect for Faisal's audacity. "Follow me."

Arkady Belisnokov stared at Faisal as he entered the room. Faisal thought Arkady's eyes would bore a hole right through him. "Sit," he said. "What are you looking for?"

"I want to buy some weapons, weapons that will kill thousands."

"You are crazy! What makes you think you can do that and what makes you think I can get you such weapons?"

"I know I can do it; I already have plans and people in place to carry it out. I just need the means to do it. I think you can help me get what I need because I have funds that you want."

"How much funds do you have?"

"How much do you need to get me the items?"

"Exactly what weapons do you want and where do you plan to use them?"

"I need five weapons that will be used in five different cities across the world." Arkady looked even more intensely at him with the question unsaid. Faisal continued, "No, none in Russia."

"None in our friends' countries, either, I hope," replied Arkady.

"No, we will kill only infidels. One explosion in Washington, one in Paris, one in London, one in Jerusalem, and one in Montreal."

Arkady laughed again, heartily. "You *are* crazy! And how do you intend to do this?"

"I will take care of the how. Your concern is only getting me the weapons. I need five and I need them by Thanksgiving. That gives you a month to secure them."

"What type weapon do you want? No nuclear; I don't want the radiation blowing in the wind over my country."

"I want either chemical or bio. Either one will do the job. Large enough to kill thousands in the first days, but portable enough to hide in a normal-sized sedan."

"You don't want much, do you?" Arkady's voice dripped with sarcasm.

"Just take care of it. How much will it cost me?"

"I will contact you in two days, first to tell you if I am going to do this, and second, to tell you the cost. Give me a number I can reach you."

Faisal handed him the paper with his phone number. Arkady waved his hand toward the door and said, "Ivan will now take you back. If you discuss this with anyone, I will know it and I will enjoy killing you."

Ivan stopped just before they exited the building and asked for the blindfold. Faisal pulled it from his pocket and placed it over his eyes. Ivan tied it tightly around his head and led Faisal outside to the car. Again, the driver circled blocks and made many turns before he stopped the car where he had picked up Faisal and Ivan. Ivan removed the blindfold and they exited the car. Faisal pulled a stack of twenty-dollar bills from his shirt pocket and handed them to Ivan. Ivan smiled and returned Faisal's gun and ammo to him. He said, "Don't get caught with this. It can't be traced, but the authorities in Russia don't like to find foreigners with weapons." With that said, he turned and met his friends and left Faisal standing by himself.

The next two days were the longest of Faisal's life. He was sure that Arkady would come through; there was too much money on the table to leave it. Faisal spent most of the time eating and sleeping. At night, he visited some clubs and even connected with a couple of ladies who he knew were just after his money, but he didn't care because they were very skilled in making a man feel good and he desperately needed some comfort in this cold, depressing country. Since such things were strictly forbidden, he could enjoy these pleasures only out of sight of his Muslim brothers. At four o'clock in the afternoon of the second day, his phone vibrated. He answered quickly and heard the gravelly voice say, "Be at the pickup spot at five o'clock. If you are late, don't try to contact me again."

Faisal hurriedly donned his winter clothes and walked to the metro. When he arrived at the pickup spot, Ivan was also there. They replicated the trip, blindfold and all, and entered the same building. Faisal was led to the same room where Arkady was waiting. Faisal knew Arkady had located the weapons or he would never have summoned him back to meet him.

"What did you find for me?"

Arkady explained what he had found and said, "Will those be sufficient?"

Faisal smiled and replied, "Perfect. Will they be ready by Thanksgiving?"

"Yes, if you have the funds. Each one will cost you two million American dollars. I will require a deposit of one-half million dollars by tomorrow morning. I will give you the account information. If I get confirmation of the electronic deposit, we will continue the project. If I don't get the confirmation by eleven o'clock local time, then I will terminate the project—and you."

CHAPTER 30

Faisal shook his head to bring his thoughts back to the present and reclined on the floor of the cave, lying on his sleeping bag. *I've got to have that treasure,* he thought. *It's right there and if I can get it, everything is in place for the great event. Arkady assures me the weapons will be ready for delivery on time. I may have to send Adar some more men. I don't understand why he can't get those chests; they are sitting there in front of him.*

He stayed to himself for the rest of the day in his cave, alternating between heightened feelings of great success and seeing himself as the new Bin Laden and the lowest level of incompetence, imagining that all his plans would disintegrate because Adar failed him.

The more he dwelled on his thoughts, the more agitated and depressed he became. He had a meeting in four days with his teams from the targeted cities. He would either give them the go-ahead or tell them the project is on hold. His future—and maybe the future of his people—depended on a positive action plan on that day.

I'll do what it takes to make it happen; it will work out! he promised himself.

The decision to do something energized him and he rose, grabbed the sat phone, and moved to the cave entrance. He waited while the phone made contact with the satellite. When he saw it display a ready state, he pushed the button to encrypt the conversation and pushed the numbers for his call. He spoke only these words: "We are ready to move." He didn't even wait for a response before he terminated the call.

CHAPTER 31

Director Frazier left Nova Scotia with a promise to keep them in the loop. Before he was in the air, he had directed his staff to go back and take another look at the helicopter trip with Dr. Bronson on board. He set a time of five hours from now to meet with his department and he expected that all information would be organized and shared at the session; all files related to the disappearance of Bronson were to be sent to him immediately as they were obtained. If there was a chance at all that Bronson were still alive, then Frazier would do all he could to rescue him. He hated to lose good people and Dr. Bronson was definitely a good person. Beyond that, he was the one person who had the knowledge and skills to take military camouflage to the next level. He agreed with Seal; it did sound like science fiction—and only two years ago, it was—but it was today's reality. He had not shared with the group in Nova Scotia how extensively it was already being used. But, as marvelous as digital interactive camouflage was now, Frazier knew that what they already had only scratched the surface to what was just over the horizon.

His phone dinged to alert him that a message was waiting. He accessed the text, which read, "Files being sent to your email account."

He opened his laptop and signed in. As soon as the computer had booted up, he opened his email account and saved the files to a new folder on his desktop. For the next three hours of flying, he studied the information related to Bronson and his fatal trip.

CHAPTER 32

We anchored at the same spot we had been earlier in the day. Our dive gear was still on the deck, so within fifteen minutes, we were ready to hit the water. The sheriff did not come back with us and Bear decided to wait on the deck unless we alerted him that we found something important. Bill began his inspection of this bluff just like he had done the first time. We had almost gone the length of the bluff when he suddenly reversed his direction, almost running into me. He motioned to me and slowly lowered himself in the water. I followed him as he entered the same opening we had been in earlier. It looked just like the rest of the cliff to me. Bill gave a 'thumbs-up' and I moved in for a closer look. He paused in front of a large, flat-looking rock. I almost didn't see it, but when I changed my angle of vision, I could see that there was a cable attached to the rock. It was a small, steel cable and was so much the color of the background rock, it was almost invisible against it. I looked carefully at it. *This would not be visible from the surface and, really, unless a diver was looking for something like this, it wouldn't be seen from five feet away from it. I didn't even see it the other time we were here.*

The cable was attached to the bottom left of the rock and had been anchored to the bluff about fifteen feet to the right and about five feet above. Bill pointed and said, "There's the pivot point." At the top of the rock almost in the center was what looked like a huge iron spike. Bill pushed against the rock, but it seemed solid and didn't move an inch. We followed the cable to its end and saw a loop that had been formed in it.

"They attach another cable to this and use a winch to pull the rock and open the access. Pretty clever and not likely to ever be discovered," I said.

"The tunnel has been there for years, maybe hundreds of years," Bill said. "The cover may have been attached recently; we have to assume that the group we are searching for did that. We need to get back to the boat. Mark this spot with the GPS on your phone."

I retrieved my phone and accessed the app. With a click, the spot was marked and would lead us right back to the same spot. "Done!" I said. We finned our way back to the boat and removed our dive gear. We told Bear and Seal about the rock covering and how we thought we could open it.

"That opening may not go to the treasure, but I would bet my last dollar that it does," said Bill. "We need to get it open."

Bear replied, "We don't have a winch on board."

Bill said, "That's all right. We can use the boat to pull it open. Do you have a cable?"

"Not with us, but we can get one and a winch back at the office."

"Then let's go do it," I said. "We need to get that tunnel opened and explore it before they get all the treasure out."

"Can you find the exact same spot when we get back?" asked Seal.

Bill looked at him, "Yes, Phil has it marked on his phone."

CHAPTER 33

Adar watched the boat speed away. As soon as it was out of sight, he gave the signal for everyone back in the water. He hoped they had at least an hour and a half before the other boat returned, if that was their intention when they sped away. They quickly attached the cable to the loop and gave the signal to winch the tunnel open. As soon as the cover cleared the opening, they headed down the tunnel.

They were still looking for Clue Three. Adar instructed his men to go back to the same places he had assigned them before and to start over. "Look for anything at all that doesn't look natural or any piece of rock or anything else that could be related to the number three. It may be large or it could be so small that you can hardly see it. Look quickly but look carefully. We have to find this clue! Now go!"

The men hurriedly dispersed to their assignments. They felt the implied threat from Adar if they were not successful. Adar went back to the center of the room where he'd found Clue Two. He stood at its side and stared down at the image. The most noticeable part of the image was the two knights mounted on the single horse; both had shields with the Templar cross on them. They were also carrying the spear or lance. It was pointed forward and slightly upward. Both men were dressed in knight's armor. The symbol was created in a circle. He could see nothing that stood out or seemed to be more important. It was just like most of the Templar seals he had looked at online.

He started moving in a circle around the seal, looking for the slightest hint of something not natural to the floor. He walked a pace or two, then dropped to his knees to look from a different angle. Then he repeated the process, over and over. *This is crazy*, he thought. *There has to be something to point me in the right direction. What could it be?* He continued the search, looking for the clue itself or for an arrow to give him some direction. *Arrow; arrow. How would that look? A shaft with an arrow head on it? But where and what would it look like?* It suddenly dawned on him! He turned back toward the center of the room and pushed through the water as quickly as he could. Stopped and looked down. *That's it! It has to be! That's the arrow*, he thought. He was staring at the spear from Clue Two. He looked at the end of the spear and eyed the path it was pointing. Adar picked a reference point on the wall so he could stay on the line and dropped to his knees and began a real search. For the first time since they had found Clue Two, he felt he knew where to look and it gave him a renewed burst of energy. He looked for the slightest line and ran his hand over the floor to see if there were any markings that could be felt but not seen.

He made it to the far wall without finding the clue. He was sliding his hand along the seam between the floor and the wall when he felt the slight knob protruding from the wall. He pushed it but it did not move; he pulled it and it did not give. He tried to slip it to the left and it would not slip. He attempted to slide it right and it seemed to move slightly. He stopped. *Was it my imagination?* he thought. He tried it again, and again it seemed to move marginally, then caught on something. He felt all around and there was nothing else there. He put his hand back on the knob and begin pushing and pulling, over and over, like someone trying to get a car moving in the snow. One way, then the other, then again, and again. Finally, he broke it free. The knob slid to his right and then stopped. He tried to pull it again, and this time it slid toward him.

He lifted the flat piece of metal and looked at it. It had some holes in it and an image on it, but was so corroded that he could make nothing out on it. He rubbed it but was unable to clear it. He looked at his watch and knew that their air supply was getting low, so he stood up with the plaque and spoke into his microphone. "Let's head back to the boat."

They secured the tunnel and gathered on the boat deck. Adar said to them. "Be ready to go back to the site in an hour. Get new tanks on deck. Go now and eat and meet back here in an hour. We are making progress and he showed them the metal plate.

They gathered excitedly around him. One of the men asked the questions all of them wanted to know. "Is it the next clue? What does it say?"

Adar replied, "I don't know yet. I have to clean it up first, but I do think it is the clue."

The men went below to eat and get the fresh tanks ready to go. Adar went to the kitchen. He looked through his cleaning gels and chose one that would remove rust and patina from metal. He coated the disc with the gel and let it set for five minutes as the directions stated. He then took the plate to the sink and scrubbed it with a rough cloth. At first, nothing happened; he kept rubbing it. Finally, the residue began to flake off. Adar attacked it with renewed vigor. When he had gotten it as clean as he could, he dried it with a towel and held it up to the light. "Yes," he exclaimed. "This has to be Clue Three!"

On the plate was a symbol made of three interlocking triangles, all contained within a circle. There was a hole in the center of each triangle; each one was shaped differently from the other two. On the back was some writing, He could make out a word that looked like "align" but the rest of the directions was worn away. He reasoned that he would have to align the disc up with a spot in the room, but where? *Maybe it would be clearer at the site.*

CHAPTER 34

Bill and I discussed the underwater finding on the way back to Lunenburg. I remembered our conversation with Director Frazier and said, "You promised the Director that you were going to call Jack to see if he could help us."

"You're right; I'd forgotten that. I'll call him right now." He accessed his contact list and keyed Lauftis. "I'll put him on speaker so you can add to the conversation if you want to."

"Hello, Bill. I was just about to call you. How are things going there?"

"We've not made much progress yet; just gotten more mysteries connected with it."

"Have you found the treasure?"

"No, but I think we have discovered a water route to it. We had to leave it and we are on the way to get some equipment we need to get into the tunnel."

"What are the other mysteries you alluded to?"

"Jarrod Frazier flew up here to meet with us. You remember him, don't you? Anyway, he's the new Director of the C.I.A. and it seems that the treasure hunt here is connected with a big world-wide terrorist plot."

Lauftis replied, "That doesn't surprise me. I didn't think a couple of Middle Easterners would simply be treasure hunters."

"With the stakes so high, the Director suggested that I recruit you to Nova Scotia to help us. Your passport's still good, isn't it?"

"Yes, it's still good, but it's been awhile since I chased terrorists."

"That's okay, it's . . . "

Lauftis interrupted Bill, "Yeah, I know; it's like riding a bicycle—you don't forget how."

"We're just supposed to stop this group here from getting the treasure; they want to use it to fund their other terrorist activities. The C.I.A. will handle the heavy work. Besides, it would be good to work with you again."

"I guess I could, but you and Phil have got to come talk with Mokuk again, first. Before you get into the treasure burial site. He's got some information for you and says it is critical that you know it before you find the treasure. That's why I was going to call you; he insisted that it be done today."

"He can't tell you?"

"No, and he won't talk on the phone. He says he was holding back on you when you were here earlier and he won't be satisfied until he tells you what he knows. You all get here tonight and I'll go back with you tomorrow."

Lander looked at me for confirmation and I nodded yes. "Okay, we'll be there tonight, meet with him in the morning, then you can come back with us."

Lauftis replied, "Sounds good. Text me your arrival time and I'll meet you in Duluth again. See you." And he ended the call.

I had two calls to make, so I made the most important one first. "Hey, Cyndi, how's it going?"

"Going well. I've gotten Director Frazier access to our Dropbox files and I'm still getting information and messages from around the world. When will you all be here?"

"We're on our way now, but we've got to leave again. Bill just talked with Jack Lauftis and Mokuk needs us to come see him. He says he has critical information for us before we can access the treasure."

"Aren't they the men in Minnesota? Can't Jack just get the details from him and tell you?"

"That's what we suggested to Jack, but the old chief won't do that. He insists that we come to him. So, we are going to fly down there again tonight and come back tomorrow. Jack said if we did that, then he would come help us. Director Frazier said he had worked with both Jack and Bill in special ops."

"Okay, if that's what you need to do. Do you want me to call the airport or get online to make your reservations?"

"Yes, that would be great. It'll take us about two hours to get to the airport, so get the first flight you can after that and book us from Minnesota about noon tomorrow. Their time."

"Okay, I'll do that."

"Thanks. I've got to call the sheriff and tell him our plans. I'll see you in a bit."

I hung up and called the sheriff. I don't think he was happy we were leaving for a day, but I assured him I would bring some good information back—and some help for us. That seemed to satisfy him.

As soon as I opened the door, Chelsea met me with tail wagging, wanting to go out; I swear I don't know which one is better trained; it seems as if Chelsea has me well-conditioned. Cyndi said, "You'll have to hurry. You have just enough time to catch your flight." So, I took Chelsea out and told her to be quick; as usual, she looked at me and continued her sequence of walking, stiffing, and squatting; but she did hurry—sort of.

Cyndi said, "I made you all a sandwich and a coffee. Get your toothbrush and get gone." She sounded a little too happy when she said, "Get gone," but I'm going to give her the benefit of the doubt.

We parked the Jeep and stopped in front of our loading gate ten minutes before the first call for our flight. Bill didn't know it but we were racing to see who could get to sleep first. I finished second again.

Jack picked us up in Duluth and we stopped at the same restaurant to eat breakfast. My pancakes were good; I really like pancakes, especially if they can hold a lot of maple syrup. On our drive to the Reservation, we brought Jack up to date. He said, "We checked all the motels for those men; they must have stayed in their car or camped because nobody at any motel remembered their staying there. As far as we could tell, they left town after they killed Wilson. We put out a BOLO on them, but never heard anything at all."

I thought it would be too early to go see Mokuk, but Lauftis took us straight there. Carrying his rifle, Magisi met us outside his house and immediately led us to Mokuk. We found him waiting for us. He looked even more tired and haggard than the first time we had seen him; his robe was wrinkled and his eyes were drooping. His voice was barely audible as he greeted us. "I appreciate your coming back here. I have to apologize to both of you." He looked at Bill and me. "I wasn't completely honest with you when you were here before. Jack has told me more about what has been going on in Nova Scotia and its connections to possible terrorist plots. I think this will help you and I hope it is not too late to stop them." He held out a small book. I took it from him and looked closely at the cover. It was an extremely old leather-covered book about six inches by eight inches in size and about one-half inch thick. Any title on the front or spine had long ago worn away.

"I led you to believe that the one chest that I have is all that our people know about; for the most part, that is true. Our tribe does not know the complete story. Only I and Magisi—and Jack now—have the truth. That book will tell you what I know. Take it and read it, but please make sure that I get it back. I hope that knowledge will help you and I will trust you not to share that information with others. No one besides the Truth-Keeper has ever seen this book.

"I feel as if you must have this information. We had a paper with directions to find the treasure; it is gone and I suspect that it must have been Ahmik who stole it. If so, then the men he was with have it. In order to get the treasure, one must successfully work through five steps. If they are not followed in sequence, then the treasure cannot be recovered. I did not think anyone could complete those steps so I did not say anything to you about them. However, the discovery that the directions were missing changed my mind. The directions gave instructions for finding the ocean access to the hiding place and it provides the second clue. From that point, each clue will give a hint for finding the next clue. When all steps have been completed, a huge fortune will be available."

"Why have you not collected this treasure for your tribe?" asked Bill.

"Because it is not ours to use, yet; it is almost time. The Knights who placed it there gave my ancestors much gold and trusted them to keep the rest buried until it was time for them to claim it. Only our tribe's Truth-Keeper knows of its existence. Now, you must go and stop the thieves." He stood, bowed, and lifted his arm to dismiss us.

I put the small book in my pocket and we left and headed toward the airport at Duluth. I wanted to see what was in the book, but Bill said, "We'll look at the book on the flight back to Halifax; we'll have plenty of time to discuss it there. Mokuk told us a lot of what it says, I think."

We arrived at the airport an hour and a half before our scheduled flight. "Maybe they have an earlier flight we can transfer to," I said. "Let's check it out."

We approached the ticket counter and smiled at the girl behind it; she looked about fifteen. On the wall was the flight schedule and I saw that there was an earlier flight to Halifax; it was scheduled to leave in fifteen minutes. Holding out our identification, we explained that we would like to move our flight up if seats were available. She touched her keyboard, clicked a series of keys, and said, "You're in luck; we have three seats on the flight about to leave. I can get you in first class, all seats together, but you'll have to pay an upgrade fee."

That sounded good to me, so I asked, "How much?"

"Only forty-five dollars for each of you. Better seats, more room, and a meal."

"Let's do it," said Jack. Bill and I quickly nodded agreement.

The customer service agent took our tickets, made the changes in the computer, and handed us the newly printed ones. "You will be loading in five minutes. Thank you for flying with us."

We stood by the counter and waited. At exactly the five-minute mark, she picked up the mic and said. "The flight to Halifax is now loading at Gate Three. There were so very few people flying out of Duluth that we didn't need to load in waves; we walked through the doorway with seven other people; the flight attendant at the entrance looked at out boarding passes and directed us to first class. We entered the section and saw that we were the only passengers in first class, which I thought was good as we could talk freely without worrying about others hearing what we said. We found our seats, sat down, and buckled our seat belts. Within ten minutes, we were accelerating down the runway. The plane ascended and leveled off and the chimes announced that we could move around if we needed to. As with all airlines now, it was suggested that while in our seats we keep ourselves buckled in.

I handed the book to Bill. "Here, look over this before you get to sleep."

He took the book and opened it. He turned several pages and said, "Hey, what language is this written in?" He shoved it back to me.

I opened the book and Jack looked over my shoulder. "It's English," I said.

"It's no English like I have ever seen," retorted Bill.

"Actually, it's Middle English, which began in the twelve-hundreds. It was a blending of Old English with mostly French language with German roots. Didn't you ever read Chaucer's *The Canterbury Tales*?"

"Is that the story of those pilgrims traveling together to somebody's tomb?" asked Bill.

"Yes, they were going on a pilgrimage to the tomb of Thomas Becket in Canterbury. They met at an inn and decided to ride together. To help pass the time, they told each other stories. There were almost thirty travelers and, originally, Chaucer's plan for the narrative was to have each of the pilgrims tell two stories on the way to Canterbury and two on the way back. However, he never completed it and the story ends after only twenty-four tales with the group still on the way to Canterbury."

Jack said, "That's right. And, if I remember my lit class, some of those stories were pretty risqué."

Bill said, "Maybe I need to go back and read them. Anyway, you are going to have to translate this book for me."

I replied, "I will; it's a good thing it's Middle English and not Old English."

I turned to the first page and looked at the words there. "Actually, if I read it aloud, you can probably understand it. The spoken Middle English sounds more like Modern English than the written Middle English looks like our modern language."

I began reading:

"This is the narrative of our journey to New Scotland. We are the order *Pauperes Commilitones Christi Templique Solomonici* – the *Poor Fellow-Soldiers of Christ and of the Temple of Solomon*."

I remarked, "That was the original name of the Knights Templar." Then I continued:

"On the night of 12 October, in the year of our Lord 1307, eighteen boats sailed away from the coast of France. We were forced to flee for our lives. King Philip was going to have all in our order executed and all our properties confiscated. The stormy night gave us cover as we sneaked away, our boats filled with horses and supplies; five boats contained our wealth and history. We knew in all likelihood we would never see France again. Thirteen other boats split up and traveled to areas of England, Scotland, and Spain. The boats with our treasures made their way to New Scotland. I am Omar and I was on one of those boats to New Scotland.

"We had anticipated that one day we would have to flee Europe, so we had already sent a few of our members to New Scotland months ago. They were to establish a colony and befriend the natives living here. The other task was to create a hiding place for our treasures should we have to escape with it. There had been no communication with them since they left France; we did not know the fate of our brothers. After weeks at sea, many of them fighting through heavy storms and rough waters, we sighted the land mass of New Scotland and we sailed into a sheltered cove to get away from the rolling seas.

"We anchored off shore and I took a party of four of my best men with me. Waiting on shore for us were ten men. I was overjoyed to see that three of them were part of the group we had sent months ago; in the time they had been here, they had become friends with the natives, a group who called themselves Lnu, meaning 'human being' or 'the people'. We had a good reunion with our members. The natives were friendly to us and welcomed us to their land. I removed from the landing boat a chest of gold coins and through a type of sign language told them it was our gift to them, a gift that I expressed was very valuable and that they needed to keep locked away so thieves would not steal it. They gave us food and led us to an island which they said was ours. They had used it for hunting, but said that it was their gift to us to seal our friendship. We thanked them and within a few days, we had started building our shelters. It was already cold there and snow was lying on the ground.

"Our knights who had settled there before we arrived had created a hiding place for our treasure and we wasted no time in getting it secured. We anchored our boat near a rocky bluff and waited for low tide. When the waters were at their lowest, we were led to an opening in the rock. We entered and came to a fork in the tunnel. One tunnel led downward for a few feet and then met a rock wall. The other one sloped upward. We took it and steadily climbed for a hundred feet; at that point, the tunnel turned left and began sloping downward. Because the highest point of the tunnel was above the level of the waters at high tide, this part of the tunnel remained dry. After a walk of several hundred yards, the tunnel opened into a large circular room. This was a perfect place for us to hide our treasures; it took us three days to unload our boats and carry the chests to the underground cavern. Once they were hidden, we decided to make them even safer by creating a series of traps. We dug a shaft from the surface to the room; if someone found our treasure, we thought it would be by digging it up. At various levels of the shaft, we incorporated traps so that if thieves were trying to get to our treasure, the trap would trigger a flooding of the shaft and room. If they got past the flooding, then the next trap would cause a cave-in and block their attempts. We put the traps in place and filled in the shaft.

"Then we went back to the treasure room itself and set some obstacles so that the only way to retrieve our treasure would be to follow a series of clues. If they were not all done in the correct sequence, then the treasure would fall into such a deep shaft that it would be lost for all time. The following pages give the directions for safely getting the treasure. It is my intention that this book be kept safe always in the hands of the leader of the Order.

"Clue One: The treasure is located at Latitude 44.31 Longitude 64.18. It is the island closest to the inner circle of the mainland. Find the northeastern rock bluff. At low tide, find the opening in the rock wall and enter it. Walk through the tunnel and find the inner circle. You will see the treasure chests, but do not try to take them off the shelves on which they are sitting.

"Clue Two: Move to the exact center of this room and find the Templar seal etched on the floor of the cave. It is the symbol with two men on a single horse. Stand facing the direction that the lance points, Look at the spear. It is pointing at the location of Clue Three.

"Clue Three: Follow the direction that the lance points to the confluence of the wall and floor. You should feel a slight knob there. Slide the knob to the right and you will then be able to pull the metal disc from the wall. On the disc will be a triquetra within a circle."

"What's a triquetra?" asked Lauftis.

"It's three interlocking triangles. The Knights Templar used it as a symbol for mind, body, and spirit.

Religious cultures have used it to represent the Holy Trinity. It is also known as a trinity knot."

I looked at Bill. "I'm surprised you knew that."

"I've seen it in some of the Native American cultures," he replied.

"Okay, back to the book." I found my place and continued: "Each triangle in the triquetra has an irregular slot cut out of it. Take the disc to the right of the top shelf. You will see and can feel similar shapes protruding from the wall about waist high. Line the shapes up with the holes in the disc and push the disc tightly against the wall. Using the knob on the disc, turn the disc in a clockwise manner. This will result in a section of the wall opening to the side of the disc. In that opening you will find Clue Four.

"Clue Four: In the crevice will be a flag hanging from a flag staff. Remove the flag and staff. It is imperative that you replace the disc from Clue Three back in its original slot. Then take the flag and the staff to the middle of the shelf that holds the treasure. Find the slot between the two shelves and place the end of the staff in the slot. Lift the flag staff and an opening will appear just below the slot. From that opening retrieve the key to the locks. You must take the flag back to its hiding place and close the opening before you use the key.

"Clue Five: Use the key to open the locks holding the treasure chests in place. You must open them in the order here: Begin on the left and open each lock of the odd-numbered chests: 1, 3, 5, and continue to the end of the shelf. Then begin on the left and unlock each even-numbered lock.

"You may now remove the chains from each box. Once you have done that, the treasure may be safely moved.

"Warning: If Clues One and Two are not followed, the treasure room will be flooded and then a cave-in will block access from the surface. If Clues Three, Four, and Five are not correctly followed in sequence, the shelves holding the treasure will sink and will never be attainable."

"Wow," said Lander. "That's a pretty complex project for men of the fourteenth century."

"If you remember, the men of the Knights Templar were considered the most advanced of the time. They were far ahead of the society they lived in." I was remembering some of what I had read about them. "There are a lot of what we consider engineering marvels from early cultures. This may be just another one of them. We know the money pit was designed by great minds because it has successfully foiled all attempts to crack its code for hundreds of years."

Jack spoke up. "There are stories about other such hiding places for my people's ancestors. It is told that the men who settled there with them showed them how to hide their treasures. One such location is the cave of our Truth-Keeper. The site in Minnesota is said to be a copy of one in Nova Scotia."

"We need to get to that cave; we have to beat the terrorists to that treasure!" I no longer had any doubts that it really existed and my two partners clearly agreed with my sentiment.

I took out my phone and took pictures of the directions. "We may need this when we get to the hiding site."

"Your memory's going now?" laughed Bill. "What else is in the journal?"

I quickly scanned the remaining pages. "It looks like it is a history of the Oak Island settlement. How the knights infused their knowledge into the culture of the natives. And, oh yeah, other knights were able to join them there. You need to read it, Bill, Good information for your classes."

"You'll have to translate it for me. I'm not sure I can get much out of this Middle English."

Both Jack and I laughed. Jack said, "Maybe you needed to pay more attention in your lit classes."

Bill pointed at Jack and retorted, "Yeah, like you did."

CHAPTER 35

As soon as the plane landed, I called the sheriff. Lucinda answered and said he was not there right now. I explained what I wanted and she said she would call both the sheriff and Bear and have them meet us at the marina in two hours.

She called me back in an hour and said, "Change of plans. Director Frazier has a video conference set up for you all at two o'clock. Get Cyndi and meet the sheriff here at the office as soon as you can."

We were almost home, so I decided to wait until we got there to tell Cyndi. When we walked into the house, Cyndi called out, "I'm about ready; take Chelsea out and feed her."

"You're about ready for what?" I asked.

"Lucinda called me about the video-conference meeting. She said you probably wouldn't tell me until you got here; she knows women need a little time to get ready and men rarely think about things like that."

"A *little* time!" I said. Actually, I didn't say it, but I did think it. Chelsea scratched my leg. It was clear what she was thinking: "I'm glad you're home." Or, maybe it was, "Enough talking; take me out!" I chose to think the first.

I took Chelsea out and she did what she always did: walked, sniffed, and squatted. She did this three times and led me back into the house. I sat her food and water out and went into the den. Cyndi was already there; Bill had introduced Jack to her and was telling her about the trip and the old journal.

She said, "It sounds like the natives and the knights set up a new colony here in Nova Scotia."

Jack looked at her and replied, "Yes, they did. They lived together in peace for years; many of the knights took brides from the natives. Most of our tribe now have DNA from both groups. I have traced my lineage and I am a direct descendent from one of the knights called Omar."

"He was the leader of the knights who came to Nova Scotia, wasn't he? I think the journal said it was written by him."

"Yes, he was the one who created the journal."

I thought a minute before replying, "Then that's why Magisi called you Sakima or chief," isn't it? Because of who your ancestors are."

"Yes, he calls me that in private and let it slip in front of you. After I got out of Special Forces, I traced my ancestry and discovered that I was descended from

Omar. Magisi knew this and talked with Mokuk; Mokuk then let me read the journal, so I have seen it before now."

"So, you knew how to get the treasure and chose to leave it in place?" asked Cyndi.

"Yes, for now. My people are in the process of setting up a council that will determine how to best use the treasure. There are other tribal documents that specify how the wealth is to be distributed. When we get the right people on the committee, then our plans are to access the treasure. We may have to accelerate this now to keep the new group from stealing it. Bill has been keeping me in the loop regarding them."

Bill said, "We need to get going; we have thirty minutes to get to the sheriff's office."

When we walked into the office, Lucinda smiled and pointed at the coffee mugs sitting on the counter. The steam swaying from the liquid showed that the coffee was hot and ready. We each grabbed one; Lucinda pointed Cyndi to the tea. "Go on in. Most everyone is here."

We had twelve minutes before the video meeting was to start, so I showed the book to the sheriff, Bear, and Seal and told them the directions to retrieve the treasure were located in it. I explained that we couldn't actually let them see the contents of the book; we had promised Mokuk that we would not let anyone else see the pages of the book.

I heard a ding and Lucinda came into the room. She moved to the laptop on the table and clicked a couple of keys. The attached projector came to life and an image slowly evolved on the screen set up against the far wall. Director Frazier was staring at us. He nodded and asked, "How's it going?"

We all acknowledged him and he said, "I have asked a couple of people here to sit in on this meeting. Charlie Pollock is the Director of National Intelligence." The silver-haired man to Frazier's right nodded to them. "On my left is Bob Spencer; he is in charge of the teams we have sent to the targeted sites. It should go without saying this connection is secure."

Bill took charge in our group and introduced everyone.

Frazier took the lead there and spoke: "Bring us up to date on what is happening in Nova Scotia. Include any information you have, even if you think it may have no bearing on our problem. And start at the beginning. Assume Pollock and Spencer have heard nothing."

I knew that wasn't exactly true, but Frazier felt like we may have left something important out when we had talked with him. Pollock and Spencer would have been briefed by Frazier any time he got information.

Sheriff Pfieffer began and took them through the early events, beginning with the discovery of the body, the exploration of Oak Island, the murder of Lively, and Cyndi's work to realize the connections to a larger terrorist project. "I'll let Lander or Kent take it up here and tell you about their trip—or trips—to Minnesota."

I nodded to Bill and he took up the story, beginning with our first trip to the Reservation. "As Director

Frazier knows, Jack Lauftis was in Special Forces with us and is a member of the Reservation there."

Spencer interrupted and asked, "How did the Reservation in Minnesota get connected to Nova Scotia?"

Bill continued, "I was getting to that. The first man murdered in Nova Scotia was from the Reservation; his name was Ahmik but he changed it to Liam Foster. He met a Syrian while he was in prison and told him about a treasure that was buried on Oak Island. When the Syrian was released, he picked up a partner and they went to Fond du Lac to meet up with Ahmik. Ahmik was a member of the tribe and he had stolen a gold coin and a map that showed where the treasure is located. They killed another man in Minnesota and then came to Oak Island with Ahmik. Once the terrorists had the map, then they didn't need Ahmik anymore and they killed him."

Frazier asked, "Have you been able to track the terrorists yet?"

I replied: "No, we still haven't seen the boat. I'm sure that they are using the latest in digital interactive camouflage. It just disappears after someone spots it. The Coast Guard here has even tried to locate it with radar, but nothing has shown up."

Bill asked Frazier, "What about Dr. Bronson's disappearance? Have you had a chance to review it?"

"We're looking into it, but don't have anything conclusive yet."

"I'll let Bill brief you on our last trip to Minnesota; we just got back this morning," I said.

Lander explained who Mokuk is and about the connections between the tribe and the ancient knights. "It appears that Lauftis is a direct descendant of the leader of the Templar Knights who escaped to Nova Scotia. We have located a map with directions to the treasure, so we are anxious to get to the cave and secure the treasure before the terrorists get it."

"Do you need additional help up there or can you all handle it?" asked Pollock. "With Jack joining you, I'm not sure we could improve the team by sending someone else."

Lander was quick with his answer, "No, we're in good shape here. We know that they have found the room, but don't think they have successfully worked through all the steps to free the chests."

"We'll come back to that in a few minutes. I'm going to let Agent Spencer bring you up to speed on the terrorist angle."

We all looked at Spencer. He was not a tall man, but he was as powerful-looking man as I have ever seen, His chiseled face sat below a close haircut; no facial hair at all. He had dark eyes that were so intense that it seemed he was seated across the table glaring at us instead of sitting thirteen hundred miles away.

He looked at each of us, then spoke: "We have identified five locations around the world that seem to be targets for a major terrorist attack sometime in the near future; we feel like the bad guys are shooting for Christmas. They think that a deadly event on a Western religious holiday would send a message. From the chatter we are getting, it appears that this attack is being planned by a new group."

When he had said, "We have identified five locations . . .", my group just looked at each other because we knew Cyndi had identified those locations and, in fact, we had told Washington about them.

Bill interjected, "That makes sense and is likely the reason that the treasure up here is so important to them. I doubt that their coffers are full. Do you know what's planned?"

Spencer looked at Pollock. "Permission to speak freely?"

Pollock nodded, "Yes, this group may know more about what is going on than we do. Please tell them what you know." It was nice to know that Pollock wasn't taking the attitude that they were the ones who with all the intel.

Spencer continued: "We don't know all we need to at this time. Identifying the leader has been especially hard. So far, he has eluded all our attempts at discovering where he is operating from or even who he is. That's why we would like you to let his agents obtain the treasure."

We all looked at each other, wondering if we had heard him correctly. "What do you mean 'let them obtain the treasure'?" Bill put the question we all had to him.

Spencer looked at Frazier, who answered Bill. "Let them get the treasure and lead us to the boss. You'll get the money back when we take him down. Our most important goal is to stop this new terrorist leader before he kills hundreds, if not thousands, of people. Think about this and decide, but it'll have to be a quick decision."

To give us time to consider his request—if it was a request—I asked another question. "You said hundreds or even thousands of potential casualties; do you know what weapon he is going to use?"

Pollock said, "From the talk, there seems to be someone looking for five biological or chemical weapons. We can't verify that it is the same guy at this time, but the fact that we are looking at five world targets seems to indicate that; I don't believe in coincidences."

"Do you have a name?" Lander asked.

Pollock replied, "We are hearing some refer to him as Faisal; that's all we know right now. We don't have a picture of him; he doesn't show up in any of our data bases. It seems that he has no former operations nor even any street creds right now. But that would change in a hurry if he were able to pull these attacks off."

Bill responded to Frazier's earlier question. "As far as allowing them to get the treasure, that will have to be a decision by Lauftis and Mokuk; the treasure seems to belong to the tribe. We will discuss that and get back to you."

"Let us know by a.m. tomorrow. Regardless of your decision, we are still pulling out all stops trying to get to him before he gets the funds." Pollock continued, "Lander has Frazier's contact information. We'll wait for your reply," and terminated the video session.

We all sat for a moment, then finally Pfieffer said, "What are we going to do?"

Bill looked at Bear and spoke, "Before we decide on anything, do you all have GPS tracking devices and, if so, can we get access to some of them?"

Bear looked at Seal, who replied, "Yes, we have them. If we need more, we can get them within a couple of hours. Our office in Halifax keeps them in stock. We have so many teams going into isolated and dangerous territories that they are a staple for our operations. What are you thinking?"

"A couple of things. First, I have an idea about our invisible boat. We can't see it nor can we track it with radar. We know that they will come back to the cave to get the treasure. I thought that I could hide out at the bluff and wait for them. When they come, I would be underwater and could see their boat from that angle; I don't think the digital camouflage would work below the surface. I could sneak to the boat and attach a tracking device to it. That would solve our problem of being able to find it whenever we wanted to."

"That's a good idea, Bill; do you think it would be safe to swim up to the boat underwater," I asked.

"I think so. They will be focused on getting the treasure; they will leave one man on the boat, but he'll never see me underwater."

"That should work," said Jack. "But I'll be with you. What about the other tracking devices? What were you going to do with them?"

"That depends on your answer to the next question." We all knew what the question was going to be, but he asked it anyway. "What about Frazier's request to let the terrorists get the treasure?"

"I've thought about that. It's a lot of funding for our tribe and we certainly don't want to lose it. But I know Mokuk would want us to do what we could to keep innocent people from being killed. He told me to use my judgment in any decisions we make regarding the treasure. It would be a huge risk, but if we have a viable plan to get it back, then we have to work with the C.I.A." He turned toward Bill. "Then you want to arm the treasure chests with tracking devices, also, don't you?"

"Yes, I do, if your decision is to use it for bait. Bear, can you check on getting the tracking items?"

Seal answered him, "I've already texted the request to Shark on our boat. He is checking our stock and if we need more, he will contact Director Armand at the Halifax office. If the helicopter is there, he will have them to us within an hour."

"You're good, I don't care what Bear says," I said with a grin on my face.

CHAPTER 36

Faisal stood behind the one-way glass and watched his teams enter the conference room; they came in mostly singles, but a couple of them had two men together. They seemed subdued and talked little with each other. They represented terrorist cells from each of the five targeted cities and were some of the most cold-blooded men on earth. They not only would kill if they needed to, they enjoyed it, especially when the targets were infidels. He knew that, if given his choice, each man there would select the American city as his target. He also knew that none of his selected disciples would hesitate to carry out his wishes; after all, they would be doing this in the service of Allah and great rewards awaited those who died in the cause. He had instructed them to wear the clothes most representative of the city they came from; he did not want a group of men spotted going to the same destination, all wearing robes and calling attention to the fact that they were Muslims. All had western clothes and most wore suits. They could have been attendees at any of the many conventions of the most successful corporations.

This meeting was being held in an isolated region of Afghanistan and he had posted guards around the lone building; no one would get close to him that did not show the proper credentials. The structure had been built as an Islamic training facility almost twenty years ago and was made available for meetings for any of the many extremist groups participating in the jihad. He entered the room and all noise stopped immediately. He approached the raised platform and stood before them, his new robe flowing down to his sandals. His long hair and his beard had been washed and brushed for this occasion. Although he had met individually with each person there, this was the first time he had assembled them together. Each man thought the planned event was only for his city. Faisal thought to himself, *They will be impressed with the planning of this great moment and he would see his prestige rise to new heights. Maybe they will think of me like they revered Bin Laden.*

He raised his arm and shouted, "Allahu Akbar!" This is the Islamic takbir and is used in many ways, most noticeably by extremists to mean "God is great"; it is used interchangeably with the more common phrase "Allah Akbar".

As one, the audience replied, "Allah Akbar!"

Faisal repeated this four more times, each time raising the intensity of the crowd until they were geared to a frenzy. He would need this level of commitment from them to carry out his plan. He raised both arms and signaled silence to the men; they immediately became quiet and Faisal said, "Please sit."

There were no chairs in the room, but that was no problem for this group; they quickly folded their legs beneath them and sat in the typical meditative posture, with their arms resting on their knees and their eyes locked on Faisal. This had been intentional on Faisal's part as he wanted the men to have to look up to him; after all, he was the new supreme commander and they were mere followers.

He spoke: "We are given the command to continue the work of Allah. We must fight for his cause and we must kill the infidels who oppose him. You are a select group and will be given the opportunity to carry out a great judgment against our enemies. As such, there are abundant rewards that await you, rewards that any Muslim would gladly die for. Are you ready to stand for the battle?"

The reply was as he expected: "Yes, we are ready! Yes, we are ready! Allah Akbar! Allah Akbar! Allah Akbar!"

They grew silent as he again spoke. "We have selected your city as our great target; we will simultaneously hit Washington, London, Paris, Jerusalem, and Montreal. We will kill thousands—maybe millions—and the world will see that the jihad is successful. So many will die that the rest of the infidels will realize that they cannot deter the great victory march of Allah and they will fall to their knees asking for mercy. But there will be no mercy! We will slaughter all our enemies!"

They rose as one and shouted, "Allah Akbar! Allah Akbar!" over and over.

Faisal let them repeat the phrase for a long two minutes, then lifted his hand for silence. "Who is our premiro in London?" He used the old jihad term for general.

A man stood to his feet and averted his eyes as he looked to Faisal. "I am Allah's servant in London," he replied. He was a small man, not intimidating at all. However, his wiry frame belied both the agility and strength hidden under his casual dress clothes. He worked in the offices of one of London's most influential financial businesses; he had been in place for years and no one would suspect him of even being tolerant of extremist Muslims.

Faisal said, "Allah will reward you greatly for your obedience. Do you have your people in place?"

"Yes, they are in place and are reviewing training. We are also identifying the best location to place the weapon. Have you yet decided whether it will be biological or chemical?"

"No, my supplier is attempting to locate five great weapons, all alike. We want to kill the inhabitants of each city in a like manner. That way, there will be no doubt that the attacks were all coordinated by the same group. Identify the top three prospects for each type weapon; when we get the bombs, we will narrow them to the best spot." Faisal shifted his head. "Where is my general in Paris?"

"Another man stood and proclaimed, "I am Allah's servant and your general in Paris. We are ready; we have the best three potential targets identified and we are now practicing for placing the weapon in the right place. Allah Akbar!" The Paris leader was a high-ranking official in the local gendarmerie. No one in the police department had any hint of his affiliation with the Islamic movement.

Faisal nodded to him and said, "Allah will reward you. What about Montreal?"

"I am here, my commander." A thin, dark man wearing a long overcoat stood. "Montreal is ready to go, praise Allah. There is a spot for each type weapon identified and my team is meeting weekly, renewing their training tactics. Montreal will fall to Allah's army." The Canadian was a corporate officer in the state government offices located in Montreal.

The man from Jerusalem was the next to stand. "We are ready. It will be hard for me to keep my group silent until the moment; they are anxious to kill the Israelis. It will be an honor to bring this unholy place to its knees. Allah Akbar!" he said, and sat back down. He was a well-known private detective and had been an invaluable source of knowledge to the jihadist movement.

Faisal had saved Washington until last. If he proved successful in the American capitol, then the world would cower at his feet. "Who is my general in Washington?"

All eyes in the room watched the lone man stand. His Brooks Brothers' suit and shined shoes fingered him for corporate success and his confident persona allowed him access to most of the most exclusive rooms in the capitol city. His name was known by many and it was not uncommon for his face to appear on national news coverage media outlets. Many in America would have recognized his voice when he spoke. "I am here! I have prepared for and waited for this for years. We will be ready for the strike."

Faisal continued to talk to the men for the next forty-five minutes. He led them to believe that the funds to purchase the weapons were already secure. He told them: "The timeline is set now. I will have the weapons by Thanksgiving, the end of the third week in November. We will time the strike for Christmas day, when all the infidels are in their homes watching their silly television shows and all the kids are playing with their childish toys."

The man from Washington spoke up. It was a question that no one else in the gathering would have had the gall to ask. "Would it be better to do it on a day when many people are gathered together at work places or perhaps a major sporting event?"

Faisal stared at the insubordinate man from America. The stupid culture of the world power taught that underlings could—and should—question authority. The man was conditioned to speak his mind; after all, he was a leader in his organization. Finally, Faisal answered him in a sarcastic voice, "If it were a typical bomb, you are right. But neither a bio nor a chemical weapon requires the congregation of people to be effective. Whether it is air-borne or some other type of distribution, perhaps a water supply, it will reach thousands of victims spread out over the city. The demonstration of our power on one of their religious holidays will be a slap in the face of the so-called Christians and will show the world the power of Allah. He looked around the room; his gruff reply to the American seemed to have the desired effect on the others, so much so that he expected no further question to his authority.

"I will talk with you again as Thanksgiving Day approaches. By then, I will have the weapons to get to you. Caution your people not to say or do anything in public that could lead to suspicion; remember that the infidels have spies all over the place. Arrangements will be made to get the weapons into your cities. They will be delivered to the safe houses you are using for your secret meetings. Remember, Allah will reward your bravery in war. Allahu Akbar!"

He watched them stand to their feet and in chorus reply, "Allah Akbar!" And he turned and left the building.

CHAPTER 37

"What do you think, Jack? What are we going to do about the treasure?"

Lauftis looked at Lander before answering. "Before I decide for sure, let's go look at the cave. I need to get a perspective on the treasure to make sure we can get it back. I do know we have to stop the terrorist threat. The money is not worth the lives of thousands of our citizens."

I agreed with him, but didn't say anything right then. We looked up as we heard the footsteps approach. Bear and Seal were coming back into the conference room. They had met Shark at their boat and checked out the supplies.

"We have only three GPS tracking units on the boat, but the office is sending us a box of fifty new ones by helicopter; they are also sending us a winch and a cable. It should be here within the next fifteen minutes. Do you still want to go back to the bluff?"

Lander answered for us. "Yes, the quicker the better. Do you have dive gear for Lauftis? It'll take an extra-large helmet for him." I looked at Jack's head and wasn't sure whether Lander was digging at him or not.

"Yes, we've got gear for all of you. Let's go to the boat and start getting things ready for the dive. By the time we do that, the helicopter should be here."

"Okay, let me go in and tell Cyndi what we're doing."

I walked back in and Cyndi spoke first. "Lucinda will run me home after a while; I'll see you all when you get back from the bluff." I don't know whether we have been married long enough that she can read my mind or whether she slipped a recording device under my skin while I was sleeping. She kissed me—or maybe I kissed her—and I went back to meet the boys.

By the time we had selected the gear and had it laid out, we heard the helicopter. It hovered over the boat and the officer on the passenger side lowered a bag to Bear standing on the deck. He released it from the cable and the cable immediately was pulled back to the open doorway. It snaked down again, this time carrying a heavier load. Bear guided it to a stop on the deck, unhooked the package, and gave a thumbs-up to the copter. The cable was rewound and the helicopter followed its blades up away from the boat. Seal backed the boat away from the dock and headed for the open bay. As usual, we kept a lookout for the other boat, but saw no sign of it. After a high-speed approach, Seal stopped the boat just about where we were the last time.

While we donned our dive gear, Bear and Seal readied the winch. The boat had connection plates on every side of it so a winch could be anchored wherever it was needed. This time they attached it to the shore side of the boat. I followed Bill and Jack into the water and turned on my GoPro Hero4 attached to my helmet. I accessed my iPhone and followed the blue line of the GPS directions to the spot I had saved at the target. Jack looked over the covering and connected our cable to the loop secured to the rock. He nodded ready and I radioed Bear to start the winch. We watched the cable snake through the pulley and saw the cave opening as the cover slowly rotated from closed position. I kept my video camera on the rock and when Bear saw it was open, he stopped the winch. We could finally access the tunnel.

Lander located another spike that had been driven into the rock and rotated it so that it acted as a stop to hold the rock in the open position. We let Jack lead the way. There was a current going into the tunnel so it was relatively easy for us to enter deeper into the side of the mountain; we had to be careful not to get our gear damaged by a sharp rock at the side of the tunnel. We kept a watch to be sure that there were no side tunnels that would confuse us getting back to open water, but there were none. After a few minutes, we emerged into the treasure room. We had agreed not to touch anything at all until we analyzed the situation, so we began at the wall where we entered and moved clockwise around the circular area. We stopped when we saw the treasure chests. *Right there sits more money than I'll make in my lifetime,* I thought. *In fact, it's probably more that all of us in the room would make together in our lifetimes.*

The sudden voice startled me until I realized it was Lander, "Look at those treasure chests! If they have what I think is in them, there is a lot of wealth there."

He verbalized what I was thinking and I replied, "But, look at the shelf; I think one of the boxes is gone. It looks like there was another one sitting on the very left, there where the shelf has broken off."

"It has already been taken, or, if the warning is right, someone tried to take it without working through the steps and it disappeared like the book said it would."

Jack said, "Let's look at the clue in the center of the room." Bill and I followed him to the middle of the space. We stood on the floor and let the debris we had stirred up settle, then we looked at the image that slowly came into focus. It was just as the book had said, two knights on a single horse and a lance or spear held at an upward angle in front of the horse. Jack moved across the room, going to the spot where the spear pointed. He bent and ran his hands along the bottom edge of the wall where it met the floor of the cave and found the slot where the third clue had rested.

"It's not here. They have it," he said.

"That means we can't go on to Clue Four," I said. "What are we going to do now?"

"We're going to put the tracking devices on the chests and then we're going to leave the cave for the terrorists," said Jack. "Come on, let's get this done quickly and get out of here before they come back."

We finned our way to the shelves holding the treasure. Jack held out a box to both Lander and me. "Here, put a tracking unit on each of the boxes." He looked carefully at a chest and said, "Be careful, not too much pressure. We don't want to move the chest at all; it might trigger a slide that would take all the chests out of our reach." We watched him pull a tiny transmitter from his box; he removed the covering that activated the device and stuck it to the back of the chest, just under the hinge. The clear transmitter became almost invisible and, unless one were looking for it, it would never be found. With the three of us working, we were through with the task in under five minutes and we hurriedly retraced our steps to the bay. As soon as we were in open water, I told Bear to use the winch to cover the opening. Again, I held my camera on the rock so he could see the procedure. We released our cable and, using the ladder, we climbed back to the deck of the boat. We told Seal and Bear what we had done.

Bear said, "Are we ready to leave?"

Lander said, "You are, just as soon as we ease back into the water. We're staying here to wait for the other boat. It will be back shortly; they are probably watching us and as soon as we leave, they will go back to the cave." Bill and Jack ducked down and crab-walked to the shore-side of the boat.

"Hey, I'm going to. If they come back, I'll stay on shore and watch for you," I said.

"Okay, follow me in the water; we have to stay submerged until we get to the edge of the bluff where we can hide. I saw some trees there; that's where we are heading."

"Bear, I'll call you when it's safe to come back to get us," I said.

We dropped almost silently into the water, slowly sank until we were about ten feet below the surface, and started swimming. About a minute went by, and, then, we heard the roar of the Coast Guard boat as it left the area. I hoped that the terrorists thought we were all on board. It took about thirteen minutes to reach the edge of the bluff, where the shore bent away from us. We eased out of the water and sat down behind some trees. We adjusted our spot so that we had a clear view of the water close to the cave opening.

"We might as well rest, but don't get too relaxed; it won't be long before they show up."

"Do you really think they will come back here?" I asked. "How do they know we are not still there?"

"I would bet my last dollar that their boat was sitting right out there, with them watching us all the time. And, if they were, as soon as they know the Coast Guard boat has gone, they will be back in the cave. There's too much money there and too much if riding on it for them to give up. They'll be here within the next ten minutes. I'll bet you a Starbucks on that," he said, looking at me.

"You're on," I said.

"Here they come," said Jack.

I looked out over the water and scanned the surface. "I don't see anything," I said.

"You won't see anything, except maybe that sign in the water." He pointed to the water where there were ripples being displaced.

I watched the small wave make its way toward the bluff. "Why can't I hear the motor?"

"They're using an electric motor, like a high-powered trolling motor. It'll push the boat slowly, but make no noise at all, or if anything at all, a slight whine."

We watched as the invisible boat made its way up close to the bluff and then waited until all was still around it. "They're in the water now; let's go," Jack said, looking at Bill. "Phil, you stay here and let us know if something happens; use text messages to communicate with us if you need to do so. We should have plenty of oxygen to get us there and back." They had slipped into the water without a sound before I could even acknowledge him.

I stayed out of sight behind the trees and watched. Even though I knew where the boat was and where Bill and Jack were going, I saw nothing that indicted anything or anyone was there. It had taken us thirteen minutes to come to this spot, so I figured it would take them about thirty minutes to get there, attach the tracking units, and get back. At thirty-five minutes, I began to worry that something had gone wrong. At forty-two minutes, I was startled to see Jack suddenly standing beside me and Bill emerging from the water about five yards from my spot. We settled down for a while as we could do nothing but wait for them to leave. I started to ask them how it had gone, but Jack cautioned me with a finger over his lips and said, "Quiet. Sounds travel over water."

Three hours passed before there was any activity. The anchored boat suddenly came to life. We could see it and the motor sounded like we were at the speedway. It sped away and before it was out of sight, I had texted Bear to come back for us.

CHAPTER 38

As soon as the Coast Guard left the area, Adar directed his boat be moved into position, but with the camouflage active and the power supplied by the electric motor. He did not want to take a chance on anyone seeing them approach the spot. As soon as they were in the right spot, he led his men back to the treasure room, stopping only long enough to connect the winch and move the rock covering. He had given his men instructions about what to look for and, as soon as they entered the room, they split up and began the search. Adar had reasoned that the disc had to fit on a section of wall that had the bulging shapes that would align to the holes in the disc. He was excited about the chests just sitting there for him, but he also knew that his time was quickly running out. And he knew what Faisal would do to him if he didn't come through with the solution.

He again had taken the floor, so he went back to the center where he had found the first emblem. In the murky water, the only way he could identify bumps in the floor was by feeling them. He removed his fins and walked across the bottom, feeling with his toes. When he felt the least uneven surface, he dropped down and ran his hands over the section. There were many such places in the floor, but it helped that he was looking for three knobs that would align with the holes in the triangular emblem in the disc. After forty minutes searching, he thought to himself, "This is like looking for a needle in a stack of hay," or whatever the Americans call it. He had outfitted his men with double tanks this time so they would not have to give up the search so quickly.

He had told his men to call him anytime one of them felt something unusual; he had been summoned to check out eight different sections, but none of them had the three requisite bulges. His men were becoming agitated. They said nothing to him but he could read the frustration in their body language. But he managed his impatience. Allah was testing him by placing the treasure right in front of him and not letting him have it. He thought it was a trial that all true leaders went through and he would not let Allah down. They continued the exploration, combing through almost the whole room.

He saw movement in the corner of his eye and moved his head to see what had gotten his attention. Juhall was waving excitedly to him. Adar marked his spot and went to Juhall, who pointed at a section on the wall. Adar looked, shook his head, and looked again. *Was it possible*? he thought, as he ran his hand over the shapes there. There were three distinct bulges in the wall, spaced out in the shape of a triangle. He quickly grabbed the disc and fitted it to the wall. He couldn't believe it; the holes in the disc aligned perfectly with the bulges on the wall. He just stood and looked at it a moment. *Now what do I do?" he thought. "Nothing's happening with the treasure.* He pushed against the disc, but it didn't give an inch. He pulled on it and the disc slipped off the wall. He replaced it on the wall and looked carefully at it. His eye focused on the knob sticking out from the disc. He grasped it in his right hand and tried to move it to the side. No luck here, either. *Maybe I can use the knob to turn the disc, like a steering wheel.* He didn't want to break the knob off, so he put only a little pressure on it, but it did not move. *Harder, but be careful.* He braced himself with his left hand and really put more leverage into turning the disc. It began to move, slowly at first, then, more easily. When it had revolved about three quarters of the way around, a section of the wall about a foot away began to open. He continued to spin the knob and the crevice opened to reveal something inside.

Yes! he thought. *I am Adar, Allah's servant.* He stepped to the new opening and shined his flashlight into the crevice. The inside was only about six inches wide and five feet tall; its depth was about a foot. Standing in the space was a flag staff with a banner hanging from the top of it. He reached in and lifted it out. He spread the flag and saw the emblem of a red cross in the center of the background, a background that was at one time white, but now was a dingy shade of yellow. *Clue Four,* he thought. *Only one more to go!*

CHAPTER 39

When Bear picked us up, I told him to go back to Pfieffer's office. When we arrived, Cyndi was still working with Lucinda. She went into the office with the rest of us: Jack, Bill, Bear, Seal, and me. Pfieffer was standing by his window. We took seats and Pfieffer said, "Any luck?"

Lander began, summarizing what had happened. "We got into the cave and found the treasure—or at least we found treasure chests. We could not look in them yet."

"Why not? That would have been the first thing I wanted to do, to actually see the treasure . . . if it really is there," said, Pfieffer.

Lander continued: "The book from Mokuk warned us not to try to get the treasure before all the steps have been accomplished. In fact, it looked like one of the chests was gone. Adar could have gotten it, but I really think it he lost it when he tried to get it before completing all the steps in order. So, we didn't want to risk losing any more of the treasure.

We found the first clue in the room; it was one of the Knights Templar's seals or emblems, an image of two knights on a single horse. They were carrying a lance, which the book told us would point us to the next clue. We searched the location it directed us to. There was supposed to be a disc there, but it was missing."

I spoke up, "Adar has to have it. He probably found it and hasn't figured out how to use it to find the next clue."

"Or maybe it was so rusted over, he had to take it with him to clean it up to be able to read it. You remember we had to do that with the coin you found," Cyndi said as she looked at me.

"Nevertheless, we hit a roadblock in retrieving the treasure. We discussed it and Jack has decided to let the terrorists get the treasure and lead us to the ringleader of the planned attack. There is just too much potential for loss of lives worldwide; we've got to help stop the bigger plan."

Pfieffer said, "But what if Adar loses us when we try to follow him? We don't have enough people to be ready to follow him if we don't know how he will leave the area."

Jack answered him. "We put tracking devices on his boat and also on every one of the treasure chests. We can follow them with our smart phones."

Cyndi said, "So you did finally see their boat. How did you get the tracker on it?"

I said, "After we closed up the tunnel entrance, we all got back on the boat. Bill, Jack, and I used our dive gear and slipped over the side of the boat. Bear left the area while we stayed underwater and made our way to some trees at the edge of where the bluff begins. We hid out there waiting for the extremists to come back. We were sure they would, just as soon as they knew we had gone. They're under the gun to get the treasure out of the cave. So, we just stayed out of sight until they returned."

Cyndi said again, "So you finally saw them."

"No, not exactly, we didn't see them. They even used an electric motor to get their boat to the bluff so we didn't even hear them coming."

"So, if you couldn't see them or couldn't hear them, how did you know they were there?" I expected her to relate this to something about a falling tree in the forest, but she didn't—you know, the one about if a tree falls in the woods and there is no one there to hear it, does it make a sound?

"We saw a slight bow wave as the boat moved into position. If we had not seen the water move, we would never have known the boat was there; the camouflage is that good. We gave them time to get into the cave and then Bill and Jack swam underwater to the boat. I took the hazardous duty and stayed on shore to be the watch dog."

Bill took up the narrative: "It was amazing; we could see absolutely nothing related to the boat above the water line. But as we approached the area under the water, we could see the boat clearly. We placed two tracking devices on the boat in the event one of them malfunctions or in case they discover one, we have a backup. That was all there was to it. We started to try to board the boat, but decided they probably had left someone on board and we didn't want to scare them away. We went back to where Phil was waiting and we remained until they left. Bear came back to get us and we came straight here."

"The trackers are all working." I held up my iPhone so they could see the positions identified on it. "The boat is in off the bluff right now and all these other dots are the treasure chests. They still do not have them out of the cave yet."

"Let's hope they take the valuables out in the chests and don't just get the treasure and leave the chests there." We all looked at Seal as we considered his words.

"We need to call Director Frazier and let him know we will let Adar take the treasure and lead them to the leader." As he spoke, Bill moved to the satellite phone that Frazier had left us to contact him with. He checked to be sure encryption was on and he toggled the speaker button so we could all hear. In about twenty seconds, it was answered.

"Frazier here. How are things in Canada?"

Bill told him, "Lauftis has decided to work with you on using the treasure as bait; we are going to let Adar get the valuables out and you can follow the trail wherever it leads. But, that's a lot of money for his tribe and you have to be able to get the treasure back to him."

I explained about the tracking devices we had planted and the complete invisibility of the boat.

"So, they *are* using Dr. Bronson's interactive digital camouflage," Frazier said. "I've got my best people on Bronson's disappearance. That would be awesome if we found him alive and could get him back to continue his work with us. And, yes, we will attempt to guarantee that Lauftis will get his treasure back."

I thought, "If it is only an attempt to guarantee, then it is not a guarantee, is it?" But I didn't say that aloud. No use to muddy the waters any more.

I turned my thoughts back to listening to Frazier again. "Let us know immediately when Adar retrieves the treasure. As soon as he gets it, he will leave the area. We have to be able to track him to his meeting with his boss. We have additional intel that man is the Faisal that is looking for the WMDs. We need to stop him before he gets his hands on those weapons."

"But you also need to know where those weapons are coming from, don't you?" asked Lauftis.

"They have to be coming from Russia. We know that former members of the KGB have access to many of the former Soviet Republic's weapons and they are getting rich by selling them to the highest bidder."

"Can you talk with President Putin? Surely, he does not want his country's weapons being used in other parts of the world. He was a member of the KGB so he probably knows if any of his former comrades are putting weapons out in the black market."

"We have been in contact with him and he says that he will try to discover if a previous operative is the potential source for Faisal. But don't hold your breath that he can stop it. The underworld and the gangsters in Russia now are powerful organizations and seem to be invulnerable from any operation against them. They are the ones who have taken advantage of the new capitalism there; they have become rich and seem to be hands-off for the government.

"What about your teams in the targeted cities? Have they been able to gather any news about an upcoming attack?" Bill asked. "Do we even know for sure what the targeted cities are?"

"We're confident that there are five cities in Faisal's sights: London, Paris, Montreal, Jerusalem, and Washington. In London, we are shadowing two different groups; either one of them may be our target. There is some social media chatter about something spectacular in the near future, but we can't nail it down any further. So far, neither group has done anything out of the ordinary.

"In Paris, there is always talk about upcoming disasters, so it's hard to tell if there is anything of substance mixed in all the garbage. Our group there could be any one of the crowd on almost any street corner. We're looking, but in Paris, it will be hard to identify the right ones.

"In Jerusalem, the Mossad assures us they are on top of things. The Israeli Secret Services are among the best in the world; I feel good about the defense mechanisms there. It will be hard to perpetrate a major event in Jerusalem.

"Montreal is working to identify any extremist groups in the city. They have good people assigned to the project. Montreal will work closely with us in attempting to defuse this situation before it becomes a deadly threat.

"And, of course you know about how Washington responds. We are taking the threat seriously and the C.I.A. is working with the F.B.I., Intelligence, and Homeland Security to render this group impotent."

Lauftis said, "You all are working together? When did this start?

Frazier replied, "Well, it just started . . . I think. I am told this will be the new normal here. If we are going to deter all the new threats, we will have to have better collaboration."

"Let's hope so. For too many years, the different initials there have spent more effort protecting their own territory than trying to protect the country." Only Lander could get away with saying something like that in front of the C.I.A. Director.

Lauftis said, "You indicated that authorities in those target countries have been alerted?"

"Yes, we have a video conference call each afternoon to debrief our activities. They are all on board and are treating this as a legitimate safety concern."

"Is the Homeland Security Advisory System still in place?" Bear spoke up, "Is that the procedure for alerting the public about the danger level of potential threats? The alerts are color-coded depending on their risk level, aren't they?"

Frazier replied to him, "Yes, you are right. But we no longer use the HSAS. It has been replaced by the new National Terrorism Advisory System. The color-coded procedure was begun in 2002, and, at that time, was considered to be a great way to alert the public. However, the use of several different colors caused a lot of public confusion and sometimes too much anxiety for the specific threat. The new NTAS—as it is called—is more easily understood by the public."

I asked, "How is it different? You still have to provide information about perceived threats, don't you?"

"Yes, we do. When we have credible information about a threat, an NTAS alert will be shared with the public. Sometimes it may include specific information about the nature of the danger, but not always. Sometimes there is classified information that prohibits that. The alert may include specific steps that people or a community can take in order to help protect themselves."

"Are all threats taken the same way? If there is no longer a color code accompanying the threat, how do people know how serious it may be?"

"Good question, Cyndi. We consider any credible threat as being serious. However, a threat may be released with the label of imminent or elevated, depending on the perceived consequences of the threat. Those labels are easier for the public to understand without having to remember what each color represents. We also are now asking the public to become much more involved. You may have seen the new tag line: 'If you see something, say something'. With almost everyone walking around with a smart phone now, it is imperative that we instill in them a responsibility to report any unusual activity or suspicious persons."

Lander asked, "Have you issued a public alert for this threat yet?"

"No, we haven't. According to our intelligence, we have until the Christmas season before it becomes an imminent threat. If we released something now, it would not only alert the public, it would warn the terrorists that we were onto them. They would go silent while still planning the attacks. Our job to find them would become exponentially more difficult."

Pfieffer spoke up. "That's true. That's the reason we really haven't told our community here what is happening at the treasure site."

Frazier continued, "There's a fine line between a public's right to know and the possible negative consequences if that knowledge is shared too readily. Many people don't get it and most of the media just wants to sell information. That's tough, but that's the way it is. It sounds like you all are doing the right things there and we appreciate it. Keep me abreast of anything—and I mean anything—that happens related to this case. Call me anytime, day or night, if you need or want to. This is the most critical threat the world has ever known from a terrorist organization. We have to do whatever it takes to stop it. If you need anything at all, let me know and you'll have it as quickly as I can get it to you."

Frazier ended the call.

Chapter 40

Faisal approached the counter and smiled at the ticket agent; he sat his small carry-on case at his feet and handed her his documents. She said, "I'll need to see your identification and your passport." His hand went into the left inside pocket of his gray suit coat and came back with the paperwork, which he placed in front of her. She picked them up and looked carefully at him and his picture I.D. Faisal had gotten rid of his long hair and beard and was dressed in a dark blue conservative suit with a white shirt and muted patterned tie. "Thank you, Mr. Wabby. Have a good flight. We'll be boarding in a couple of minutes." Faisal moved to the side to wait for the boarding call.

This I.D. was only one of about a dozen that he kept. He also had credit cards in Michel Wabby's name, but intended to use only cash for the trip. He would like to carry and use only cash, but some hotels and car rental companies insisted on seeing a credit card. So, he carried one. The fact that it was not really his was none of their business.

Six hours later, he exited the Charles de Gaulle airport in Paris. Standing on the sidewalk, he looked around for his ride. A taxi driver approached him and asked, "Do you need a taxi?" Faisal shook his head no. The driver said again, "Do you need a ride? I'm supposed to pick you up, Mr. Wabby. Follow me."

Faisal walked behind the driver, who stopped at a black and white taxi labeled: *De Gaulle Taxi Service*. He got into the back seat and was whisked out of the airport. They drove for thirty-five minutes and the driver slowed in front of a house at the end of the cul-de-sac. He turned into the driveway and pulled the car into the garage, where he punched the remote and the garage door closed. Only when it was completely down did he open his door and say to Faisal, "This way." He opened the door from the garage into the house; Faisal followed him in, through the kitchen, down the hallway, and into the front room. The man sitting there in the chair said, "Thank you, Lawrence, that will be all. Wait for Mr. Wabby in the car." The driver nodded and reversed his route through the house to the car. When he heard the door close, the man spoke. "Welcome, Mr. Wabby. There are drinks or coffee in the kitchen."

"No, thank you. I do not wish any drinks at this time."

"Please, sit down."

Faisal sat in a leather side chair and looked at his host, a man called Robechet. The man had dark hair running toward gray around his temples; his eyes were intense and focused on Faisal. Although he had a slight bulge around his waistline, he looked strong enough to handle himself with most people and, in fact, he proved this almost daily in his job as a supervisor in the Parisian Gendarmerie. Faisal judged him to be in his mid-forties. He said, "Tell me about your preparations."

Robechet answered: "I have eight good men on my team here in Paris. We have met three times since your call to action."

"Have you assured that the meetings have been unobserved?"

"Yes, we have taken precautions. We met in a safe house and each man followed protocol to get to the house. I utilized guards outside the house to assure we were not compromised."

"What about the plan? Tell me about the target."

"If the package is chemical, we will deliver it to the water supply. I have keys to the water house. The source supplies water to all of Paris and the surrounding areas twenty-five miles outside the city. We estimate a potential population of four million people in the area served."

"What if it is biological?"

"If so, then our target will change. Paris has one of the best mass transit systems in the world. Its subway system, the Metro, has sixteen lines serving over three hundred stations. We can use the air filtration system for the Metro to disperse a bio-product. The Metro services many tourists in a day's time, so if those people are infected and the disease has an incubation period of a few days, they will go back to their homes and spread the disease. The potential for the bio-weapon is even greater than that of a chemical bomb."

"Very good, Robechet. I will be in touch. You must maintain secrecy and be ready to go when you are contacted." Faisal stood and immediately went back to the garage. He had another flight scheduled, so he commanded the driver to hurry.

He visited the airport business lounge and stopped in front of the shredder. A minute later, Michel Wabby ceased to exist.

He made his way to the ticket counter and showed his papers. "I hope you have had a good trip to Paris, Mr. Geren, and will come back to visit us again. Here is your boarding pass."

Faisal's new I.D. and passport carried the name of McKenzie Geren, a business executive from Idaho. His ticket showed a destination of London. In about one hour, the full-capacity jet was touching down on the runway. He got into the car with the driver waiting for Mr. Geren and was driven to the outskirts of London. He slipped into the house and sat down with Thom Bidson, an official in the London financial district. Faisal asked Bidson to summarize his plans for the weapons.

"If the bomb is chemical, we will utilize the London water distribution system. London has a population of over eight million people and millions of them have contact with the public water supply daily. I have a man in place working for the municipal water works and he can make the diffusion.

"If the device is biological, then we will disperse the spores though the London Underground system known as The Tube. It is one of the largest subway systems in the world and has a filtration system that we will access. There is a man working there that will plant the device for a price of one quarter million dollars."

"Tell him we will pay one hundred thousand dollars, no more. He will do it." Faisal stood up and said, "Be ready when I call."

Faisal checked into the airport and got his ticket, this time as William Abbey. He took his seat and slept until he landed at Ben Gurion Airport. He was met by a taxi driver and taken to the north suburbs of Jerusalem. The Israeli private detective was waiting for him in the safe house. The agent was in his mid-thirties; his intense daily circuit training was the reason he was in the best shape of his life. He was casually dressed in sweat pants and a Gore-Tex jacket. When questioned how he planned to use the device, he said, "I hope it is biological; once started, it will continue to replicate itself. But if it is chemical, it will also work. Either one of them can be infused in the water supply and dispersed to the almost one million people who live in and around the city. "We are ready; we are ready," he kept repeating as Faisal left the building.

At the airport, Faisal entered the restroom and, standing in a stall, he put on a dark wig and a fake mustache. He stripped off his top shirt and tossed it in the trash can. His tight long-sleeve pullover shirt emphasized his slender frame and showed off his six-pack abs. He approached the ticket agent and after showing his passport and picture I.D., he received his one-way ticket to Montreal. "Thank you, Mr. Davis, for flying with us. Have a nice trip."

Shaun Davis entered the plane and found his assigned seat. As soon as the jet lifted off the runway, Faisal reclined his seat and slept until the pilot announced the approach to Montreal. This was a lot of flying in a short amount of time, but Faisal felt as if he had to make personal contact with his operatives to confirm their status and impress on them the importance of staying careful and focused. Andrew Libechet met him and took him to a coffee shop that had no customers at this time of the night. Libechet's plans mirrored those of most of the ones he had already talked to. There were a lot of ways a chemical or biological weapon could be activated, but for maximum effect, either the water supply or air-distribution system is the best. Faisal finished the coffee and discussion and Libechet took him back to the airport.

He entered the U.S. as Robert Jeffrey and flew to Ronald Reagan Washington National Airport, where he was met by a wimpy little man who drove him to one of the city's many upscale hotels. He was already registered as Jeffrey and had only to show his I.D. to get his room key. As soon as he entered the eighth-floor room, the phone in the room rang. He picked up the receiver and the voice told him to come to room seven-thirteen. He visited the restroom and then walked one floor down the stairs and knocked on the door. It opened and the tall, handsome man bid him to come in. Cary Logan was a well-known television personality in the D.C. area and was recognized almost anywhere he went. He handed Faisal a drink from the mini-bar and asked, "How did the world tour go? You've been almost around the world in the last day."

"Everything is in place and all are ready. We just have to get the weapons now."

"What about Oak Island? Is Adar going to come through there?"

"He still claims he will be successful. He has located the treasure but he says that it will be destroyed unless he works through all the steps outlined in the clues. Do you still have a buyer for the treasure?"

"Yes, if it is as advertised. My man is anxious to get his hands on the coins and jewels. He will pay almost anything we ask for it."

"We are close, my brother. This is what we have worked for all our lives. Let's get some sleep and we'll continue this discussion in the morning."

CHAPTER 41

Adar examined the flag and the staff carefully, looking for a clue how to use it to get to step five. He checked it again, running his fingers over each section to see if there were any indication of a hidden fragment there. Nothing! "What do I do with the flag," he thought. He stared at the flag as if to will it to answer him. He stood and propped the flag back in its hiding place and turned to look at the treasure. As he turned back, his eye caught the glint of something on the bottom of the crevice. He bent to retrieve it. It was some kind of paper with some writing and an image on it; not exactly paper, maybe a piece of skin. He remembered that men used to write on sheets made from sheepskin, sheets called vellum. He shined his light on the sheet and read, "Find the slot under the top shelf and use this staff to find the key to the treasure. Replace all previous clues. Odd in order, then even."

"This is it," he thought excitedly. "The treasure is mine! They can't stop me now."

Adar lifted the flag staff and carried it to the center of the top shelf. He looked under the ledge for the slot. He could see nothing. He slid his hand along the surface, feeling for any type opening. *There! I can feel it.* He hurriedly placed the end of the staff in the slot and tried to move it. He expected it to leverage another hiding place where the key to the locks would be found. It wouldn't budge, no movement at all. He removed the flag pole and reinserted it. He still could get no movement at all. *Maybe this is not the one,* he thought. He propped the flag on the shelf and began looking again, searching for another slot. He spent almost thirty minutes looking, but could find no other opening for the staff. *Now what do I do?* He felt defeated, not for the first time in his life.

Finally, he glanced at the piece of vellum and read it again: "Find the slot under the top shelf and use this staff to find the key to the treasure."

"That's exactly what I did," he thought. "The directions couldn't be clearer; I followed them to the tee."

He looked at the paper again. And saw it. "How did I miss that?" He read the rest aloud, "Replace all previous clues." He looked down and saw the disc still lying on the floor where he had placed it. He picked it up and walked to the spot where he had found it. Bending to his knees, he pushed the disc back into the slot and made sure it was in all the way. He went back to the shelf and picked up the flag staff and inserted its end into the opening. He slid his hands up on the shaft and pulled. This time, the top of the pole moved downward and an opening appeared below the slot. He dropped the flag staff and put his hand in the new opening. Adar closed his fingers around the key and pulled it free. He raised the key to the first lock, then stopped. "I'm not going to make the same mistake," he thought. He picked up the flag and pole, went to the crevice where he had found it, and placed it back inside. When he removed his hand, the opening closed.

His men stood watching him as he moved back to the first treasure chest and inserted the key.

CHAPTER 42

Faisal met Logan for breakfast in one of the hotel's restaurants. They moved to the far back corner of the dining area and sat down. Their waitress brought them water and coffee and asked, "Will you be eating the buffet or do you want to order from the menu?"

Logan answered her, "From the menu. I'll have the Western Omelet with wheat toast, no butter."

She looked at Faisal, "And what about you, Sir?"

Faisal replied, "I want two eggs, over medium, crisp bacon, and sourdough toast."

She left and Logan said, "Are we really going to do this?"

"Yes, everything is falling in place. Adar says he has solved the puzzle to get the treasure; all he has to do now is get it out of the cave and to me. The new camouflage has worked perfectly."

"What are we going to do with the scientist now? We told him we would let him go if he cooperated with us."

Faisal knew this was going to be where they disagreed. "We can't just let him go; he knows too much."

"He thinks the whole plot is one run out of the Middle East. We are working off his radar. Once the attacks are successful, he can't link us to anything. Besides, we may want his services again someday."

"You may be right; I'll consider it. But we'll have to terminate our group working with him. There can be no loose threads that point to us."

"Your disguise has worked perfectly," Logan said. "No one has any idea that you are my younger brother. As far as they are concerned, you were killed when your helicopter went down with Bronson on board. Even Bronson thinks you were forced to crash with his stand-in on board. Making him watch the crash assured him we were serious when we told him what we would do to his family if he didn't work with us."

"Getting him to help us was a stroke of genius," Faisal said. "It was Allah's plan when he allowed you to be at the Washington press conference to hear what Dr. Bronson was working on."

"I don't think Allah has anything to do with it— neither do you. It was our luck and our long-term planning that put us in a position to make our move."

"Do you have any regrets about our decision to work with the terrorists?"

"No, none at all. When Washington denied me my opportunity to go into Special Forces, I vowed then to get even with them. Just like you; you were never satisfied to be a chauffeur, even if were in a helicopter. Uncle Sam wouldn't use our talents, so we will use them on Uncle Sam."

Faisal agreed with him, then went back to Adar, "Can we trust Adar to get us all the treasure that he recovers?"

"No, we can't trust him, but I have that covered. I insisted that he video the entire room with the chests; then number each one and video it as he loads it."

"Can he video it under water?"

"Yes, I sent him a camera. The new GoPro will work to those depths. He has already sent me the file that shows how many treasure chests there were in the room. Unfortunately, he got impatient and lost one of them. He will send me the video of him loading the treasure. In the first video, I saw that each chest had a Templar seal on it, so we'll know if he tries to get into a chest before he delivers it to us."

"What if he takes the treasure and runs? There are a lot of places he could go where we might not find him."

"He's committed to the plot against the infidels as he calls them, so he'll stay with the plan. Besides, he has a tracking device inserted under his skin. If he tries to remove it, it will release a poison that will kill him instantly. As long as he has it, I can track him anywhere in the world on my phone. In fact, I have an app that will let me remotely trigger it if I need to."

"Good touch! My brother is sharp. How are we going to get the treasure from Nova Scotia?"

"I have arranged for delivery by land to the U.S. The border with Canada and the U.S. stretches for thousands of miles and not all of the border is protected. We will use the same delivery method used last year to move the illegals into the country. The same driver will do this for us."

"How much will it cost us?"

"He thinks he is doing it for a percentage of the package value; I told him the trip would be worth two hundred thousand dollars to him. And, we are going to arm his delivery van with the digital camouflage. Dr. Bronson almost has a van ready for us."

Logan looked at him and said, "That's a lot of money for one trip across the border."

"Yes, it is, but we'll get it back, all except the deposit. We'll give him fifty thousand dollars up front to buy his allegiance to us."

"How are we going to get it back?"

"Actually, he'll never get the rest of it. He won't need it after he delivers the goods to us. He'll be another loose end we take care of."

Logan recognized the significance of Faisal's reply and, this time, agreed with the need to make the driver disappear.

Faisal said, "You said you have the buyer lined up. Can we trust him?"

"Yes, he is very anxious to get the coins. His clients will pay a fortune for the wealth of the Knights Templar. He'll get much more than he'll pay us for it.

But we don't know how much it is worth until we get those chests and see what's in them."

Faisal said, "We're still going with our own plan, aren't we?"

"Of course; we will consider it our retirement package."

CHAPTER 43

Adar looked at the video camera and then turned the key to the first lock. Faisal had outsmarted him when he demanded a video be taken of all the chests and the removal of them. That threw a monkey wrench into his plans to skim off some of the loot for himself. But with the video record, he had no choice but to adhere to Faisal's wishes. There were twenty-four chests—well, twenty-three now that the one had been lost—with a fortune in them.

He heard the lock click and the body of the lock fell away from the shank; he removed the chain that held the chest in place. He started to move the chest, but remembered the warning: "Odd in order, then even". So, he went to every odd-numbered chest and took the chains off them; then he started all over again with the even-numbered ones. He laid all the locks on the floor and directed the four personal underwater vehicles be lined up below the shelves. He lifted the first chest from the ledge and placed it on the first PUV. Although the chest was full and heavy, in the salt water, one man could easily handle the weight. As soon as the first PUV was loaded, he directed that it be taken to the boat, emptied, and brought back. He could get only two chests on each vehicle; it took each vehicle three full trips to get all the treasure on board. After the last PUV exited the tunnel, he signaled to Juhall to close the opening. Standing on the deck of the boat, he looked at the chests, lined up like a row of boxcars on a railway track. It was all he could do to keep his men from opening a chest to see what was really in it; he knew as loyal as they were to him, it was still the fact that he used his Glock to emphasize his request to leave them alone that they obeyed him.

He ordered the men below to bring the crates topside. He would secure each chest in a crate that would be locked. He had one key to the locks and Faisal had the other. It took about thirty minutes to get the treasure chests locked in the crates and carried below. He then sent the video file to Faisal. Within a few minutes, he received a one-word text, "Excellent". He felt like a great weight had been lifted from his shoulders and, though he still had to meet the man who would deliver the cargo to Faisal, he had met the new deadline to get the treasure aboard. Now, all he had to do was elude the Canadian Coast Guard and those pesky Americans and his job was done. And with the digital camouflage system, that should pose no problems. After all, they had been driving right by him for several days now and they had no clue he was even there. He had enjoyed watching them searching for him and had even laughed so hard one time, he was afraid they had heard him.

The boat moved away from the bluff and eased into the cove where he had found refuge for the last few days. The men anchored the boat and made sure the camouflage was active. When everything was secure, Adar called his men together and congratulated them on a job well done. He would stay put until he received word that it was time to go meet the man who would move the treasure to the U.S., so, with time to spare, he left one man to stand watch and let the others go below to get some much-needed rest. He went to his private cabin, removed his soiled clothes, and took a long, hot shower, letting the steam work its magic on his tired, aching muscles. Finally, he stepped out of the shower, put on clean clothes, and lay down on his bed. He stayed awake for a while and thought about the great treasure until he was overcome with sleep where the great treasure took over his dreams. In two hours, the vibration of his phone brought him out of his slumber. He keyed the talk button and listened to the directions. He said, "Understood."

CHAPTER 44

Bochere backed the white van to the dock; it was a three-year-old vehicle that had been modified for maximum efficiency for someone who made a living on the wrong side of the law. It had a turbo-charged motor that could move it on a highway up to one hundred twenty-five miles an hour; it had no windows in the cargo area other than the rear one and it was tinted so dark a person could not see through it. The van had a heavy-duty suspension system and all-wheel drive so that it could go off road. It had a GPS navigation system build in, had a radar detector, and had blue-tooth phone capability. But the modification that got his attention was the DIC or digital interactive camouflage. He had been told about it when the van was delivered to him just this morning. He had a text that told him that Adar would explain how it worked. He looked out over the water, wondering where his contact was; he saw nothing at all. He would wait no longer than fifteen minutes for him to show and then he was out of here. After eight minutes of watching, there was still nothing. Suddenly, the boat was there, sitting fifteen feet in front of him. It scared him because he was sure it had not come into the isolated bay while he was searching for it.

He watched the large boat ease into the empty slip. Three men stood on the deck, two of them holding long rifles, the other a Russian Bizon SMG. He recognized it as the weapon made for law enforcement and Special Forces. This particular one was chambered for nine by nineteen parabellum rounds; it could hold fifty-three cartridges and no doubt could be set for single shot, three-round bursts, or fully-automatic fire. He recognized Adar from the image sent to his phone, so he left his automatic weapon in his pocket and stepped out where they could see he was no threat. No words were spoken and within twenty minutes the cargo had been moved from the boat to the back of the van, where it was stacked beneath identical crates that held automobile parts. The whole cargo was then covered over by a blue tarpaulin. Adar explained to Bochere how to activate the digital interactive camouflage. Bochere was fascinated by the technology and realized how effective it had been while he had been looking right at Adar's boat and saw absolutely nothing. The boat accelerated away from the dock.

Bochere activated his phone and tapped out the number. When he heard the acceptance of the call on the other end, he said, "Package delivered. Twenty-three pieces."

Faisal replied, "Confirmed. Continue to the drop."

CHAPTER 45

As soon as he dropped the delivery, Adar called Faisal and said, "It is done; the goods have been delivered to the van."

Even though Faisal knew the answer, he asked, "How many crates did you load into the van?"

"Twenty-three, of course. I have none of the chests left with me."

"You know what to do now, don't you?"

"Yes, I will take the boat to the drop in Newfoundland and complete the next directive."

Adar took over the driving of the boat. He eased away from the dock and accelerated. He left behind the treasure-drop site, an old abandoned factory on the Northern coast of New Brunswick in the Northumberland Strait, which separated New Brunswick from Prince Edward Island. He pushed through the choppy waters at fifty knots and soon saw the coast of Newfoundland appear to the northeast. He felt safe this far away from Mahone Bay so he did not activate his camouflage. Although he had been told he could move at full speed with it on, he still was leery of it working correctly at high speed.

Adar slowed the big boat when he was ten minutes from his destination. His radar detected no other boats in his area, but he still took the time to run a visual check himself. When he saw no one, he slid the motor control to idle and called Juhall over to him. He backed up and told Juhall to take over the steering. When Juhall placed his hands on the wheel, Adar eased up behind him. He raised his right arm. In his hand was a double-edged, serrated knife—an S.E.K. military dagger and dive knife. Its three-point-nine-inch blade had ended many lives over the past three years. Adar actually favored using the knife over that of his handgun. He slipped the knife over the shoulder of the man and before Juhall could react, he had plunged the blade into his neck and sliced both to the right and left, severing the carotid arteries and the vocal cords at the same time. Before the blood was shooting from the neck, Adar used his left hand, pushing the towel he held to Juhall's neck to keep blood from staining the surface of the boat. Within a few seconds, Juhall expelled his last breath and Adar dragged him to the side of the boat. He checked one last time to be sure he was not being observed and eased the lifeless body over the side. He watched him sink and knew that by the time the sharks were through with him, there would be nothing left to identify.

Ahmud and Falad were below. Adar keyed his radio and spoke into the mic. "Ahmud, would you come up here for a minute? Bring some binoculars with you."

"What's going on?" said Ahmud, as he joined Adar at the side of the boat.

"I thought I saw someone watching us, over there. See if you can see them with the glasses." He pointed toward the shore of Newfoundland. He slowly moved to the rear of Ahmud. He waited until Ahmud was focused on the coastline.

"I don't see . . ." He never finished the sentence as the blade cut his speech off. Adar watched as his body joined that of Juhall beneath the North Canadian waters. He turned and saw Falad observing him from ten feet away; he had seen everything. Adar slid his handgun from his shoulder holster and as Falad turned to run, he pulled the trigger three times. Adar was an excellent shot and the first bullet had ended Falad's life. Adar ran to the lifeless body and pulled it across the deck; he struggled to lift it over the edge and gave it one last push. Falad made a small splash as he hit the water.

Adar smiled and thought to himself, "That was easy enough." He moved back to the boat controls and checked his GPS for directions. After twenty-two minutes, he eased into the isolated cove where Faisal had directed him to leave the boat. Following directions, he locked everything up and stepped out on the deserted dock. He called Faisal and said, "I am finished! The boat is secure and the men have been taken care of."

"Great job, Adar. Now, go find the truck I have left for you. You will go into the woods to your left. Go north for three hundred yards, where you will find an old fire trail. Turn left and you will see the truck after two minutes' walk. Take the truck to the safe house; you have further directions there. Now, before you go, remove the battery and the SIM card from the phone you have and toss them all in the sea."

"I am going now. Allah Akbar!" He threw the pieces of the phone into the deep waters and set off to find his ride."

Several hundred miles away, Faisal watched and waited. After ten minutes, Adar's implanted tracker confirmed that he was deep in the woods. Faisal nodded to his brother and pushed the button on his phone. In Newfoundland, Adar fearfully glanced at the sudden sharp pain under his skin, drew his last breath, and dropped to the forest floor.

Faisal said, "You are correct, Adar. You are finished."

Cary Logan smiled at his brother. "Loose ends—we can't leave them."

CHAPTER 46

Bochere **double checked his load and made** sure that the real cargo was stacked underneath the other crates and tied down the blue tarpaulin that covered it all. He wondered what he was carrying this time, but had not asked. Bochere was smart enough to stay quiet and collect his massive fees for his trips. After a few more of these type hauls, he would be able to retire. He stretched and stood behind the van and relieved himself; he had a long drive coming up and didn't want to have to stop for a restroom break. He lifted his thermos, removed the lid, and poured strong coffee into his driving cup. He buckled his seat belt and began the four-hour journey. He had made this trip a number of times before and knew what to expect. He eased the van onto the dirt road and turned toward Botsford. At the roundabout, he took the first exit, following the sign for access to Trans-Canada Highway Two. There was very little traffic, so he made good time and at Exit 19-B, he merged onto TC-2 W toward Saint John, Fredericton. Staying within the speed limit of one hundred ten kilometers per hour, he completed that leg of one hundred sixty-six kilometers in a little over an hour and a half. He followed his route to highway NB-4 and arrived at his destination right on schedule. The Canadian/U.S. border was almost within his sights now. He pulled his van into a St. Croix diner and parked up front where he could see it from the dining room. He locked the vehicle and went into the restaurant, found a booth where he had line of sight to the van, and sat down. He ordered the specialty of the diner, Hungarian Goulash, which had become his favorite dish. Bochere took his time and enjoyed the meal, then finished it off with blueberry cobbler and coffee. He went back to his ride and drove across the road to the gas station, where he filled up. With a full tank and a full stomach, he drove north a short distance and turned into a parking area for access to Lake Spednik. He backed into a parking spot and looked around; all was quiet and he cracked his window for some fresh air, reclined his seat, and lay back to sleep. He had arranged for a private ferry to take him across the lower end of the lake into the U.S. and he was not supposed to be here until two o'clock A.M. It would cost him a whopping five hundred American dollars, but he could afford to pay it for this particular trip.

At one-forty, Bochere was awakened by the vibration of his phone. He stepped out of his van and carefully looked all around. When he was sure he was alone, he got back into his driver's seat and started his vehicle. Keeping his lights off, he eased out of the parking lot onto the maintenance trail that led to the lake; he paused at the edge of the ramp and confirmed that the boat sitting there was his ride to the other side. The boatman collected his fee in advance, then guided Bochere onto his deck. He chocked the wheels of the van, then reversed his diesel motors, and idled away from the dock. He moved slowly across the lake to keep his noise level down and used no running lights at all. He knew the schedules of the border patrols, so at times, he completely stopped and shut down his engines. Finally, they reached the other side. Bochere confirmed that he would wait for him to return and then he snaked through the old logging road until it connected with Vanceboro Road. Bochere saw no one around, so he flipped on his lights and turned west on Vanceboro. He was in the U.S. and drove to Lambert Lake, only about ten miles away.

Faisal was waiting for Bochere in the parking lot of the lodge on the south side of the lake. He drove up, backed into a parking spot near the woods, killed the engine, and sat motionless for five minutes. After they were sure Bochere had not been followed, Faisal and another man approached the van. They met at the back and watched while Faisal quickly changed the Canadian tags for American ones registered in West Virginia. Bochere gave him the key to the van and he opened the door and looked at the cargo. Satisfied all was there, he handed Bochere the key to his car and slipped him an envelope. Bochere knew not to question Faisal, so he shoved the envelope inside his pocket and walked to the car. He got in the car and turned back toward Vanceboro and his ride back to Canada.

Faisal drove the van back onto Highway 6 West. When he reached the entrance to the interstate, he stopped briefly at the parking area of the truck stop. He accessed the app for his tracker and looked at his brother. He pushed the button and the car they had given Bochere disintegrated in a huge ball of fire. He said, "No loose ends."

He drove the van onto I-95 South toward his next meeting.

CHAPTER 47

Everyone around the table was watching the image on the wall. My iPhone was connected to the projector that duplicated its screen on the whiteboard. Sitting around the table were Lander, Pfieffer, Bear, Seal, and Cyndi. I sat beside Cyndi. Also connected via video conferencing were Frazier, Pollock, and three more men that Frazier introduced as Brett Daniels, Liam Figgs, and Robert Randolph. Daniels was from Intelligence and Figgs and Randolph worked in Special Operations.

"That was a great move, putting the trackers on the treasure chests. We can follow the money right to the buyer now without worrying that they will spot us tailing them," Frazier said.

The group had been assembled for the last several hours, watching the progress of the treasure as it was moved from Nova Scotia. They could tell almost exactly where the boat was anchored and they had seen the route Bochere had taken to cross the border, overlaying the route on the image of the land seen through Google Earth.

Lander said, "The treasure has been moved to the U.S. I bet that Faisal is the one who picked up the package on this side of the border."

"What makes you think Faisal is now in the U.S.?" Frazier looked at Pollock as he asked the question. "We've had no intel that he has entered the country."

Lander responded to him: "A good operative can get into any country if he wants to, almost at any time he wants to. I would think he would want to handle the treasure disposal all on his own. He came in via one of the secondary international airports, disguised and under another identity. He's the one driving the van right now."

"What makes you think it's a van?" asked Bear.

"A white van is the most anonymous vehicle on the road. It's big enough to carry the load and it's common enough to be just another vehicle on the road. Faisal is driving a white van with no side windows and modified for speed and toughness."

"What's our next move?" asked Lander. "When are we going to close in on them?"

Frazier spoke up. "We'll let Faisal make the exchange with the buyer first and then leave. Then we'll hit the buyer and get the treasure back. When Faisal leaves the buyer, we'll put a tail on him and let him lead us to the brains behind the planned attacks."

I asked, "If we don't know where Faisal is going to make the exchange, how can we have someone there to follow him?"

Lander spoke, directing his remarks to Frazier. "We have the trackers now. You can put a drone on him to track him, can't you? In fact, I would bet you already have a drone on the car. A drone can stay high enough to not cause suspicion, but is fast enough and accurate enough to track him anywhere."

Pollock entered the conversation. "I want to remind everyone here that this operation is not officially occurring. Nothing is to be repeated outside this group. Does anyone have a problem with that?"

There was no dissension to that, so Frazier answered Lander. "Yes, we have access to a drone, and, yes, there is one tracking the treasure right now. We are assembling hit teams at one hundred-mile increments in the direction the van is traveling. As he passes one of the teams, they take a helicopter and leapfrog ahead of the next team. We'll have a team ready to move as soon as the driver of the van makes a contact. At no time will a team be longer than fifteen minutes away from the target vehicle."

Lauftis said, "If you have a drone locked on them, can't it send you an image of the vehicle?"

"Yes, we should be getting one pretty quickly. I have instructed the drone operator to collect pictures and shoot them to us."

We watched the dots as they continuously moved south. Lauftis said, "Every once in a while, they leave I-

95, but they always get back to it. What do you think they are doing?"

Bill replied, "They are staying off the toll portions of it; they don't want pictures of the van at the toll booth. They're working around the pay sections."

I heard a ding and looked around to see who had gotten a message, but saw no one in our group pulling up anything. Pollock said, "We just got a picture of the vehicle. I'll post it up on the board." The image from my iPhone disappeared and was replaced by one from Washington.

We looked at the image. "It's a white van!" Seal spoke what we all were thinking. Lander was the only one not surprised by the picture.

"Can the drone get a close-up of the driver?" asked Lauftis.

Frazier replied, "Not as long as he is in the van. If he stops and gets out of the van, we can get one. I've got the controller on notice to do that ASAP."

"What about a tag number; can it get that?"

"It got a close-up of it, but it was covered with mud so it was not legible."

"He'll have to stop for gas, food, and to go to the restroom pretty soon; he's been driving for almost five hours now. Even a man will have to stop some time." Cyndi looked at me as she spoke.

We turned toward the door as Lucinda came in. She was carrying boxes and said, "You all are probably getting hungry, also. I've got pizzas here—pepperoni, mushroom and cheese, and supreme. There're drinks in the kitchen—iced tea, soft drinks, and coffee."

We all stood up and Pfieffer said, "It's a good time for a break. You know where the kitchen is; the restrooms are farther down that hall."

The group gathered back around the table, eating pizza and watching the tracker dots on their constant migration south. "They seem to be stopping," said Lauftis. We watched as the dots seemed to circle and then settle to a stop.

"Where are they?" asked Pfieffer.

We looked at the overlay on Google Earth. "They are on Highway One just north of Hampton, New Hampshire," said Cyndi.

Frazier spoke up, "The drone has a visual of the driver and is sending the image to us." We watched as the driver's image filled the screen. "There were two people in the van. We are seeing them now." Two head shots appeared; both wore Washington Nationals' caps.

Pollock said, "Both were wearing caps pulled down over the tops of their faces, but they must have heard something because they both glanced up briefly. It wasn't long, but enough that the drone got copies of their faces. Their images are being scanned by our facial recognition software. If they have any history, we should get a hit on them pretty quickly."

Our pizza forgotten, we sat in anticipation.

We stared at the board as the new display filled it. "This is unbelievable," said Frazier. "We have identified both men in the van."

Lander said, "One of them was the helicopter pilot, wasn't it?"

Pollock replied, "Yes, but how did you know that?"

"It's the only thing that made sense. We all feel as if the terrorists are using the digital interactive camouflage developed by Dr. Bronson. If Bronson really did not die in the crash, then it's logical that the pilot was in on the fake crash. Who is he?"

Pollock said, "I'll let Daniels answer that. He is Assistant Director, Intelligence."

Brett Daniels had been in the meeting with us all day, but to this point had not spoken. "He is Rick Logan. He has been in the service for eight years and tried out for Special Forces, but could not pass the grueling fitness tests. He has flown helicopters for the last five years, but never in a combat situation. He has called himself a chauffeur."

"What about the other man? Have we identified him?"

Daniel replied, "Yes, it is his brother, a well-known TV personality in the Northern Virginia area. Cary Logan was in the marines years ago, but left the service under a cloud. He was never officially charged with misconduct, but it was generally believed that he was guilty of some atrocities in the Middle East."

Lander said, "So we have a couple of brothers holding a grudge against the U.S. Do they have families?"

Daniels answered him, "No, they don't." He looked at the paper just handed to him. "For the last four years, they have lived together. We are pulling all information on them we can get."

CHAPTER 48

The Logans ate quickly and got large coffees to go. After a hurried visit to the restroom, they walked back to their van. Rick—or Faisal—handed the key to Cary. "Your turn to drive; let's stop next door and fill up before we get on the road again. We've still a long drive to South Carolina ahead of us."

They filled their van with gas and headed south on Highway One toward Hampton. "It's a longer drive, but let's still stay away from the toll sections of the interstate. I know you like to speed, but keep it on the legal side; we don't need to get stopped and some local cop get curious about what we are carrying."

"I know," said Cary. "I'm not going to take any chances now. Too much is at stake." He pushed buttons on the sound system for Sirius XM and chose channel six; hits from the sixties filled the van. Six hours later, they were navigating the series of the three big cities, New York, Philadelphia, and Washington. "I hate all this traffic," said Cary.

Rick roused from his nap. "I know; I do, too. But maybe in a few weeks, it will not be so bad," he said. "Get us on the other side of D.C. and we'll stop to eat. We need gas pretty soon anyway."

CHAPTER 49

"They've stopped again," said Pfieffer. "Where are they now?"

"Thirty miles southeast of Washington. Just entered Virginia," replied Lander. "Hey, maybe they are going to see you," he said, pointing at Frazier on the monitor. Frazier's group was in Langley, Virginia.

"I don't think so," replied Frazier. "But it would save us some time and trouble if he would just come on in."

Lander asked, "Does either of them have any history or connections to Virginia? I know that is where they live, but they wouldn't be taking the treasure to their home."

"Not that we can determine. We are just going to have to follow them to their contact." Pollock pointed at Frazier, "He has scrambled two more teams to be ready if he stops in Virginia."

Lauftis asked, "What about contacts? Have you checked their phone records?"

"Their registered phones show no suspicious calls. They have probably used throwaways for this operation."

Lander asked, "Has anything unusual shown up at Cary's work? Have you talked with anyone there?"

"We've not yet explored that. We don't want him to know we're onto him. We need to get the treasure back before we spook them."

Lauftis said, "That's a good idea. I appreciate your commitment to get my tribe's valuables returned. But at the decision point, don't let that reluctance lead to tragic results."

Pollock replied, "Oh, you can be sure we won't. The safety of our cities is the most important goal we have."

Lauftis asked, "What about Faisal? Do you think one of them is Faisal?"

Pollock answered, "It looks like that may be Rick. Faisal showed up on the radar after the helicopter crash. Since that time, Rick has not been seen or heard from. Cary has continued to work his job at the television station; he may have been able to work with his brother, but he didn't have the time to fill the lead role."

Lauftis replied, "Is Rick the brains behind the planned attacks?"

"Probably not; he is in all likelihood one of the top lieutenants for the head man. He's not been in the game long enough to have the street creds to pull off a major attack on his own. We are hoping that he can lead us to the main man."

Bear said, "They're on the move again."

CHAPTER 50

Rick got behind the wheel again as they left. He had napped enough that he was relatively fresh and the hot cup of strong coffee would provide the caffeine he needed to stay alert. Finding a busy gas station, he stopped and filled the tank. He looked to be sure that his back tag was still partially covered with mud so no one could see a complete tag number. He drove around the block a couple of times, making unannounced turns to be sure that no one was following him. Seeing no one, he pointed the van at I-95 again and entered the south ramp. "The last leg of the journey," he thought to himself. He had less than five hundred miles now and, since they had left the toll sections behind, he would be able to stay on the interstate. As long as he stayed within the speed limits, there was little likelihood that he would be stopped. He glanced at Cary; he was already asleep.

He stayed in the flow of the traffic and made good time. Soon he was seeing signs for Richmond. Another seventy miles brought him to the North Carolina border. Just north of Fayetteville, he saw signs for a Pilot Travel Center. The sign said Dunn, North Carolina and he took the exit to Sadler Road. Cary roused as he pulled into the parking lot. He hid his van beside an eighteen-wheeler and told Cary, "I've got to make a pit stop and get some more coffee. You wait here and guard the van while I go in. Do you need to visit the boys' room?"

"No, I'm fine. But bring me some coffee and a cinnamon roll. Do you want me to drive?"

"No, I'll be okay once I get back."

Rick stayed on I-95 south for another hour. He looked at Cary and said, "We've got to make a decision here. We can stay on ninety-five until we get past Lake Marion. Or we can take state and local roads. That would be the shorter distance, but would take about the same amount of time. What do you think?"

Cary replied, "Stay on the interstate as much as possible. Small towns sometimes are too curious about who is driving through."

"I agree. The interstate it is."

An hour later, Rick saw the signs for Santee State Park. He took the exit and turned south on State Highway Six. He followed the curvy two-lane road southeast until it approached Lake Moultrie. His navigation system kept him on Six as it curved south and followed the shoreline of the lake. Finally, he saw the walled-in property he was looking for. He stopped at the closed gate and called the number he had been given.

"Yes?"

"I have your new chests you ordered." He followed the script he had been furnished. If there was any deviation at all, he would not be granted access.

"What color are they?" asked the voice.

Rick replied, "They are brown, a deep mahogany with gold inside."

The gate slowly swung open and the van moved and followed the curved driveway through tall old oaks and pines and stopped in front of a white plantation-style house.

Cary and Rick stepped out of the van onto the brick-cobbled drive. Cary immediately saw the three men standing by trees; they each held an automatic assault rifle chambered for thirty-nine mm rounds. The man standing in the doorway held a semiautomatic handgun at his side. It was the Glock 17, a nine by nineteen Parabellum model. He looked at us and said, "Mr. Faisal?"

Rick returned his stare and replied, "I am Faisal. Take me to Mr. Whitney."

"Do you have the cargo?"

"Yes, I do."

"Bring a sample with you to show him."

Faisal moved to the back of the van and leaned into the rear cargo area.

"Keep your hands where my men can see them."

Faisal laughed at him. "How can I keep my hands in sight if I need to get into the back of the van to get you a sample?"

The guard answered by nodding to his men, who moved to the back of the van. Faisal reached into the van and moved a corner of the tarpaulin aside. He pulled the top two boxes off the end and set them aside. He slid the heavy chest toward him and unlocked it. Raising the top, he reached in and selected three gold coins. He shut the chest and closed the door. He locked the van and looked at the man who was still standing on the covered porch, "Let's go see Mr. Whitney." Rick and Cary walked up the steps to the porch and moved toward the door.

"Wait!" said the man.

The men with the assault rifles closed around them. One of them handed his rifle to the man on his right and moved in front of Rick. He quickly and efficiently checked him for weapons. Finding none, he moved to Cary and confirmed that he carried nothing dangerous. Whitney had warned Rick about trying to see him with a weapon, so the Logans had left their handguns locked in the van. It was a matter of trust—the honor among thieves—that allowed collaboration between those who would not adhere to the public law.

"Now, you may follow me."

They followed as Whitney's man led them through the house. Cary and Rick looked around at the furnishings. The whole house was appointed with antiques—expensive, Cary was sure. On the walls hung oil paintings, some with a Master's signature. Rick would have bet they were authentic. The thick Persian rugs over the hardwood muffled their heavy steps. The man stopped in front of a closed door, knocked, and, then, opened the door.

He motioned for Rick and Cary to follow him in; the three guards stayed in the hallway. The man closed the door and led the way across the room. "Mr. Whitney," he pointed.

Cary looked at him and said, "You have a beautiful house, Mr. Whitney.

Whitney glared at him; his eyes were dark and angry. "Let me see the sample," he growled.

Rick handed him the three gold coins. Whitney held them up to the light. He slightly gasped and said, "You have more of these?"

Rick proudly answered: "Yes. We have twenty-three chests. Ten of them are filled with these gold coins and five have a mixture of fine gems, diamonds, rubies, and emeralds. The other eight house a collection of books and information about the early Knights Templar. That history may be worth as much as the coins and stones."

Whitney glared at him. "Nothing has value unless there are willing buyers!"

"But we know you have buyers . . . or else you would not have had me bring these items to you."

Whitney just looked at him. Finally, after forty seconds of silence, he replied, "Yes, you are right; I have buyers. If we can confirm the amounts, I will give you the amount we discussed. Let's go look at these chests."

CHAPTER 51

The group stood around the table, all eyes on the trackers that had stopped moving. "They are there," said Lander. "Do we have a confirmed location?" He addressed that question to Frazier. It had been a long day and one could see the weariness in the faces.

"Yes, they are at a house on Lake Moultrie. We are getting a team in place now; they are ten minutes out."

"Don't do anything until the Logans have left. We need him to lead us to the head man."

They watched as the trackers began to move, one at a time. "They are unloading the chests," said Lauftis. It won't be long now." They counted twenty-one trackers being moved into the house.

Finally, Lander said, "It looks like they are keeping two of the chests for themselves. They were moved away from the back of the van."

Pollock responded, "Yes, it looks like their greed overrode their obedience to Allah. They won't get the great rewards."

I whispered to Cyndi, "No houseful of virgins for them."

She replied, "Good, I'm rooting for the virgins."

Frazier said, "Rick and Cary won't leave until they get confirmation that the funds have been electronically deposited to their accounts."

Pollock replied, "You're right, but if this is a true purchase transaction, that won't take long. Funds should have been placed so that they could be immediately transferred."

CHAPTER 52

Whitney could hardly contain his excitement. This was the greatest discovery of hidden wealth he had ever known; it may even be the most valuable ever found anywhere. He had to have it and would have paid whatever it took to secure it. The ten million dollars asking price was a fraction of the true worth.

The man looking through the stones looked up and addressed Whitney. "These gems are real, but they are not the highest quality. We can sell them on the market but not at highest grade." Whitney recognized the code phrases and realized that the gemstones were truly at the high end of quality.

Whitney looked at Faisal. "You asked for ten million dollars; I will give you nine million. If the stones were top quality, the whole amount would be worth ten." Whitney would have paid three times the ten million, but was determined to get the treasure for no more than nine and a half.

"I need ten million to carry out our project," Faisal replied.

"I don't care about your project! I will give you nine and a half million dollars. If you don't want that, then load the chests back up and get out of here!" Whitney had observed the pleading anxiety in Faisal's voice and knew he would accept his final offer. "In two minutes, I will either transfer the money to your account or have you escorted off my property." He turned his back on Faisal and went to his window that looked out over the lake.

Rick whispered to Cary, "We have to take this; it's too dangerous to try to find another buyer. Besides, I'm not sure we would leave here alive if we turned him down."

Cary replied, "You are right. We would be executed here and he would get the treasure anyway."

Rick spoke to Whitney. "You are getting a bargain, but we will take your offer. Transfer the money. Here is the account number." He handed Whitney a slip of paper. "As soon as I have verified the deposit, we are out of here."

CHAPTER 53

Frazier was talking to someone on his phone. "As soon as the van has left the area, get in there and secure the treasure." He listened a moment and then responded, "The drone sent us pictures; there are at least four guards there. Three of them were carrying assault rifles, so go in there fully loaded and expect resistance. This is a national security operation, so do what you have to do."

He ended the call and turned back to the video screen. "We have an assault team ready to go. They'll use a helicopter to get onto the property. As soon as the Logans have left the area, they have the green light to go. The drone will stay with the van."

The group watched the two trackers in the van move away from the property. When it was a mile away, Frazier called the pilot, "They are gone. Go now!"

About five hundred miles from Langley, the pilot banked his helicopter and accelerated. Within three minutes, he was hovering over Whitney's lawn. It took thirty seconds for the eight members of the assault team to be on the ground, sliding quickly down the cable. All ready looking for resistance, two of them faced in each direction as their boots hit the turf. Weapons were up and ready and set for three-round bursts. Immediately, almost simultaneous shots rang out and three figures sank to the ground, all with head shots. The team spread out, with two of them running to each side of the house. Two kneeled in place, providing cover for the last two of them sprinting for the front door. Stopping at the porch, they gave cover for their comrades to join them. One of the men pulled a small brick of C4 explosive from his backpack and molded it to the door lock. The leader spoke into his throat mic, "Are you in place?"

The two clicks answered him and he spoke again, "Okay, everyone's in place. On my count . . . three . . . two . . . one. Go now!"

Everyone on the porch took cover and the soldier detonated the explosive. While it was still smoking, he kicked the door and it sprang open. He rolled inside, coming to rest with his weapon pointed to the right. The next man followed, clearing the left. The third man in took the front.

"Right clear!"

"Left clear!"

"Front clear!"

Almost immediately, they heard the same responses from the rear of the house.

Each of the assault teams was to clear the house to the right of their entrance ways. By doing this, they would not confront each other while they searched the house. After clearing the first floor and finding nothing, they met in the kitchen. The leader said, "There is a basement and one floor on the second level. We'll take the basement; you guys take the second floor. Be careful; we don't know what is in here."

Half of them moved to the stairs going to the second floor. Going blindly up steps was the most dangerous in assault maneuvers; the head was the first part of the body exposed and the most lethal body part to be shot. Almost no one survived a head shot. After all the earlier noise, there was no advantage in trying to remain quiet, so the team spread out and attacked the stairs, running as swiftly up them as they could.

The other group moved to the door for the basement stairs. The leader paused at the top and called out, "We know you are there! Give yourself up immediately!" He waited for ten seconds, then repeated the warning. "Give yourself up immediately! I'll give you five seconds to respond." No one moved and he heard no noise.

He removed a flash bang grenade from his pouch, pulled the pin, and dropped it into the basement. There was a huge explosion and a bright flash of light. He led his men down the steps with weapons drawn. He saw movement to his left and put two holes in the forehead of the big guard.

He heard the weak voice call out, "Don't shoot; I give! I need help."

"Stand up with your hands above your head. Now!"

"Okay, okay." The man struggled to his feet with his hands as high as he could reach. His face was bloody, blood flowing freely from his nose.

"How many men do you have?"

"Three were outside. The only one inside was my personal guard, the one you shot here." The leader turned and motioned to his men. They quickly went through the basement, then came back to the leader.

"All clear. No one else is here."

The leader spoke again into his mic, "What about floor two? Any resistance up there?"

"No one up here. All clear."

"Get this man tied up and out to the lawn." The leader radioed his pilot, "Ready for extraction in five. Should be clear."

"Anyone see a group of boxes?"

"Over here, Captain."

They gathered at the spot he indicated. The captain counted the boxes and pulled his phone out and hit the fast response number.

CHAPTER 54

Frazier **answered his phone. "How many** boxes?" He paused, then continued: "Okay, take the boxes to the front lawn; there will be another chopper joining you. Place all the boxes in it. Take the survivor into custody as a potential national enemy combatant under the National Security Act. Don't let him talk to anyone or make any phone calls. There will be a clean-up crew there to sanitize the house and grounds. No one is say a word about this operation. Did you get his phone?"

He waited for a minute while the soldier found the phone and said, "Yes, I have it here."

"Check the numbers on his contacts. Faisal's number will be the last call he received. Send me all the numbers and contact names; also get me a printout of all calls within the last month, incoming and outgoing."

Frazier looked at Daniels. "Get me a trace on Faisal's phone ASAP. I want a printout of everything associated with that cell."

Frazier turned to face the video screen. "Operation completed. Twenty-one boxes, all still full, were recovered. The buyer is in custody; his guards were all eliminated. We will send the chests back to you via government jet. By the way, do you want them delivered to the reservation in Minnesota? If I understand it, the treasure is the property of the tribe there."

Lauftis faced Bear and said, "Will that be okay? The tribe has documentation that shows ownership. All the knights that brought the treasure to Oak Island took tribal brides and were infused into our community. We have been planning for a few years to come claim our heritage."

Bear replied, "I think that will be okay. But you will need to file the necessary papers to make it legal."

Frazier replied, "Then we will deliver it to Duluth. I'll let you know an arrival time so you can arrange to pick up your cargo. Two boxes are still with Logan in the van. We are keeping the drone on him in hopes that he will lead us to the lead terrorist. As soon as we corral him, you will get those two."

CHAPTER 55

Cary said, "You changed the plan. Is it wise to keep two of the treasure chests? We had agreed to hold on to one of them."

Rick replied, "Why shouldn't we have it? We're the ones that delivered the treasure. Besides, we got enough from Whitney to purchase the weapons. Once the attacks are over, we will retire and live in comfort the rest of our lives. I've got to call Arkady, but first, let's find a motel and get some sleep. I'll call him tomorrow."

"Good idea, but I've got to eat first. You're so skinny you don't need much, but I have to have my meals."

They drove back toward the exit they had taken from I-95 and found a Cracker Barrel. They parked the van in front of a window so they could see it from inside. Cary ordered the daily special—Chicken and Dumplings—and Rick selected Fish and Chips. Thirty minutes later, they pulled under the awning at a Best

Western. Cary went inside to register and came back shortly and pointed down the line of rooms. "We're the last room on the bottom floor. We can park right outside our room. Take the van down there; I'll walk."

Rick backed the van into the parking slot, keeping the back door just outside the window to their room. They made sure the van was locked and Rick activated the alarm system. Cary was already inside and when Rick came in, said, "I've got dibs on the shower."

Rick said, "Go ahead, but don't take too long. If you do, I'll be asleep when you get through."

Thirty minutes later, both men had showered and were fast asleep. The next morning dawned bright and cloudless. Rick awoke first and looked at the van still parked safely in its spot. Neither man had heard the stealthy visit last night. The van now had a tracking device stuck to the frame under the front wheel well. There was also a small fly on the roof that would sit stationary until the door was open, then flit inside and find a spot to ride. Activated, it would allow the C.I.A. to monitor the two men, sending both audio and video. It was so lifelike that it would take a botanist to discern the difference; it was named Super Fly. The high-flying drone would stay with them, but now in a backup role.

They decided to go back to the Cracker Barrel for breakfast. Once they were back on the road, Cary asked, "When are you going to call the Russian? The quicker we obtain the weapons, the better I'll feel. Maybe we need to accelerate the plan and not wait for Christmas."

"You want to strike now, don't you? Patience was never one of your virtues."

"Yes, I want to get it all behind us so we can get on with our lives. I plan to make good use of our share of the treasure. Early retirement will be good."

"I'll see what Arkady says about the bombs. We lucked out on the treasure and got it much quicker than I anticipated. Now that we have the funds, we may be able to move it to Thanksgiving. I have to see where our lieutenants are with their planning. I'll call them after I talk to Arkady."

"Thanksgiving is only a few days away. How far is Dr. Bronson in his work? Is the fabric ready to use?"

"That's where we're going today. We need to talk with the good doctor. We need that fabric for our attacks. With it, our men can just walk up to the distribution point and no one will ever realize that they are there."

CHAPTER 56

When Super Fly started broadcasting, **Frazier** reconvened both groups—his and the team in Nova Scotia. When he saw the high-definition video and heard the enhanced audio coming from the van, Lander said, "This is amazing. I knew you were working on new surveillance techniques, but had no idea it was this advanced. Talk about the 'fly-on-the-wall'. We have it here, in spades!"

When they heard the destination for today was to see Dr. Bronson, they were ecstatic to learn he was still alive. Daniels immediately left the room and came back a few minutes later. He announced to the group, "I have teams getting ready to rescue Dr. Bronson. I also have a team tasked with insuring the safety of his family, who still don't know he is alive."

Lauftis asked, "What's your plan of action for the rescue?"

"We'll play it the same way we did yesterday with Whitney. We know that Faisal is not ready to terminate Bronson; he still needs him. So, we will follow him to the location, wait for him to leave, then go in and snatch the scientist."

"Sounds like a plan to me," said Lander. "Do you have any idea yet where he is being held?"

"No, but . . . wait; listen; Logan is talking with his Russian supplier now." Everyone got quiet and stared at the screen. Both video and audio were as clear as if they were standing beside him.

"How are you, my Russian friend? Are you ready to do business?" He was silent while he listened to the reply. "Don't give me that B.S. I know that you have access to what I need. I have money that you need— good American dollars. I will give you nine million dollars for the five weapons." He listened again, and made a face at Cary. Cary pointed to his ear and Rick hit the speaker icon. Both sides of the conversation were now audible.

"I can't get ten million. If you can deliver them to me in two days, I will raise the price to nine and a half million dollars—if they are biological. If they are chemical, the price stays at nine million. That's American dollars, not those cheap Russian rubles. You ship me the cargo and I'll transfer the funds to your account—half when you ship and the other half when I receive it." Another pause.

"How do I get them to you?"

Faisal continued, "I have a boat anchored off Newfoundland. Come in from the north and you can get through to the boat. Use a fishing trawler to clear customs there."

"We can't just carry five bombs on a boat into Canada. The Canadians are too observant."

"Okay, then I will meet you at your embarkation point and place a disguise on the items. They will never be found. Let me know when and where to meet you and I will take care of them."

We watched Rick as he listened to the reply from the Russian, "I'm not sure we can do it this quickly."

Finally, Faisal said, "I want them two days from now. Let me know tonight where and when you are ready to ship them and I will be there tomorrow. I want these weapons and you want my American money." He ended the call.

Frazier said, "I believe Super Fly has already proved its worth. This is the first real test we have given it."

"I agree. I don't know what it cost to develop it, but whatever it was, it was worth it." I think we all agreed with Lander's assessment.

Our attention went back to the van when Cary asked, "Where are we going? Where do you have Bronson stashed?"

"He's in a lab in a remote section near the coast of South Carolina, not too far from here. We'll be there in less than two hours."

In Langley, Daniels left the room for the second time, this time with Pollock. Ten minutes later, they returned.

Pollock said, "I have had a conversation with Alex Polovonov. He is the Director of the new KGB. I alerted him to the pending transaction. If we discover the location of the site, he wants to be there. He's determined to stop the sale of Russia's weapons on the black market and he wants to work with us to stop this potential global threat."

Lander asked, "Does he know a former KGB agent that may be involved in this operation?"

"Unfortunately, he knows many that could be the suspect, but without a name, he can't identify any one person that it may be. Many former KGB operatives have moved into the underworld and some of them have leadership roles in the new gangster communities. If we hear a name, he wants it immediately."

Lauftis asked, "Can we trust Polovonov? Russia has been trying to move farther away from the U.S. There are many in Russia who would like to see a resumption of the cold war. They want Russia to regain its standing as a world power and, to do that, they think they have to diminish the influence of the West."

Pollock replied, "I explained to Polovonov that five major world cities were in the crosshairs of this new threat with millions of potential fatalities. I stressed the fact that if the attacks occur and the world finds out that the weapons had originated in Russia and that the KGB had been notified, and had done nothing to try to stop them, it would set Russia's plan for dominance and influence back many years. And, I did tell him, if the attacks occur, the world would know about Russia's lack of involvement. A tape of our conversation would just happen to be leaked to the media. He will help us."

I never liked backroom politics or persuasion by coercion, but realize that sometimes it is the only way to get things done. This was one of those times and I said, "Good job, Mr. Director."

Daniels spoke up, "I have a team on standby in Charleston. It looks like Rick and his brother are headed that way. We have a helicopter available and can be airborne with five minutes' notice."

Pfieffer said, "I don't think anything new will happen until they get to the lab. Why don't you all take a lunch break? Get out of here for few minutes. I'll stay and watch the drive and let you know if there is any change. You've got an hour or maybe even an hour and a half before they get close to the coast."

We all welcomed the break and were getting hungry, but the best benefit was just the getting out and walking a few minutes. There was a diner in the next block, so we walked over to it, had a good meal, and were back in the conference room in about forty-five minutes. The sheriff was glad to get the meal we took back to him.

"Anything happen while we were gone?" Lander asked.

Pfieffer replied, "No, it's been quiet. Cary has been sleeping in the van, so there's not even been talk between Rick and him. Nothing new out of Washington. Frazier has his people trying to identify possible lab sites near the coast of Charleston, but so far, nothing."

We all sat again in our self-assigned seats; it was just like being in church. The van was still on I-26 headed southeast. Rick drove under a freeway and took the first right exit to I-526 East—the bypass known locally as the Mark Clark Expressway—toward Mt.

Pleasant. He stayed on it until he came to Highway 703, took that exit, and pointed the van south on Ben Sawyer Boulevard. The van crossed the Ben Sawyer Bridge onto Sullivan's Island. Logan turned right, went two blocks, and turned right again. He slowed in front of a large block building with a few cars in the parking lot. He shook Cary's shoulder and said, "Wake up; we're here. I'll stay out here; Dr. Bronson thinks I am dead and we want him to keep thinking that for now. Put on your wig and face mask so he can't recognize you."

Daniels already had his team in the air and he directed the pilot to land at Fort Moultrie, just a few blocks away from the destination. Everyone would remain on alert in the helicopter and be ready to leave as soon as the van pulled away from the lab. He made a call and then told his team they would have two large SUVs available; it would be easier to drive to the lab than to have the helicopter land in the front lawn. There would be less disruption and a smaller chance of innocents getting hurt. He directed the teams to the waiting cars.

We lost both the audio and video on Rick as soon as he left the van. The drone picked up the video and showed Cary entering the building through the main front doors. We sat on the edge of our seats, willing that Dr. Bronson would not be harmed during the visit. After twenty minutes, Cary exited the building, carrying a package, and moved hurriedly back to the van. He opened the rear door, deposited the package inside, and then moved back to the driver's seat.

"How did it go? Was the doctor still cooperative or did you have to convince him again?"

"He is still with us; he doesn't want anything to happen to his family. I reminded him again how much fun we could have with his wife and daughters. He'll do whatever we ask."

"Do the other people in the building suspect anything?"

"No, they think Dr. Bronson just leased the lab to work on his secret project. There's always someone here doing that. Having a state-of-the-art lab out here away from everyone was a good idea. There is always a waiting list of scientists wanting to lease a lab for a short time so they can work privately."

"Did he have the new fabric ready?"

"Yes, the science has been verified. He's creating more as we speak. He gave me some samples, enough that we can hide the weapons we get from Arkady."

In Langley, Pollock immediately left the room and called Polovonov. When he answered, Pollock said, "Arkady."

"Arkady! I might have known it was him. He is ruthless and would sell his mother for the right price; I think he did sell his sisters. I'll see if I can locate him."

CHAPTER 57

As soon as the van crossed the Ben Sawyer Bridge going north, the SUVs were rolling. In three minutes, they parked at the front entrance to the building.

The men had already been briefed and, before the cars had even completely stopped, they were out and sprinting toward the front door. This would be a tougher assignment because they had to assume that people other than those immediately with Bronson were innocent; they were not even sure that the people working with Bronson were all bad guys, although there had to be some guards to keep him in line.

When the team got to the door, they slowed to a walk and entered the lobby. They each had a spot to check and did so within five seconds. Seeing a receptionist at the desk, one of the men moved to her. "We're here to see Dr. Bronson. Can you direct us to him?"

"There is no Dr. Bronson here. I'm sorry."

"He may be working under a different name." He flashed her his I.D. and said, "I am Cronos. We know he is here. Came here a few weeks ago. He just had a visitor that left five minutes ago."

"That would be Dr. Camo. I don't know much about him. He stays away from the rest of us. He has one assistant and the two men who always seem to be with him when he leaves his lab."

"Have you heard any of their conversations? Or has Dr. Bronson said anything to you?"

"No, he nods a greeting, but he looks like he doesn't want to speak—or maybe he's afraid to speak? Has he done anything wrong?"

"No, but we need to see him . . . now! Take us to his lab. But, first, do you have pictures of the scientist and his assistant?" He knew that most reputable organizations maintained photo I.D.s of their staff.

"Yes, I have digital photos of those two; I don't have pictures of the other two, the ones that seem to guard Dr. Camo." While the receptionist accessed the photos on her computer, Cronos turned to his men and said, "One assistant, probably innocent. Two guards; take them down." The receptionist pointed at her screen and Cronos continued, "Look at the two photos; the older one is Bronson and the other is his assistant. Let's go."

The woman led them through a door which she accessed with a password. They walked down a long gleaming white hallway with spotless floors. "Dr. Camo wanted to work in the last lab on the right. He said it would provide him with the most privacy. She paused in front of the door and asked, "Is he expecting you?"

Cronos replied, "No, but he will be glad to see us. After you unlock the door, you need to return to your front desk. Wills here will see you back there."

She unlocked the door and Cronos turned the knob. He paused for a minute while Wills escorted the girl down the hall and back to the lobby. When she had exited the hallway, he turned to his men and whispered, "On my count. Per the plan, right, left, forward. Okay, three . . . two . . . one . . .!"

He pushed the door open, stepped forward, knelt, and checked right. There was movement. He paused just a fraction, until he confirmed that the man was not the scientist or his assistant; he saw the man pull his hand from his shoulder and start to lift a handgun. Cronus pulled his trigger twice, the silenced bullets both finding the center of the man's forehead. From his left, he heard the "crack, crack" and heard another body hit the floor.

"Right, Clear!" he said.

"Left, Clear!"

"Front, Clear!

They kept their weapons at their side and moved to the center of the room.

"Dr. Bronson, are you here? You are safe now. We are here to take you home."

"Don't shoot; we are here." Two men stood up behind the table where they had been hiding.

"Dr. Bronson, let's get you out of here."

"I need to get my things."

"Are there more guards besides the two that were here?"

"No, there were only two. But they'll hurt my family if I go with you."

"No, they are safe; we have them protected."

At that, Bronson broke down. "Is it really over?" he asked.

"Yes, it is finished. Let's go home."

CHAPTER 58

"**We got him out!**" Frazier made the announcement to all the participants. "He's okay, and so is his assistant. The two guards were taken out."

"That's great news," said Pfieffer, speaking for us all. "When are you going after the Logans?"

"We're still monitoring them as you can see. I think we are going to let Faisal lead us to his Russian contact tomorrow. Polovonov assures me that he will be at the site and has invited me to join him. We are expecting Faisal to confirm the site with Arkady later today. Faisal has some coverings made from the digital interactive camouflage; he will take them to Russia. Polovonov will take the suspects and will regain the weapons for his country. This will be a major accomplishment with the two countries working together and Polovonov will undoubtedly be awarded a medal for his country. He will realize he could not have done that without the cooperation of the U.S. It will be good to have him 'owe us one'."

"Did Dr. Bronson know what the plans were?" The question came from Pfieffer.

Frazier thought a moment, then replied, "No, we don't think so. They threatened to rape and kill his wife and daughters if he refused to help them; we will not pursue action against him. We are debriefing him at the present time. And we have given the good news to his family; they couldn't believe he is still alive."

Frazier toggled a switch and the two men in the van filled the screen. It was apparent that they thought everything was going as planned; they were almost giddy and were hyped up with their success. Rick finally said, "I'm going to call Arkady again; I don't want to wait on him to call me. I want to get the rest of this done. They can't stop us now." He held his phone so he could see it and dialed the Russian.

"Yes?"

"Do you have a location for me?"

"I am working on it."

"No, I know you; you already have a site and time . . . for tomorrow. Tell me where to meet you. And you do have bio-weapons, don't you?"

Arkady laughed. "You think you know me! You are an arrogant American. But, of course, all Americans are arrogant. Fly to St. Petersburg. Twenty miles east of the city limits is a private airport. We will meet there at five-thirty local time. The airport will be closed and no one will be there except my pilot. I will have a driver meet you at the Polkovo Airport at four o'clock. Be there on time or I will not meet you. Also, come alone. And, yes, they are bio."

"I thought you were going to bring them into Canada by boat. Why are we meeting at an airport?"

"I'll send them to Greenland by helicopter. From there, I'll use a boat to take them to Newfoundland. I want one half of my money tonight. I will send you a text with the account number; I can't take a chance on telling you over the phone—you'll mess it up."

"It will be done. I'll see you tomorrow."

CHAPTER 59

Frazier and Pollock left the room and returned in ten minutes. Pollock said, "I have updated Polovonov about the meeting. He invited me to observe, but I am sending Daniels to meet him. The KGB Director said not to expect Faisal to return from the trip." We all understood the deeper meaning of the words and had no problem with the terrorist being eliminated. "He asked me to send him an image of Faisal so that they would be sure they were targeting the right person."

"Will Cary go to Russia with his brother?" asked Lauftis.

"No, I don't think so. We'll keep a team on him and, as soon as Rick has left the country, we will take Cary."

"And get the remaining two chests," I reminded Pollock.

"Yes, we will get those back safely. The trackers on them are still active so we can find them no matter where the men go."

"Do we have time to go home and get some sleep? Rick is not meeting Arkady until tomorrow afternoon." Bear looked worn out as he spoke. I looked around the room and could say the same thing about all of us. It had been a long couple of days.

Lander replied, "No, not if you want to see what's happening. Remember that Russia is nine hours ahead of us. Rick is going to have to catch a flight quickly in order to get to St. Petersburg for the meeting. We can alternate nap times here while someone stays awake to monitor the activity."

Frazier chimed in, "And, as soon as Rick is on the plane, we will take Cary. I hope he can identify the terrorist cells in the targeted cities."

Pfieffer asked, "Do you think he will be willing to do that?"

Frazier replied, "He will be willing to if he can. Anything Cary knows, we can obtain. We'll be able to break him pretty quickly."

Lucinda opened the door and brought in a tray of sandwiches. Lauftis looked at them and said, "They have a Subway here in Nova Scotia? Where is it?"

Lucinda replied, "There's one over on Montague Street. Drinks are in the kitchen." She looked at me and smiled, "You know where the coffee pods are."

After a good Italian B.M.T. and a coffee, I felt almost human again. While we ate, we watched as the Logans drove to Charleston International Airport. Rick looked around to be sure no one was observing him and pulled his travel bag from the floor behind his seat. It took less than ten minutes for him to completely change his appearance.

"I'll call you as soon as I have met with Arkady. Get a car and meet me in Halifax tomorrow night; from there, we'll go to the boat in Newfoundland. Leave the chests in the van and take it to the garage we rented and lock it there; it will be safe until we come back to get it."

He stepped from the van and entered the concourse. Standing at the ticket counter, he said, "One way ticket to St. Petersburg, Russia on your earliest flight. I also want a return ticket from St. Petersburg to Halifax, Nova Scotia for tomorrow night, local time."

She keyed in the information and said, "We have a flight leaving in forty-eight minutes from this gate. I need to see some identification and passport."

Faisal handed her the documents. She verified the information, printed the boarding passes, and said, "Have a nice flight, Mr. Smith." She passed him the paperwork.

Faisal looked at her and smiled, "Thank you. Have a nice day." He sat down to await the boarding call.

As soon as Rick had entered the airport, Cary drove the van to the garage. It was a reinforced block building with steel doors. He eased the van into the building and backed it up to the far wall so that no one could get in the back door. He locked it, set the alarm, and exited the shop. He closed the hardened steel lock and double-checked it to be sure it was secure, then he walked around the corner and found a motel, a Holiday Inn Express where he paid cash for one night's stay. He ate next door, then showered. He set his phone to wake him at five o'clock in the morning and went to bed. He thought, "I can't believe it's about over." And then went to sleep.

CHAPTER 60

Two hours later, Cary was jarred awake by the light coming on and the man standing over him. He opened his eyes and looked into the barrel of a Glock handgun.

"What the hell! What do you want?" He tried to sit up but was halted by the motion of the gun.

"Just stay where you are for a minute. Where is your weapon?"

"I don't have one. Just take my wallet. I won't try to stop you. Do you know who I am?"

The next thing Cary was looking at was the identification badge with the symbol of the C.I.A and another one with Homeland Security; names were listed as Adam Young and Dalton Evans. Young said, "We know who you are, Mr. Logan, and we know who your brother is. We know what was in the van and what is still there. We know about the planned terrorist threats, and we know that your brother Rick—or

Faisal—is on his way to Russia to meet with Arkady. We are taking you into custody as a threat against the United States. Now, again, where is your weapon?"

Cary dropped his head and pointed at his pants lying on the chair. "In the pocket."

Young said, "Get his gun and his phone. And get the keys to the garage where he parked the van."

Evans took the keys to the door and handed them to another agent. "Just around the corner. White block building. Get the chests out of the van."

Cary asked, "I need to make a call."

Evans from Homeland Security said, "I'm sure you do, but you will not make a call nor will you talk to anyone."

"You have to allow me one call," said Cary.

"No, we don't, not when Homeland Security is involved. It may be a long time before you talk to anyone you know. Now, stand up and get your clothes on—and don't give me an excuse to waste you right here."

The agents placed cable ties on his wrists and sat Logan on the bed. In about five minutes, the door opened and the man said, "We have the items out of the van and in the back of the car."

Evans led Cary outside and pushed him roughly into the back seat of the black SUV, a Chevy Tahoe that was a favorite of federal organizations. He was pressed to the center of the backseat and Young and Evans sat down beside him, one on each side. They placed a blindfold over his eyes. The other two agents got in the front seat. The Tahoe sped out of the parking lot and turned north away from Charleston.

"Where are you taking me?" asked Logan.

Evans responded. "To a room so dark you may never get out of it. I'm going to say this once and it may be your only chance to continue to live. When we get to our destination, at some point there will be another man come to question you. He will want to know who and where the terrorist cells are. We know they are in London, Washington, Jerusalem, Paris, and Montreal. You will supply him the names. Your brother is on the way to St. Petersburg and will never get out of Russia, so he cannot help you. If you choose not to help us, you will be classified as an enemy combatant."

That got Cary's attention. He recognized that enemy combatants were routinely shipped to Guantanamo Bay in Cuba; terrorists could be held for years at Gitmo before a trial is even considered. His fear seemed to be slowly suffocating him.

Evans continued: "The U.S. Patriot Act provides us the tools we need to deal with scum like you. You will have one chance to help yourself. I would advise you to take advantage of that opportunity."

The rest of the trip passed in complete silence, a planned tactic designed to amp up the overwhelming fear that already possessed Cary. They drove for three hours before turning the car into a tree-covered, one-lane road and bounced across the rough trail. The driver put the car into four-wheel drive and crawled up a muddy hill before stopping at a rustic log cabin. The men got out of the car and looked around; there was no sign of civilization in any direction. Cary was led into the cabin and the blindfold and cable ties were removed.

Young said to him, "Don't even think about making a sudden move. I would like nothing better than to put a bullet between your eyes; give me the slightest excuse and I will gladly do it. I ought to do it anyway because you used Dr. Bronson's family to threaten him. You're a tough guy, going to rape young girls and women." Young's eyes bore right through Cary. "Go over there and sit. Don't say a word to us."

Cary went to the chair and sat down. He could feel his own fear gripping him; he was seeing his plans for the good life he had had just a few hours ago evaporate before his very eyes. If he could have ended his life right then, he would have gladly done it. Death was a better option than what he would face in the next days. He thought about trying to escape and letting them shoot him, but he was too much a coward to do that. He would be no willing martyr.

Evans felt his phone vibrate. He looked at the caller I.D. and answered. "When?" he asked. He listened, then responded, "I'll be there in thirty minutes." He motioned Young to his side and whispered, "That was Frazier. I am going to pick him up. His copter will be at the highway junction in forty minutes. Keep Cary here—and safe. We need information from him."

Young replied, "Yes, Sir. Against my better judgment, but he will be alive when you get back."

He was looking forward to watching Frazier question Cary.

CHAPTER 61

St. Petersburg was a gloomy city, set in the cloudy, foggy climate of November. The huge jet landed and Daniels was one of about fifteen people to get off here; the other passengers on the crowded plane were going on, *to a much better destination*, Daniels thought. He eyed the ones heading for the exit. There he was—Faisal was the second passenger in line to step off the plane. Even though he knew the disguise he wore would keep him from being recognized, Daniels lowered his head and slumped his shoulders. He had anticipated that he may end up on the same flight as Rick and had used his makeup artist to create the cover. His red hair and facial hair were nothing like his normal appearance. The use of silicon pads on his face completely transformed the contours of his face. He followed the departing passengers out of the plane. He had no luggage, so he went to the exit where his ride was waiting for him. He had told

Polovonov he would be using the name Ivan Irvin and he spotted his ride holding the sign with his name on it. He spotted Rick entering his ride. They were going to the same place, but would not share a drive. It would be a one-way trip for Rick.

His driver took him directly to the place where Polovonov was waiting for him. They shook hands and the Russian Official said, "Welcome to St. Petersburg, Mr. Daniels. If it is okay with you, we will watch from the tower. Arkady and Faisal are supposed to meet here and load the cargo into a helicopter to take to Greenland. This is what your Director Pollock told me."

"That's right. We have to make sure that doesn't happen and you reclaim the weapons to store in the safety of your country."

Polovonov said, "These men are terrorists and will not live another day."

Daniels answered him, "Yes, they are terrorists, a threat to all mankind. They are in your country and I have no opposition to your choice of justice for them."

CHAPTER 62

Tetik looked again at the two images. One of them was familiar to him, but he couldn't place where he had seen him. He was on the roof of the tower, where he had been waiting for the past two hours. The men who had entered the tower below him were not his targets and he had been assured by one of them that they would be gone after they retrieved the packages. He could then leave the area and would neither be detained nor tracked. He preferred working with no audience, but the extra money from his friend led him to accept the assignment.

He saw two vehicles approaching, one a black Mercedes and the other a dark SUV. They circled the field and then came to a stop front to front. Two men got out of the cars and met at the tailgate of the SUV. They raised the lid and bent over the floor of the baggage area.

Tetik rested the rifle on the sand bag he had brought with him. He looked through the scope and willed himself to be calm. Breathing in, then out, he held himself steady. It would take two quick shots, but an easy task for him. He waited until the men stood up and looked to the sky as if they were looking for a ride. He slowly pulled the trigger. He barely felt the recoil and even before the first bullet found its mark, he had sighted and pulled the trigger on the second. One head after the other exploded in a red mist and both men fell to the ground.

Faisal's driver took the five packages from the SUV and placed them in his trunk, then drove to the tower, where he waited for Polovonov and Daniels to join him. After Pollock had given Polovonov the details of Faisal's arrival in St. Petersburg, Polovonov had arrested the man tasked to meet Faisal and had substituted one of his men, with directions to take a longer route to the meeting so that Polovonov and Daniels had time to get there first. The Russian and the American verified the packages and shook hands. The weapons stayed with the Russian and the camouflage sheets were handed to the American. "Good job, my American friend," said Polovonov. "I am thankful for your help. Our country does not need to be known to the world as a provider of mass destruction. Perhaps we can meet again in a more agreeable circumstance."

"On the contrary, I have found this outcome most agreeable. America thanks you for your cooperation. We have saved thousands of lives with our joint effort. That is how it should be."

"My driver will take you back to the airport now. By the way, your disguise improves your appearance. It gives you a Russian look." He smiled as he said this.

Daniels took his phone and typed two words: "Mission accomplished." He hit the send button and Frazier got the message he had been expecting.

CHAPTER 63

Frazier **closed his phone and looked at Cary.**
"It is over. Your brother and his Russian supplier have been eliminated and the weapons have been returned to the government of Russia. Your one chance is now. I want to know the names of the terrorists in each of the five cities you all had targeted. I want their names and contact information. I am going to go out of the room for ten minutes." He handed Logan a clipboard and a pen. "When I come back, I will take the clipboard from you. If it has accurate information on it, we will send you to trial as a cooperative perpetrator. If the paper is blank, or proves to have bogus intel, then you will be sent to Gitmo as an enemy combatant. One day, you may go to trial, but I suspect it will be when you are an old man." Frazier turned and walked out.

Exactly ten minutes later, Frazier reentered the room and went to Logan, who handed him the clipboard. Frazier looked at the paper and walked outside. He made five phone calls, one to each of the five cities, gave quick directions, and then made one more call to Langley. He went back to the room, looked at Cary and said, "Good choice! I have one other question. What happened to Deputy Roget? I know you had him eliminated after he was no longer any use for you?"

Logan sighed and whispered, "He is at the bottom of the ocean. Sharks have probably feasted on him. He was going to double cross us after we got the treasure."

Daniels turned to the agents in the room and said, "Get him out of here. Take him to Farmville and book him."

CHAPTER 64

Frazier looked at the screen and gave a **thumbs** up. "We have them all. Faisal and his supplier are dead; the weapons are secure under government control in Russia. Faisal's brother gave us the names of the terrorist lieutenants and we have teams right now preparing to take them down. All the treasure has been recovered and will be delivered to Lauftis for his tribe."

Pollock pointed to the group in Nova Scotia and said, "No one else will ever know it, but you all have prevented the worst terrorist disaster in the history of the world. I am speaking for everyone when I say your efforts are appreciated and the American government recognizes you for your heroic actions. You will hear from me again." And he terminated the call.

We all just sat there, too numbed by the swift conclusion to even say anything. Finally, Lucinda came in and said, "Congratulations. We need to celebrate."

We came back to life and everyone stood and started high-fiving and talking at once. Bear and Seal hugged us all and said they had to go report in. They started out the door and Lucinda came back in, carrying her purse and announced, "I'm through as a receptionist. I'm going back to work with the Coast Guard. From now on, call me Dolphin." She smiled at me and said, "Get your own coffee—you know where the pods are."

We met the next morning to debrief and tie up loose ends.

Cyndi asked, "Why did the terrorists use the old language on their boat? It's not a dialect that is in modern use."

Bill answered, "Frazier told me that he asked Cary Logan that question. According to him, they decided to use it after they saw the coin and determined the language was a form of old Yiddish."

"But I thought the Knights Templar left France," said Pfieffer.

"They did, but their first temple was in Jerusalem, so they had a lot of background with the early Jews."

"What about the connection with the statue?" asked Bear.

Lander answered, "It was the perfect symbol for the planned attacks. As you know, it is called *The Awakening*. Many think that the giant rousing symbolizes rebirth or renewal. That is the connection with the terrorists. They had hibernants—people lying dormant in place for years—waiting for the signal to step up and be a part of the operation. The murders and the fact that they were so unusual in their poses made sure that they would be headline news; the hidden terrorists were told to look for that sign."

Lauftis went to each of us and said, "My tribe will never forget what you have done. You will be an honored guest any time you want to visit us. I know that Mokuk would want to thank you personally." Bill and I took him to the airport where he departed for Minnesota. I felt as I had met a true American hero.

Sheriff Pfieffer tried to talk us into moving permanently to Nova Scotia; he even offered us a job. I was almost sorry to have to turn him down.

I looked at Bill and said, "What are your plans? You need to stay a few more days with us. We will have time now to do some sightseeing. You have to see the lighthouse at Peggy's Cove and the Maritime Museum in Lunenburg. I think the Bluenose II is in port now; maybe we can even take a ride on it."

"That sounds great," said Bill. "I also want to visit the Swissair Flight 111 Memorial. I can stay until the weekend . . . but only if you promise to not get me into anything else."

I replied, "Just fun and games until you leave."

"What do you mean? This was the fun and games." We both laughed, mostly because we both knew how close to the truth that really was.

When we entered our house, I was feeling pretty good about what we had accomplished. I looked at Cyndi and smiled. She smiled back and said, "Take Chelsea out."

The End

Thank you for reading my novel. If you enjoyed it, please consider posting a review where you purchased the book.

ABOUT THE AUTHOR

C. K. Phillips is a (mostly) retired educator who is an avid reader. *Comes the Awakening* is his first novel in the Kent/Lander series. *Echoes of Skeletons Past* is the second and *The Survival Initiative* is the third. Although he implies no comparison to them, he points to Cussler, Baldacci, Brown, and Grisham as some who have inspired him to write. He lives with his wife in Southeast Tennessee. Phillips welcomes your comments. You may connect with him:

Email: authorckphillips@charter.net
Facebook: https://www.facebook.com/authorckphillips
Twitter: https://twitter.com/Dr_Ken_Phillips
LinkedIn: https://www.linkedin.com/in/charleskenphillips

69899062R00215

Made in the USA
Middletown, DE
23 September 2019